FOR GOD AND COUNTRY

LEONA FOXX SUSPENSE THRILLER #1

TED PETERS

APOCRYPHILE
PRESS

Apocryphile Press
1700 Shattuck Ave. #81
Berkeley, CA 94709

Copyright © 2013 by Ted Peters.
Revised edition 2018. All rights reserved.
Paperback ISBN 978-1-947826-75-5
Ebook ISBN 978-1-947826-76-2

No part of this book may be reproduced in any form or by any electronic or mechanical means, including information storage and retrieval systems, without written permission from the author, except for the use of brief quotations in a book review.

FREE SHORT STORY

Get more Leona!
Join Ted Peters' readers group
to stay up to date on all things Leona!

Join today and download "Shooter,"
the new Leona Foxx short story at
BookHip.com/NJFLNJ

Catch us the foxes,
The little foxes,
That spoil the vineyards,
for our vineyards are in blossom.
—*Song of Solomon 2:15*

This is a book of fiction.
It mixes truth with lies.
Which are which?

THANKS

Like the corned beef I cook slowly each St. Patrick's Day in my electric crock pot, the story of Leona Foxx has been simmering for nearly four decades. After reading Stieg Larsson's trilogy in preparation for a visit to Sweden in 2010, my resolve to write fiction finally took hold. A threshold had been crossed. I began this new and strange writing process. The writing took on a life of its own, and I began to live in Leona's world. Leona's world, of course, is partially my world and the world of selected individuals whom I have come to know and revere. It is time to serve the dinner while it's piping hot.

Without identifying exactly what advice or spice or ingredient came from whom, I wish to thank those who contributed to this book's final recipe: Arthur Amos, Linden Berry, Juliet Bongfeldt, Kayla Carter, Erik Cederblom, Mary Anne Cooney, Matthew Crabb, Mark and Carmen Dankof, Arielle Eckstut, Mark Fischer, Kathryn Franzenburg, Elizabeth Peters Frase, Gabriel and Kristi Friekin, Stephanie Fuelling, Martinez and Gail Hewlett, Paul and Lucy Lange, Nina Lescher, Jean Mansen, Martin and Harriet Marty, Thelma Nauth, Anja Passananti, Riitta Passananti, Jenny Peters, Paul William Peters, Peg Pursell, Christin Quissell, David Henry Sterry, Alicia Vargas, Elisabeth Vergun, and the "Bookies" at Marin Lutheran Church. More. Without Karen Peters—who joined me in Leona's world to provide silhouette design, inspiration, encouragement, and editorial criticism—this book could not have flowered as it has.

Ted Peters
Berkeley, CA
Ash Wednesday 2013

*"Purity of heart is to will one thing,"
said Danish philosopher Søren Kierkegaard.
Not two things. One thing.
No double-mindedness.
No waffling. No equivocation.
No ambiguity. No nuance.
Just one thing.
Leona Foxx is about to discover
that purity of heart is impossible.
At least for her.*

1 / MONDAY, CHICAGO, 6:24 PM

LEONA PEERED out the window as the Metra passed the South Shore Cultural Center, the once elegant South Shore Country Club. Flowing auburn hair draped around a slender unblemished face, partially covering one of her electric blue-green eyes. Wearing ear buds, Leona listened intently to the Cubs' play-by-play on WGN. Even when the team was losing—which it had been for as long as she could remember—Leona was dedicated to her Cubbies. She proudly wore her oversized Cubs jacket that hid the otherwise head-turning figure of a thirty-five year old fan.

It was the bottom of the eighth inning of a rain delayed game at Wrigley Field. Leona's favorite player, Hank Greer, was stepping into the batter's box with runners at second and third. Two outs. The physical world disappeared from Leona's vision, replaced by a mental picture of the diamond surrounded by a roaring crowd at Wrigley. A swing and a miss for strike one. *God!* she whispered to herself. God had long been on Leona's spiritual speed dial. *I know you've got a giant universe to watch over. But could you send just one moment of grace to Hank Greer? All we need is a single!*

A called strike on the inside corner. *Just a single, God!*

Greer swung. It was a pop fly headed toward right field. Leona sprang momentarily out of her seat. So did 24,000 people at Wrigley.

The spinning blooper curved toward the foul line. Would it drop? No. The ball lodged itself securely in the glove webbing of a scurrying second baseman. Out number three.

Damn. Even you've abandoned the Cubbies, God!

The outcome of the game had been decided. Discouraging, but not unexpected.

Leona turned her attention toward the intersection at 71st Street where the commuter train made one of its many stops. She glanced at the storefront signs: "Food Exchange" and "Party Mart" were perched slightly askew over doorways that were once white, but now shades of cream and brown. On the door of the photography studio in uneven, handwritten letters: "No Drop-In Customers! Call for an Appointment." With a small jerk, the train was again in motion, making its way at twenty miles per hour through the neighborhoods on Chicago's south side. She packed her listening paraphernalia into her purse.

At the Windsor Park station Leona watched a handful of people exit. A young Hispanic woman pushing a baby carriage boarded. Leona pondered the expression on this mother's face, showing both the strain of negotiating an awkward carriage and her devoted concern for how the baby was taking the bumps. Just as the doors on the next car were closing, a youthful African American man leaped aboard, barely pulling his back foot through the opening in time. Once on board, he paused, then entered the breezeway separating the cars. He cupped his hands around his eyes, pressing them against the smudged windows to inspect the passengers. Evidently finding what he was looking for, he pushed the doors open and stepped into the car where Leona was seated. He did not sit down.

Perhaps in his early twenties, he stood about six foot two with even features. Clean shaven. The husky build suggested maybe 230 pounds. Recent tight taper haircut. The Nikes on his feet—Lebron X—were unscuffed. His faded blue sweatshirt did not match the generic gray sweat pants. Leona noted how nothing bulged in the pant pockets. No wallet. No keys. He leaned back against the doors with an arrogant demeanor that indicated a tough life on the streets.

The Metra Electric again lurched forward. Leona continued to gaze out the window, observing the decay of an economically impoverished neighborhood. Empty lots were strewn with partially exposed bags of garbage, beer bottles, and plastic take-out containers. Passing the U-Haul livery signaled to her that it was time to stand up and head for the exit. The approaching station sign read: "Cheltenham / 79th Street."

Leona checked her watch. She shouldered her suit bag strap and situated herself at the door. When the stop came, she stepped onto the concrete platform between the northbound and southbound tracks. Out of the corner of her eye she observed that "Mister UnScuffed Nikes" had also disembarked and was standing still, about one train car distant. Leona turned to walk slowly toward the blue exit doors at the south end of the platform. Behind these doors would be the waiting room and the final exit door to the 79th Street ramp.

Most of the commuters who had finished their workday in the Loop were disappearing through these exit doors, heading home. Home directly, or perhaps indirectly after a stop at the 24/7 Coffee Shop or one of the 79th Street bars.

Leona made a mental note: one person was not exiting. A muscular black man, twenty-ish, in a lime-colored shirt with open collar and khakis, was standing still with his back to the exit doors. A medium fade haircut with a short top. Feet parallel, fifteen inches apart. New Nikes. His arms hung straight downward. *Athlete? Former athlete?* she asked herself. He was looking her way.

Across Exchange Avenue she spotted a third young man. Black. Gangly in jeans and a baggy tee shirt, about the same age as the first two. He sported a red tam and leaned against a green dumpster next to a white panel truck. *New Nikes just like the other two? A uniform? Sale at Big Five?* A rusty car passed.

Her iPhone vibrated. Leona paused on the platform to check a text from Bud Stevens: "Church council meeting tonight. Special guest." The phone's digital clock told Leona that being a little late was unavoidable.

Leona pretended to be listening intently to a voicemail, but her actual attention was directed behind her. Her ears picked up the faint sound of small stones crunching under otherwise silent rubber-soled feet. She clicked off the phone. She let the suit bag drop from her left shoulder and the purse drop from her right hand.

He struck. Powerful hands gripped the ribbed collar of her Cubs jacket. With a deftness and alacrity that caught the assailant by surprise, Leona withdrew her arms from the sleeves, leaving the attacker with an empty Cubs jacket in his clenched fists. Leona turned quickly, her black shirt and white clerical collar now fully visible. The stunned look on the attacker's face didn't last long. A jump step. A spin. And then an axe kick. The ball of Leona's right foot caught the thug under his chin. The blow lifted his 230-pound body first upwards, then backwards. He crashed down on the concrete platform, rolled off the deck and onto the southbound tracks five feet below.

Leona had no time to regain her composure. Immediately, the muscular arms of the open-collared hoodlum wrapped around her torso. His knee kicked the underside of her left leg and she spun downward. Her right cheek slapped the pavement. Fragments of cement chips burrowed into her facial flesh like boll weevils. Blood spurted, spewing onto the concrete. Rushing adrenalin blocked her pain.

The goon was now on top of her, their eyes meeting only inches apart. He expected to read fright. But Leona's eyes were not those of a frightened victim. They spit fire, the fire of a voracious beast about to pounce on its prey. Though outweighed by more than fifty pounds, her right knee came up with the force of a horse's kick right in the thug's crotch. He winced, but only momentarily. Like snarling wolves in mortal combat, their clutching embrace seemed like a death contract for one or the other. He rolled to his right, hanging on to his prey. Leona rolled with him, over him, freed her arms, and then found herself flung toward the platform's edge. Her torso reeled off the platform over the northbound tracks. The attacker still held on to her legs as her upper body wafted perilously in mid air.

The engineer of the northbound train felt a wave of panic as he caught sight of the frightening activity ahead: the top half of a human form slung in the air above the tracks. Although the train was slowing, no amount of braking could possibly stop it before reaching the disastrous point of deadly impact.

For a moment, Leona's head turned southward and she counted in tenths of seconds the time remaining before her bloody and grotesque end. In less than one of those tenths, she prayed in a panic: *God, into your hands I commend my spirit. Amen.*

Then, a tug on her legs.

The engineer made a split-second decision. Too late for an emergency stop. Too late to prevent the loss of this poor woman's life. Even a normal stop could be a mistake. If there is gang trouble on the station's platform, then a normal stop might invite this trouble aboard. The engineer thrust it to full throttle and gunned through the station without stopping at all.

The train whizzed passed as Leona, now with her head back on the platform, stared at her assailant with an increasingly violent countenance. She had no time to ponder the mystery: *Why am I alive and not dead?*

Leona caught sight of a gold neck chain nestled under his open collar. The assailant paused. This was his undoing. Leona grabbed the neck chain, clenching a medallion in the palm of her left hand. She jerked. She jerked again. The snorting bull suddenly became a docile calf.

Keeping tension on the leash, she planted her feet. She rose slowly, holding the neck chain in a tight threat of strangulation. Her unexpected ferocity had partially unnerved the assaulter, but not enough to blunt his next move. Once the balls of his feet reestablished his equilibrium, his strong hands wrestled his chain and medallion free. He so twisted Leona's left arm to his right side that she could not resist being thrown to the platform. Once again, the thug had established dominance.

The voice from the previous attacker, at this point standing on the track bed, screamed: "She's a priest!" Even louder. "Didja see the shirt? Nobody tol' us she'd be a fuck'n priest. Let's get outa here!"

Leona on the ground froze. The aggressor on his feet froze. Then, shouting "Sheee-it!," he released his grip and jumped from the platform down to track level. The two hunters left their prey and ran—one hobbling—across Exchange Avenue. The wheel man in the red tam had already started the engine of the white van. His two partners climbed in as the van engaged in gear and sped south. Leona stared at the van. "Evanston Cleaners," on the van's panels. *What's an Evanston truck doing down here on the south side?*

By this time the train passengers had exited the platform and were crossing the tracks on the 79th Street sidewalk. The commotion behind them drew their attention. "It's a robbery," shouted one woman. One man set his briefcase down on the sidewalk and jumped across the tracks toward the activity. Another followed. Then a third. By the time the three Good Samaritans arrived beneath the platform where Leona stood panting, the van had departed. They asked in shouting voices whether she was okay. Leona inhaled two deep breaths and told her would-be rescuers that she was just fine. Nothing had been taken. Numerous witnesses were dialing 911 on their mobiles.

Leona collected herself, as well as her things. Once the suit bag strap was resting again on her shoulder and the purse in her hand, she exited and walked through the crowd of onlookers. They were concentrating on interrogating the three rescuers, so they hardly noticed Leona slip her way through the gathering to the other side. Stopping to talk to police—police who might not ever come—was something she wanted to avoid. She crossed the southbound tracks and headed west on 79th Street. Though disheveled and bleeding slightly from her cheek bone, no one would have thought from her gait that this young woman had only a moment prior escaped a potential mugging.

Leona's mind was running at full throttle. *How many other innocents in the history of Chicago have felt the strong arm of crime crash down on their heads, heads which otherwise might be held high?* This is the city of John Dillinger, Al Capone, and the Valentine's Day Massacre. This is Upton Sinclair's jungle. This is Carl Sandburg's "City of the Big Shoulders," or more accurately the city that mercilessly hurls big shoulders to the ground and grinds them into gravel. *These purse-*

snatching thugs on the Cheltenham platform are unknowingly extending a long tradition, she grumbled to herself.

Leona walked past a currency exchange on her left and the 24/7 Coffee Shop on her right, both open for business. She walked past other storefronts with covered windows and wrought-iron gates with padlocks jailing the exhausted establishments. Even though the evening sun was still shining, she had the feeling of a gray day. The monotony of inner-city death seemed to be broken only by some noticeable activity at Good Samaritan Auto Repair on the corner of South Burnham Avenue. She turned left and headed south on Burnham.

The harp ring on her iPhone drew her attention. Leona clicked. The name Angie Latham appeared on her screen. Even though Angie lived a time zone away in southern Michigan, she was still Leona's closest friend. Leona hit "ignore" and walked briskly southward.

2 / TUESDAY, AFGHANISTAN, 5:00 AM

THE RISING SUN colored the eastern horizon as the four door pickup truck rocked its way slowly up the stony road. In the crew cab of the Toyota Hilux rode four drowsy men, bobbling at each bump. The terrain did not look hospitable to the human race. Dry. Dusty. Foreboding. When the sun finally cleared the horizon and the temperature soared to a hundred degrees, the four riders closed the windows and continued their trek in air conditioning.

The driver pulled off the road and parked the vehicle. Four doors opened. Four doors slammed shut. "I think this is the spot, Manuel," said the driver squinting through his sunglasses, looking at a path that would take them up a hundred feet to a ridge. The driver was a tall, strapping and athletic looking man, perhaps in his early forties. Above his light-colored combat boots he wore khakis and a tan tee shirt. His garb along with his fair skin and short cropped blond hair with threads of gray made him nearly invisible in a background of sand-dusted shrubs and rocks.

The stocky Mexican wore jeans and a neck scarf plus the leather cowboy boots he had specially made in Nogales. "Si, Gringo," Manuel responded with a smile.

"Grab your rifle, Manuel. We'll see if you can bag your own prey." Manuel pulled a M4 Carbine from the truck bed. Turning to the other two men, the driver barked, "Bring the backups." Both reached into the truck bed and drew out finely stitched canvas carrying bags, long and shallow, zipped shut. The four began their hike up the trail toward the sky.

Long before they reached the sky they stopped at the top of the ridge. What lay before them was a valley, and beyond the valley another ridge lower than theirs. This valley too was dry. Despite the bleakness of the landscape, they could see square dried mud houses with adjacent corrals and sheds holding wandering goats and chickens. Human activity seemed to be absent, giving the brightly lit and heated valley a ghostly feeling. The four were not tourists. They were looking for something specific. They did not see it. So, they waited.

Each of the four took a turn surveying the landscape through binoculars. Later in the morning Abdullah Pashtun, the only Afghani in the group, reported that he could see some relevant activity.

"Gimmie the binocs, Abby," ordered the truck's driver. After studying the dust wake of a pickup on the far ridge, a victorious smile grew on his face. "It's almost showtime," he announced. He continued to watch and report what he saw.

An Afghan government issue pickup with two in the crew cab came to a stop on the ridge just above a small, apparently unoccupied, farm. Two men exited the vehicle. Both pulled out their binoculars and began to survey the same valley from the opposite direction. They stood side by side, in plain view, at an estimated distance of five hundred yards.

"Okay, Manuel, there's your target. The Kabul land inspector is the one on the left. I think he's from the Afghan Eradication Force. No doubt he's looking for poppy plants."

Manuel picked up his rifle and looked through the scope at the targeted person on the left. "Who es el otro man, Senor Jarrod?" Manuel asked in Spanglish to the foursome's leader.

"Parece un Americano," said Jarrod in his desperate Spanish. "Probably Army."

"Si le tiro al Kabul officer, el Americano pedira' Cobra helicopters. Nos buscara'n," complained Manuel.

"Well then, let's take them both out. I'll take care of the American," said Jarrod.

"Mi carabina no es accurate desde aqui," whined Manuel.

Jarrod turned to Abdullah and the fourth man in the crew, an American mesomorph with a shaved head dressed in fatigues. "Open those bags and prepare the special M14s."

Jarrod turned back to Manuel. "These 7.62 millimeter M14s have been modified for the U.S. Marine Corps Designated Marksmen." Manuel did not understand exactly what Jarrod had said, but he got the idea that they were getting an upgrade.

The two weapons were assembled and placed on stabilizing rocks in front of the shooters. "These babies are good up to six hundred and fifty yards," remarked Jarrod as he looked through his scope. "Take aim, Manuel." The other American helped Manuel position his hands and look through the scope.

The two shooters positioned themselves. They took aim. The two distant targets were concentrating on what they were seeing through their glasses. They did not notice the flicker of lasers on their chests. Jarrod counted. "Uno. Dos. Fire!" Both squeezed their triggers. The two shots sounded almost like one. Watching through the binoculars, Abdullah saw both targets drop their hands, spin slightly, and fall to the dusty ground. It was over.

"With the government inspector gone, the land is yours, Manuel," announced Jarrod. "You owe me."

"Muchisimas gracias," responded the Mexican, smiling and revealing his gold tooth.

3 / MONDAY, CHICAGO, 6:56 PM

Nearing the end of the block Leona arrived at Trinity Church. The building was a golden-bricked chapel with geometric stained-glass windows. Next to it sat an asphalt parking lot. Across the parking lot and opposite the church, yet on the same side of the street, stood a dirty brick house with a large windowless wall. The lower portion of the wall was covered with white painted graphite. In the back, behind the church and adjacent to the parking area, Leona caught sight of a second house, her house, the parsonage.

I wonder if I still have time. Oh, well, it doesn't matter. Gotta change quickly. She raced through the parking lot, hurried past the church, flew up the porch steps two at a time and, in her haste, fumbled unlocking the front door. Once inside she threw her purse and rumpled Cubs jacket on the couch in front of the picture window. This frowzled an otherwise tidy room, one that Leona had skillfully decorated within the budget confines of an inner city pastor.

No time. No time. Leona zipped up the stairs as she unzipped her jeans. The suit bag slipped from her shoulder. As she reached the bedroom, the bag fell to floor while she made a 180 degree turn to hit the bed, bottom first, and hurriedly untied and removed her cross trainers, followed by socks and jeans. The black clerical shirt with white collar remained. She scrambled through the bag to find her new black A-line skirt and jacket, custom-tailored by a Hong Kong tailor in Chicago, a special gift to herself. They were made to fit her shapely, athletic physique as well as her professional role as the pastor of Trinity. The matching black pants remained in the suit bag, crumpled at the bottom, the second victim of the unfortunate incident at the train station.

What a frazzled mess! No time to fix my hair. Hate being late. She slipped into her skirt, squeezed her moist feet into a pair of black pumps, and grabbed the new suit jacket.

The doorbell rang. It rang again, impatiently repeating. She shot down the stairs, donning the coat as she descended. No time to look into the mirror; no time to admire her new purchase.

Through the screen door she saw Hillar, the fourteen-year-old boy who served as her personal Quasimodo minus the hump, always volunteering to help her around the church. With his lanky teenage frame and loosely tousled blond hair, Hillar did not look like the Hunchback of Notre Dame. But Leona could not wash the association out of her mind. Sometimes she called him "Quaz," a nickname that Hillar owned as badge marking his special relationship to Leona. She forced herself to appreciate the grotesque vulture tattoo on Hillar's neck and the twenty gage stainless steel hoop protruding from the teenager's nose, testimony to his being an early twenty-first century youth. "Hurry, Pastor Lee," Hillar stammered. "The church council meeting is starting. They're waiting for you."

"I'm coming!"

Leona slipped past the young man. With a long reach Hillar closed the parsonage door behind her and felt it lock. The two marched down the cement stairwell into the church basement.

Hillar and Leona wound their way through the kitchen, passed partially-covered trash cans and recycling bins, heading for Fellowship Hall. Leona's nose caught a faint scent of rancid yogurt. Her gait slowed to an unexpected stop. Her mind carried her uncontrollably into another time and another place. A gruesome scene appeared on the stage of her mental theatre. As if in a dream, or more accurately a nightmare, she stared into the face of a man in a blood-soaked shirt lying lifeless on a gurney. She riveted her eyes intently on his, hoping in vain for acknowledgement, for contact. The dead man's eyes were static and empty, his last gaze before three well-placed bullets robbed him of his being.

The pungent odor had drawn Leona to the scraps basket in the kitchen. The pastor separated the flaps of the plastic bag, revealing globs of discarded yogurt.

Hillar's shouts brought her back to the moment. "Don't stop, Pastor. Come on. They're waiting." Hillar grabbed Leona's arm and guided her into the Fellowship Hall.

4 / MONDAY, CHICAGO, 7:10 PM

AT THE FAR end of the Fellowship Hall the tables were arranged in a large U. Next to the south wall sat a banquet table set lovingly with a pale yellow tablecloth, a flower arrangement of homegrown asters and snapdragons in the center, and a coffee pot accompanied by a variety of mugs in all sizes and colors, donated by members of the congregation. Sugar, sweetener, and powdered creamer accompanied a generous spread of brownies, oatmeal with raisin cookies, and chocolates. Seeing this array reminded Leona of how little time she had anymore for such simple tasks like baking cookies.

The council members were already seated, sipping coffee and nibbling on sweets. Bud Stevens, manning the obvious seat of authority, stood up and with commanding volume in his voice announced, "Welcome, Pastor Lee. We were just about to begin."

Leona found the only remaining empty chair—next to the one Hillar had taken—on the end of the left U arm. She wiggled into her chair. "Hi, everybody," she said with a smile of greeting. Her eyes darted around the table acknowledging each person, a guilt reaction for being late.

Multiple "Hi's" echoed around the table. Eyes stared, expressing a bit of puzzlement.

"Are you okay, Pastor?" asked Bud so that all could hear. Bud's burly build testified to decades of physical labor in the steel mill. His deep voice sounded like falling gravel, exuding power while eliciting a sense of grandfatherly comfort.

"Of course. Thanks."

"But you look like you may be bleeding. Are you sure you're okay?" Heads swiveled back and forth, watching the dialogue between council chair and pastor.

Leona felt her damp cheek. Her hand grabbed a napkin from a nibble plate and swabbed. She looked at the crimson blotch on the napkin. "Oh, it's nothing," she announced. "I had a little accident disembarking from the Metra. I'm gonna be fine. Thanks."

"It looks like a lot more than merely a little accident to me," said Thora Stevens, Bud's wife, sitting directly to her husband's right. "Should you see a doctor?"

"No, no," replied Leona with an element of stress in her voice. "It's just fine. Really." Her inner voice chanted a litany of self-criticism. *Why didn't I take two minutes to look at myself in the mirror? My hair is probably a mess. How bad are those bruises? Worse than they feel? Blood must be visible if Bud mentioned it. So much for the new black suit.* The professional dignity associated with this specially-tailored suit would be eclipsed by her disheveled appearance. *Too late to do anything about it now.* Leona wanted the attention turned away from her and back to the business of the council. "Please go ahead."

With a look of reluctance on his face, Bud called the meeting to order, shifting the focus to the agenda before them. "Let's begin with a word of prayer. Thora?"

Thora could be relied upon to oblige almost any impromptu request from her husband, or from anyone in the congregation for that matter.

"Sure. Let us pray. Our Heavenly Father, thank you for the blessings you have showered like rain on our community of faith here at Trinity. Open our eyes to see the needs of the needy and our ears to hear the voices that cry out. Fill our little church with love, grace, and hope. In the name of Jesus Christ, we pray. Amen."

A cacophony of half-whispered "Amens" reverberated around the table. The next moment was given over to coughs and the sound of folding chairs scraping on the tile floor. Finally, everyone's attention was directed to the council president.

Bud spoke. "You can see we have guests for this evening—actually three guests. Maybe all of us should introduce ourselves first."

Leona had taken note of one particular guest, the one in the last seat on the U arm across from her. She fixed her gaze on an African American man with radiant skin, golden brown reminding her of cappuccino. Perhaps in his mid-to-late thirties, built like an athlete, perhaps a quarterback. *Quite handsome,* she thought. *No. Hot! Damned hot!* But Leona criticized herself silently again. She turned her attention to the council round robin.

"Bud Stevens, president of the congregation and council chair. Former steel worker." Bud smiled, nodded, and glanced to his left. Introductions continued: J. Carter Hansen, a wiry seventy-something retired steel worker, with frameless glasses and gray hair; Kathleen Mortensen, an attractive brunette in her forties who contributed her CPA skills as church treasurer; and Brad Kuhn, a young, blue-eyed Germanic who proudly announced he had just been accepted into service as a patrol officer with the Chicago Police Department.

Leona scrutinized the debonair newcomer as he looked directly into the eyes of each speaker, making contact without being intrusive. *Mmmm. Aplomb.*

The baton passed to a shy and fidgeting Hillar, the youth representative on council. He was the only one in the room under twenty-five and the only one showing body piercing. Hillar looked downward as if introducing himself to the worn linoleum tile, "I'm Hillar, and I help Pastor Lee with youth work and stuff."

Leona smiled affectionately at Hillar while he spoke. Then she turned to the group. "As you know, I am Leona Foxx, pastor of this faithful congregation and I am delighted to see new faces around the table."

Leona was followed by Thora, whose visage and soft voice conveyed the sensitivity one would hope to find in a nurse at bedside. Next was Harriet Bolstad, a plump, slightly graying woman in her sixties, giggling as she identified herself as baker of the evening's goodies.

To Harriet's right were two of the evening's visitors: two slender, poised African American women, both fifty-ish, professionally dressed, displaying a respect for tonight's invitation. The first woman spoke in soft, deliberate words, "I'm Ruth Williams. This is my sister, Orpah Tinnen. We are joining Trinity this coming Sunday. Mr. Stevens invited us so we could meet you all, and get to know a little about how the church works. I'm a check-out clerk at the Jewel on 79th and I live on South Marquette just off 81st."

"Hi. I'm Orpah," announced her sister. "And please don't confuse me with Oprah!" Orpah's strong voice and throaty laugh gave everyone permission to laugh along with her. Leona secretly chuckled inside as she reminded herself that these were the names of sisters, Naomi's daughters-in-law. *Straight out of the Book of Ruth.*

"As long as I have the floor," Orpah began with a soothing authority in her voice. "My sister and I are grateful that we've found Trinity Church. We look forward to making Trinity our church home and making you our family in the Lord. Now, I'd like to take a moment to express my personal thanks to Pastor Lee. What Pastor Lee did for me and what remains of my family was so meaningful. She was by my side through everything."

"Would you tell us what 'everything' is?" asked Bud. "I know, of course, but it would be good for all of us on the council to hear."

"I mean the memorial service for my son. You see, he was a Navy Seal. We received news that he had died in Afghanistan. Somehow he was in a village house when a bomb fell and the roof caved in. His body was so dismembered, we were told in a letter that he could not be shipped home for a funeral. We received a military urn of ashes, which we were told were his cremated remains. I was shattered. So was Ruth. Pastor Lee held our hands. She prayed with us and walked us through the details of the memorial service. I'm so glad we could hold the service here at Trinity. It was two weeks ago Tuesday morning. It was nice to see Mr. Stevens there." Turning to look at Leona, she added, "Thanks, Pastor."

"My son also died in Afghanistan," Carter interjected. "We held his funeral here at the church too. Do you come from a military family, Mrs. Tinnen?"

"I guess you could say that. My father was killed in the first Iraq war. My husband died in the second. They were both Marines. Now my son the Seal has followed his dad. Would you call that a military family?"

A hush palled the room.

Next came Anders Martinsen, a tall thirty-year-old blond. Any voice at this moment would have sounded like an interruption of the sacred quiet. Anders proceeded to tell the group he was a divinity student working on a doctorate at the University of Chicago. He turned his head to his left to address Orpah, "I'm sorry to hear of your grief, your triple grief." Her glistening eyes thanked him.

Another quiet moment followed. The stranger's turn arrived. *Finally*, Leona thought, *I get to find out who this guy is.*

The tall, well-built African American man coughed slightly into his fisted hand and addressed the group. Leona was intrigued with the way he had put himself together: a camel hair sport coat, a crisp chocolate brown shirt accompanied by a print tie with tiny flecks of deep teal. *No box bulge in his shirt pocket. Not a smoker. No shine in his eyes; no contacts. So, either he sees twenty-twenty or he's nearsighted with glasses in one of his inner pockets.*

"My name is Graham Washington. I come here representing the bishop. The bishop's office has grafted on a new branch to its work. It's called 'Parish Listening'. I'm planning to spend a month or six weeks here with you at Trinity, listening, so to speak. I want to understand better your ministry both within the congregation and in your rapidly changing neighborhood."

"Welcome!" Bud greeted him. "And please extend our warm greetings to our good bishop when you communicate with him."

"Hold on!" snapped Leona with a scowl on her face. She turned her eyes toward the newcomer. "Why are you here without prior notice? Why was I not contacted about this in advance? I am the pastor here, after all."

"My apologies," said Graham, looking with total composure at Leona. "I tried getting hold of you by phone this morning; and I left a voice message on both your office and cell. No answer. No response. So, I called Mr. Stevens, who graciously invited me to tonight's council meeting."

"This morning?! Why not a month ago? Why not two months ago?"

"Well, all I can say is that I'm sorry for the short notice. I do look forward very much to getting to know you. Your help will be invaluable to me."

Washington is just too suspiciously suave, Leona thought to herself. She offered a simple nodding smile and turned her official attention to the chair. The group's eyes also turned toward Bud, and then Leona surreptitiously pulled out her cell phone. When she could get away without being noticed, she glanced down at the screen on her lap. Had someone been watching Leona, they would have noted frequent frowns on the face studying the cell phone screen.

Bud took over. "Trinity Church was established by Norwegian immigrants at the beginning of the twentieth century. I'm saying this for Mr. Washington's benefit, although Mrs. Williams and Mrs. Tinnen might find this interesting too. English did not become our official congregational language until 1927. If you look closely around our neighborhood, you'll see some remnants of Scandinavian history. One block north of us is a red brick church. It has on it a hand painted sign, 'Labor of Love Apostolic Church.' But if you look at the concrete front door arch, you'll also read, 'Svenska E. Kyrkon.' That's Swedish for Swedish Evangelical Church. It was founded in 1906, right Thora?"

"Yah, sure, you betcha," she added jokingly as if she were a character in *Fargo*.

Bud grinned, rolled his eyes, shook his head sideways. He was hearing an old joke, too often repeated. Bud continued, "So, a century ago this was a neighborhood where lefse and limpa were on our Christmas dinner tables."

Mrs. Bolstad laughed audibly. The newcomers had no clue why.

"But our neighborhood is in rapid transition now," said Bud to the group. "The steel company is closed. White families with children have moved to the suburbs. New people are moving here from Woodlawn to our north. Gang influence is growing. Businesses are moving out. We've got our challenges. This is only Pastor Lee's first year with us, but she is leading us bravely so that we can make a stable Christian witness in the middle of this social turbulence." He nodded appreciatingly at Leona.

"I applaud your courage," said Graham Washington. "I want to learn much more about you. I'll be listening."

A church council meeting is like a Ferris wheel. Some topics just go around and around. Momentary high points provide expanded vision. But such moments are followed by drops back into the minutiae. The meeting ended with the group reciting the Lord's Prayer and Pastor Lee's benediction. Immediately, Graham hastened to greet Leona. "Can we talk?" he said with a tone of urgency, not authority.

5 / MONDAY, CHICAGO, 9:30 PM

During the dispersal of the council meeting in the church basement, Harriet walked up to Leona and Graham. Graham stepped back in deference to allow a conversation between the two women.

"We heard gun shots on 79th again last night, Pastor Lee," said Harriet. "I'm worried. Lars has found a nice neighborhood out in Naperville. We're…"

"We need you here!" interrupted Leona. "We need you to stay in the neighborhood. This is our chance to stabilize South Shore, to make it into a model of a racially peaceful community. It's a matter of faith. I'll try to drop by and see you later this week to talk about this."

Harriet stood motionless. A full second passed before she whispered, "Thanks, Pastor."

After the goodbyes, Leona toured the church building, switching off lights and checking to see that all the doors were locked. She and Graham exited the front door and descended the steps into the asphalt parking lot. Graham stopped to study the church marquee. "Trinity Lutheran Church. Rev. Lee Foxx, Pastor. Sunday School 9:00

am. Sunday Worship 10:30 am. Saturday Morning Club Begins September 19 at 9:00 am. All Are Welcome!"

"Why do you call yourself 'Lee'?" asked Graham. "Isn't your name 'Leona?' By calling yourself 'Lee' one cannot tell whether you're a man or a woman."

"This is no accident," responded Leona. "I like the ambiguity. One day shortly after I arrived at Trinity, the office phone rang. I answered it. The man calling heard my female voice and assumed I was the secretary. He asked if he could speak directly to the pastor." Leona lifted her right hand with the thumb pointing to the ear and the pinky toward her mouth. "'Is anyone there besides you?' he asked. I looked around. 'No. I'm the only one here,' I said. 'Oh nuts!' he muttered. 'I wanted to talk to the pastor.' So I heard myself saying, 'Is there any way *I* can help you?' From then on I told everybody I would be 'Lee,' not 'Leona.'"

They both laughed. "Okay, *Lee!*" Graham enunciated.

"Actually, my long-time friends have called me 'Lee' as well."

"Then, I'll immediately become your long-time friend, Lee. Now that we're friends, let's talk like friends. If you could offer me a cup of coffee, I would like to discuss some matters with you."

"My parsonage is right back here," Leona said pointing. "Ordinarily I would not invite a strange man into my home for coffee. And, I might add, I do believe you're a stranger, and not yet a friend. During the council meeting I went to the Illinois Synod website. Nowhere on that website does your name appear. There is no desk for Parish Listening. Now, I'm not afraid of you, because I'm not afraid of anyone. But..."

Graham held up his right fist, thumb held high. Up and down went the thumb. "Not Illinois Synod Bishop Gerald Botwright. Higher."

"Do you mean Churchwide headquarters? You mean Hurley?"

"That's right: Presiding Bishop Justin Hurley himself. Want to check that website?"

"I'm on that website almost daily. I've never...Let's go in the house." The two walked toward the rear of the parking area. They climbed up the porch stairs and entered the parsonage living room.

"The lavatory is upstairs, if you need it" she said waving in that direction.

"Yes. Thanks." Graham climbed the stairs.

Leona's voice followed him up. "I'm going to check Mother ELCA's website while you're doing your business. This'll determine whether you get coffee or the boot outa here."

Graham grinned confidently. As soon as the visitor was out of sight, she grabbed her wrinkled Cubs jacket and straightened the couch pillows. Then she turned toward her downstairs computer desk.

Leona discovered why Graham was so confident once she had accessed the home page of the Evangelical Lutheran Church in America, initialed ELCA. Intermittently a variety of pictures would float up on the screen. One pictured Martin Luther sitting before a computer keyboard. The next showed the baptism of an African child. A third showed Bishop Justin Hurley all decked out in his bright red Eucharistic robe, complete with an oversized cross—*could it be a five pounder?*—hanging on a gold chain. Then, a new announcement: "Parish Listening Post Established by Presiding Bishop." The announcement included the photo and name of Graham Washington. "He was right," Leona muttered aloud.

When Graham reached the bottom of the stairs, Leona turned. "You passed the recognition test. Now, which do you want: coffee, chardonnay or cabernet?"

"I know you Norwegians like your coffee. But I prefer wine. Cab will be fine."

"I'm not Norwegian. I drink only two cups in the morning. Evenings are for a different libation," said Leona, disappearing into the kitchen.

Graham surveyed Leona's living room and adjacent dining room, admiring the simple but tasteful décor. He knew about how much she must make in salary as a pastor, so he especially appreciated how she had cleverly transformed simple into tasteful.

The downstairs rooms were a soft off-white, with accents of burgundy, gold, and a deep forest green. The mantel over the fireplace and the brick surrounding it were the same shade of white, and served as a central focus for the living room. Graham walked over to the mantel to gain a closer look at the framed photos: the pastor's seminary graduation; her ordination with a man who was probably her bishop; Leona smiling, arm-in-arm with a blonde-haired woman about the same age; a photo of Leona with an attractive older woman; and Leona in liturgical garb holding an infant. *Stories there*, Graham thought.

The couch was black leather, a bit worn, indicating it was probably a gift from a caring parishioner. Graham noticed a Cubs jacket casually draped across the arm of a burgundy corduroy La-Z-Boy that was angled in the corner of the living room, a floor lamp for reading snuggled close by. The large LED screen, positioned on the wall above and to the left of the La-Z-Boy, was best viewed when sitting on the couch. Two additional living room chairs were wood—Windsor style with wicker seats. Toss pillows on the sofa pulled the color scheme together.

The hardwood floors throughout the first floor had been freshly sanded and varnished, a welcoming sign from a congregation that was eager for a young, energetic pastor. An area rug in the middle of the living room was modern, probably an Andy Warhol, with dramatic sweeps of black, burgundy, and gold. The coffee table resting on top of the rug was an obvious hand-me-down from the 70's made of faded oak, with a shelf under the glass top filled with magazines on religion, science, and the wines of California and France. On top was a neat stack of books: Peter Jennings' *America*, Garrison Keillor's *Lake Wobegon Days*, and Dietrich Bonhoeffers' *Letters and Papers from Prison*. A slightly wilting philodendron poked out of a white porcelain pot. Two half-burned green candles were stationed at one corner.

Leona returned with two partially filled glasses of red wine. "This is a Chateau Gilette," she said apologetically. "Here in Chicago the only wines you can get at a reasonable price are imported French wines. At least this is a Bordeaux. Dry. Twenty years old. Kinda thin and tasteless, don't you think?" Leona sat down on the front edge of her La-Z-Boy and crossed her legs. Graham could not help but stare momentarily, gawking at the shapely calf on the top leg.

By this time Graham had seated himself on the leather sofa with the picture window behind him. Leona noticed how erect he sat. *He's got the posture my mother tried to make me have.* Graham swirled the ruby-colored liquid. He buried his nose in the glass and sniffed audibly. He tipped the goblet to allow a small amount to drop into his mouth and sloshed the fluid from cheek to cheek. Then he drew the liquid to the back of his tongue. He swallowed. "Not that bad." He paused. "Actually, it's great. Robust. Complex. I think I don't believe you, Lee. Thin? Tasteless? Hell no. This wine is over the top." He paused again. "I suppose you prefer the more full bodied Cal cabs, eh?"

"If I ever get a rich boyfriend," she said, nodding, "I'll ask him to buy me a case of Silver Oak."

"No parish pastor should ever be able to afford Silver Oak," Graham responded with a grin. "That violates the vow of poverty. It would spoil the image of the sincere and hard-working shepherd tending our flocks. To even have taste buds cultured for cabernet sauvignon is a sign of degeneracy."

"Should we toast the degenerate?" Leona raised her glass. Graham raised his glass. Both tipped, sipped, and issued the universal "Ahh!" of satisfaction. Graham held his wine glass in his right hand. His left arm leaned loosely on a couch pillow faced with a needlepoint design. In the center was a vivid crimson heart, and this was in turn centered with a black Latin cross. The heart with the emblazoned cross was surrounded by the petals of a white rose.

"Is this Rosicrucian?" he asked.

"No. For the sake of Athens, it's the Luther Seal. Haven't you seen it before?"

"Guess not. Oh, actually I have, come to think of it."

"What has Athens got to do with it?" asked Graham.

"Nothing. I just say the names of cities now and then. It's a habit. A tick." Leona's brows furled. She cocked her head slightly. "So, just what are you going to listen to?"

"I've got two questions. The first one is this: what happened to you shortly before showing up at council this evening?"

"And the second?"

"What happened to you in Tehran?"

Leona was stunned. After having allowed herself a few minutes of relaxation with the suspicious representative of her presiding bishop, Leona's mind underwent a lightning transformation. Her face froze. Her friendly countenance disappeared. She took tight control of every feeling. She cloaked herself with a long-practiced façade of composure. With a business-like expression and deliberate cadence, she said, "May I ask again: who are you?"

"Will you answer my two questions?"

"I hear only one question. The first one. I have nothing to say about the second one, either now or at any time in the future. Must I repeat: Who are you and why are you here?"

"Let's deal with the first question first. Then, you have a right to have me explain."

Leona paused. "Okay," her voice dropping mid-syllable. She paused again. She proceeded to construct a narrative of the trip to Chicago's Loop and her return via the Metra train. Her account seemed to Graham as detailed as it was emotionless. She was uncanny in her objectivity as she recounted for both herself and Graham every moment of the platform attack.

"As far as you know there were three and only three: two on the platform and one driving the van. Is this correct?" interrogated Graham.

"Yes, correct."

"Was the van private or commercial?"

"Commercial."

"By any chance did you catch the name of the business?"

"Yes."

"Well?"

"Why do you want to know all these details? You're not trying to grant me sympathy, are you?"

"Might the van logo have included the words, 'Evanston Cleaners?'"

Without acknowledging what had just been said, Leona pressed, "I think it's time for you to tell me who you are. Are you ready to explain?"

"We're not done with your story. Please confirm, 'Evanston Cleaners' or not?"

"Yes. So what?"

"Here's my thought. This might not have been a random purse snatching at all."

"What then?"

"I think it was a botched kidnapping."

6 / MONDAY, CHICAGO, 10:01 PM

AFTER POURING a second glass of wine for each of them, Leona resumed her cross-legged position on the La-Z-Boy. She invited Graham to remove his camel hair jacket and make himself more comfortable.

"Who are you?" she asked in a presumptuous tone.

"I earned a Masters of Divinity at PTS," he began.

"You mean Princeton Theological Seminary or Pittsburgh Theological Seminary or some other PTS? I'll bet you didn't attend Presbyterian Theological Seminary in Seoul."

"You got it the first time. Princeton. But I did not seek ordination."

"When looking for you on the web I noticed that you're not on our church's clergy roster. Nor do you recognize Luther's Seal. So, for the sake of Akron, who are you and what's this all about?"

"I'm not on any clergy roster," Graham responded. "Oh, I'm a believer all right. Biblical criticism didn't undo my faith. Although, I must say, it came close. And I just don't recall having bumped into Luther's Seal. Now, I hope these facts don't make you suspicious."

Leona glared.

Graham ignored her glare, taking a sip of wine with some fanfare. Then he continued. "What I decided was that I could serve God by serving our country. I went into government work. The widows' mites in our collection plates do not pay my salary. I'm paid by Uncle Sam."

"That's not specific enough. What kind of work does Uncle Sam ask you to do?"

"Counterintelligence and counterterrorism."

"What?!"

Graham reached into his jacket pocket and pulled out a leather wallet. He unfolded it to show Leona the oval credential. Above the eagle's head read, "Central Intelligence Agency."

"No doubt you've seen one of these before."

Leona remained expressionless. "More," she demanded.

"Perhaps you're not aware that the new CIA director, former Minnesota Senator Gerhart Holthusen, was a college friend of Justin Hurley. They're both Saint Olaf grads. It was easy for Holthusen to simply call our Presiding Bishop on the phone and make the arrangements. The ELCA thinks it has a new director for Parish Listening. But what we actually have here is a new form of church and state partnership. This is confidential, as you can imagine."

"So, why is a CIA operative here with me?"

"Trinity Church is the only church listed in my portfolio. You are the sole reason I have this appointment, and you are the sole reason for my ELCA job."

"Just what is your job again?"

"To protect you. I'm your bodyguard, so to speak."

"To protect my body? What about my soul?" Leona laughed at her own joke.

"That, too, if need be. I'm kind of an all-service spy." It was Graham's turn to laugh at his own humor.

"So, what is it you need to protect me from? I have no enemies."

"You just got mugged. No enemies?"

"A random act of inner city violence. It's Chicago, after all."

"What happened in Tehran?"

A steel-like expression came over her already hardened face. She slowly turned her stare away from her conversation partner to gaze glassy-eyed through the front picture window into the parking lot. Her mind left the room. Once again, she found herself momentarily in another time and another place. Her nose rebelled at the smell of rancid yogurt. Her eyes closed at the sight of blood-covered corpses. An old familiar internal pain returned, grasping and clawing at her psyche. She forced her attention back to the present. She turned toward Graham. "I have nothing to say."

"I know something," he said.

"Then be satisfied with what you know."

"It might be relevant to what's before us."

"You have not told me what's before us. What do you count as a threat to me? Is anybody else involved? The CIA is supposed to work internationally, not locally. Unless, of course, it has to do with national security. So, again, why are you here?"

"I understand that you have a personal relationship with our president."

"If you mean Bud Stevens, president of our congregation and chair of the church council, of course."

"No, you know what I mean. The other president. The one in the oval office."

"That I cannot confirm."

"Can you deny it?"

"I neither confirm nor deny."

"You sound like you're on trial."

"I feel like I'm on trial."

"You were once a CIA agent, weren't you?"

"I neither confirm nor deny."

"Once an agent always an agent. You know that. There's no quitting. As a baby, you were baptized into the name of the Father and the Son and the Holy Spirit. That's a life-long baptism, maybe even eternal. Then you were born again, baptized a second time. Only, this second baptism was not of the Holy Spirit. It was in the name of our country, the United States of America. You took an oath. Whether you like it or not, this is a commitment you cannot break. You are worshipping two gods, one in heaven and the other right here on earth. I represent your earthly god."

Graham was baiting her. If she were a cat, the hair on her neck would have bristled. "Get thee behind me, Satan," she said aggressively. "When I left the agency, I turned in everything and made a clean break. I have no relation whatsoever to the CIA or its mission. I went to seminary in Berkeley. Got a divinity education. And now I'm serving as pastor here in Chicago. I am doing everything in my power to forget or, if I have to, deny what happened when I was serving the insatiable lusts of the Whore of Babylon."

"Ouch. That's harsh."

Leona paused. "It's your turn."

"Well, in time I plan to tell you more. You deserve it. But in the meantime, know just one thing. I'll be hanging around. I'd like to visit, observe, comment, and most importantly, protect."

"You're not staying here!"

"No, of course not. I've got a hotel room in Hyde Park. I'm leaving, but I'll be back tomorrow. Anything cooking?"

"In the early evening I do my role play. The court sends me teenage boys on probation. Sometimes their overloaded probation officers show up, but far too seldom. If you want to *listen* to some part of my ministry, come at 6:30 pm."

"I've got paper work to do all day," said Graham. "My day will also include a visit to our Churchwide Office—you know, to Higgins Road, as we affectionately call it—and our good bishop. I'll drop into Trinity about 6:30. Can you stay out of trouble all day?"

LEONA WALKED her guest down the porch steps into the parking lot.

"We're being watched. Quiet." His voice turned to a loud whisper. "Did you see that?"

"No, what?"

"Two eyes. When the light is just right it reflects off what looks like two eyes. There, behind the garage, in the shadows."

They stopped to stare into the dark silence. For a second, the mysterious eyes turned toward them and shone in the reflected alley light. Bluish white. Both caught a fleeting glimpse.

"Looks like a wolf to me," Graham said. "Who ever heard of a wolf in Chicago? I think maybe I should go investigate."

"Probably a loose dog," said Leona, turning back to look at her human visitor. "You run on. I'm going to be fine."

Graham turned to walk away. Then, he turned back. "Do you remember the name of Orpah's son?"

"Yes. It was Magnus Tinnen."

"Mr. Tinnen did not die in Afghanistan He died in Iran. He was captured and beheaded."

"Iran?"

"Right, Iran. No one in the military would want it known that a Navy Seal was in Iran let alone that he was executed. His body was irretrievable."

"How do you know this?"

"I read the report on Magnus Tinnen at the conclusion of my previous assignment. It was a coincidence that I happened to meet his mother tonight."

Leona was stupefied. "Beheaded, you say! So, the body's ashes that I buried...?"

Graham shrugged and said, "I don't know. Maybe the ashes of a fireplace log? Fence post? Who knows?"

"Fence post!" Leona could control it no longer. She let out a wail. "I pronounced a holy benediction over a fence post! Over a lie!" Her two hands rose, palms up.

"No matter whose ashes they were, you, Pastor Lee, are not a lie. Good night." Graham departed.

Leona recognized the compliment. but it did not assuage her rising anxiety. She returned to the house and quickly changed into her jogging suit. She rifled through her front closet and pulled out a jump rope. She returned to the parking lot. With a handle in each hand she began to jump. The muscles on her face tightened. The jumping speed increased. Her entire muscle system stiffened. Faster. Still faster. She grimaced. But she continued to jump. She did not notice anything, including the two shining eyes watching her from the shadows on the other side of the parking lot. For fifty-five minutes without interruption Leona jumped at an inhuman speed.

7 / MONDAY, CHICAGO, 11:14 PM

This Monday, Leona's evening bath would be a long one. She slipped into the steaming hot tub, enhanced with lavender bath salts. In the background, Bach's Passacaglia in D Minor softly garnished the quiet. Leona played this whenever she was at her emotional edge. The mournful, resonant tones reflected the foreboding mood moving over her like a dark cloud.

The bath would help soothe her wounds. Although the lesions and bruises were minor and likely to heal in only days, in principle any wound is a reminder of our physical fragility. An unattended infected cut could become gangrenous and could eventually spell death. A single drop of blood led Leona's mind into thoughts of death. She surrounded herself with warm bath water and entertained thoughts of her future grave.

"God." She started a prayer. Her thoughts drifted. As if in a theater seat, she watched her life's past dramas. The faces of the three young men who put her life in peril at the Cheltenham station flashed on her mental stage. She relived the terrifying moment she saw the north-bound train about to decapitate her. Then Orpah Tinnen walked into the scene. Leona thought of her son, Magnus, decapitated by the Iranian military. She remembered her moment in the church kitchen, her moment of remembrance of the blood-spattered chest of the executed prisoner.

"God," she muttered. She paused. "God, you have got such a fucked up world. Why did you put me here like a pin cushion to feel every prick of its pain? Yes, I want to love your world as much as you do. But goddammit, it's hard. I'd like to ask the Holy Spirit for the wisdom and strength to trust in what I cannot see. But goddammit, I'm too pissed off to think it's worthwhile. I hope your grace covers me. Amen."

Leona considered phoning Thora to come over to exercise her nurses' skills and her nurse's compassionate heart. A glance at her watch convinced her that it would be too late to call Thora. Her wounds would be her own to nurse. By taking this responsibility alone, she would have the additional benefit of avoiding questions. She had effectively shunned calling the police about the attempted robbery. Now, she was glad she had avoided police questioning. *Could Graham be right: it was not just a mugging?* She considered phoning Angie in Michigan, but it would be past midnight there.

The lengthy soak in the hot water eased her tension. Leona relaxed. Despite Passacaglia in her ears, death thoughts departed and a mixture of pleasantries swirled in her mind. She inhaled the wafting Essence of Lavender. The Sand Man was inviting her. She gladly accepted the invitation.

8 / TUESDAY, AFGHANISTAN, 2:15 PM

THE TOYOTA WOUND its way down the mountainside nearly as slowly as it had ascended. When flat and straight stretches of roadway opened up, the Hilux speeded up. About mid-afternoon the four turned into a small farmyard. An Afghani opened the wooden gate and allowed the pickup to pass through a club of wandering and now curious goats. He closed the gate behind the truck. Then he walked around to open the crudely constructed wooden door at the entrance of a heavy equipment shed. Jarrod drove his Hilux into the shed while the shed door closed from behind.

Ceiling lights popped on. The four riders exited the Toyota and headed for a just opened door at the building's rear. This took them down a long flight of primitive stairs and into a modern subterranean room with electric lights and Western furniture.

One wall, covered with open cabinets, held an arsenal of automatic rifles, grenades, and hand-propelled rocketry. Three men in military clothing lounged, playing video games on their laptops and iPods.

The American in fatigues went immediately to the refrigerator and pulled out a cold Budweiser. Manuel and Abdullah looked at Jarrod with pleading expressions on their faces. "Yes, get yourselves some beer," he told them. Then he spoke directly to Abdullah. "I believe that the boss and I will want a party this evening, Abby. You know the kind of party I mean. Can you provide us with the refreshments? You'll be rewarded well."

Abdullah sipped his brew. "Of course, Mr. Jarrod. In fact, I can offer you something special: two young girls, both sixteen and twin sisters. They live in a small village not far from here. I've watched them grow up. Both virgins, I'm sure. No STDs. Maybe I can make an arrangement. Shall we call it a 'premium' arrangement'?"

"Sounds perfect. I'll double my normal fee if you'll add another one for Manuel. He's ready to celebrate."

Manuel smiled. Jarrod looked invitingly at the American who was about to grab his second beer. "Louie?"

"No, Jarrod," Louie said. "I'm good for tonight."

"Time to tell the boss what's happened," said Jarrod. He turned and walked toward the rear of the room. He stopped in front of a large reinforced metal door. He pressed a button and deliberately stood in front of a camera so he would be visible. "Ah, it's you, Jarrod," could be heard over the communications speaker. "Come in."

With the sound of an electronic switch buzzing, the door popped ajar. Jarrod opened the door and entered. The large heavy door slammed behind him.

9 / TUESDAY, CHICAGO, 5:30 AM

When the first rays of sunshine splintered her upstairs bedroom blinds, Leona awoke rested. Well, almost rested. As was her routine, the rising sleeper donned her vanilla fleece robe and staggered down the stairway to the kitchen to hit the "on" button on her Cuisinart coffee brewer. The pot huffed and puffed like a locomotive departing the station. Leona opened the refrigerator door and removed the orange juice. After pouring a six-ounce glass of the golden liquid, her morning mouth swallowed it in three rapid gulps. She turned to the cookie jar, a teddy bear with a removable head and seized a gingerbread man. She bit off the left leg. Then stood there, leaning against the drain board, waiting for the brewing process to conclude. Finally, she poured a cup—a green and white cup with a picture of Sparty, the Michigan State mascot, on it—to the brim with Peet's Major Dickason's Blend. With the steaming cup in hand, the MSU alumna stumbled up the stairs and staggered to her bedroom, mercifully avoiding spillage. Leona set the now disabled gingerbread man and coffee on the night table and snuggled again under the cover, a pink and blue mosaic comforter quilted many years prior by her grandmother for her mother.

Opening her Bible, she read Psalm 31 for Tuesday on her morning meditation list. She gave special attention to verses 13 and 14: "For I have heard the slander of many. Fear was on every side, while they took counsel together against me, they devised to take away my life. But I trusted in thee, O LORD. I said, Thou *art* my God." *That's me*, she thought to herself. *Or, it's what has become of me.*

Grabbing the remote, she switched on CNN. Sipping coffee and cannibalizing the ginger man, she continued her morning liturgy.

After a half hour of waking up at the speed of a snail climbing a water drain, Leona swung both feet overboard and placed her soles squarely on the carpeted floor. The next stop would be her lavender-scented bathroom, a place where Leona could become her day-self again.

After pulling her hair back into a pony tail and dressing in her sweatsuit with New Balance 967s on her feet, Leona skipped down the stairs. She opened the heavy inside door. Then she pressed the screen door outward. At her feet on the porch something shocked her. Kneeling down she found the body of a dead squirrel. Looking closely, she saw that the squirrel's neck was broken. Its body was not yet stiff, suggesting it had been placed there only a short time ago. *Who? Why? What does this mean?* Leona exited the front door and surveyed the parking lot, the church, the house and yard across the way, the alley. Nothing else seemed out of the ordinary. Yet, she was now plagued with an ominous feeling.

Leona located a shovel and ceremoniously buried the slain squirrel in her flower bed. She placed the still warm limp body gently in the dirt hole before covering it over. The pastor added a brief prayer, turning this burial into a funeral. *If I can pray over the ashes of a fence post,* she said to herself; *certainly I can pray over one of God's furry creatures.*

10 /TUESDAY, CHICAGO, 6:30 AM

ONCE THE RITE WAS COMPLETED, Leona took off jogging. At 79th Street she turned toward Lake Michigan. She ran across South Lakeshore Drive, heading toward Rocky Ledge Park. In only minutes she had turned to run north. At five foot eight, shoulder length auburn hair, long athletic legs, and running with a rhythmic gait, Leona added an ornamental beauty to the natural green landscape.

Leona did not think of herself as an addition to the landscape and seascape. She felt she belonged to it and it belonged to her. *Space,* she thought. *The land is green. The sky is blue or, better, bluish gray. The water is bluish green. I can't see beyond the blurry boundary where the water merges with the sky. It's all bigger than me. Yet, somehow it is me. Will all this be here when I'm gone? All this was here before I came. Does my being here now make a difference?*

We think of Chicago as a place. But it is also a time. It was about twelve thousand years ago that a southern finger of the last great ice field began to curl and scrape the earth's crust, leaving a massive gouge. The melting ice filled the evacuated cavern, giving birth to what our geologists tell us was the giant ancestor of today's Lake Michigan. This behemoth body of water covered what is today metropolitan Chicago to a depth of sixty feet. After a few thousand years of evaporation, a mound of dry land emerged between the receding lake and the Des Plaines and Chicago rivers. Chicago's potential rose, so to speak, as the chaotic waters receded. This primordial history has now slipped into the less than conscious memory of the rocks and sand which underlay square mile after square mile of asphalt and concrete. Such a deep past seems lost to the night of time. Yet, not completely. On many occasions Leona had asked questions about what might have taken place when picking the tiny crinoids from among the pebbles at the great lake's edge.

Thoughts about our origin and destiny are never completely unconscious. They endure just on the edge of our awareness, framing our focus. Leona's focus was on the disturbing drama of the dead squirrel on her front porch. Regardless of her mental focus, her flying feet were carrying her northward toward the Chicago skyline. Five miles north. Five miles back south. Both directions on the asphalt path laid out for joggers, walkers, and baby carriages.

At the turn-around point in her run, Leona paused to sit on a park bench. The resting jogger took a draught from her water bottle as she hit the speed dial button on her mobile. Soon she and Angelina Latham—Leona's nearest and dearest friend since their days together at Dearborn High School—were engrossed in conversation.

"Do you remember Sheila Hutchins?" asked Angie.

"Yes, I think so. Wasn't she the one dating Richard Lawler at Dearborn High?"

"Yes, that's Sheila. She actually married him. I can hardly believe it. Well, I ran into Sheila at Starbucks."

"Starbucks! Ugh. Why not Peet's?" Both laughed. Angie continued. "Well, let me get back to Sheila. She reported that Patty Scarpace died."

"Oh no! How awful! I always liked Patty. What happened?"

"Evidently it was a combination of ovarian and breast cancer. The diagnosis came too late to save her. She deteriorated rapidly and died in a matter of weeks. I am devastated. I sat right behind her in Mrs. Karpinski's English class in ninth grade. I didn't hear about the death in time, so I missed the funeral. You can check out the obit on the *Detroit News* site. Sad, eh. So sad."

"Yeah. Sad. I feel like I've lost touch with so many people. You're my only link to the old crowd."

Angie smiled through the phone. "Your Goddaughter lost her first tooth."

"Congratulate Maddie for me." Leona felt an emotional twinge, realizing for a moment that Angie's youngest child was five years old and she, Leona, was still not married.

Angie paused. "Now, Lee, bring me up to date with you?"

Leona provided Angie with a brief account of her mugging, leaving out most of the violent details and minimizing the seriousness of the event. Angie had a way of over-dramatizing and then worrying. Leona also shared both the facts and her perceptions of the church council meeting, careful to make sure that Angie understood how important her ministry at Trinity was. Angie had married right out of college and had chosen the life of a mother and—twice at this point—the role of wife. Leona loved Angie like a sister, but they lived in totally different worlds. Leona mentioned meeting Graham.

"Tell me about this guy, Graham, Lee."

"Well..."

"Is he good looking? Hot?"

"I'd say..."

"Wedding ring?"

"No."

"Mustache?"

"No."

"Beard?"

"No."

"Body piercings?"

"No."

"Tattoos?"

"No."

"What do ya mean 'no'? How do you know?"

"Well, no *visible* tattoos, for the sake of Antwerp."

Angie interrupted. "Gotcha! I get the feeling that he's triggered a little something in you, right?"

"Much too soon to say."

"Lee, do you have any contact with, well, your secret love?"

"No. None. Remember, Angie, he's not available to me. I've got to keep him out of my mind if I can."

"But Graham's apparently available."

"How's Harry?" asked Leona, trying to switch topics.

"Oh, for a second husband, he'll do. But dragging him out of his man cave is more painful than extracting a tooth."

"Remember, Angie, husbands come 'n' go but a girlfriend lasts a lifetime."

"BFF!" said Angie. "Best Friends Forever."

Both were quiet for a few moments. Angie had learned that quiet did not mean absence in Leona's case. It meant thinking was taking place. She waited patiently.

"I'm disturbed, Angie," said Leona. "This morning when I opened my front door I found the warm body of a dead squirrel. Broken neck. What could this mean?"

"Is somebody trying to frighten you?"

"I hesitate to think that. Yet, it is kind of ominous, isn't it?"

"It worries me, Lee."

"Well, Angie, gotta get back to my jog."

"Keep me posted about this Graham character."

"Will do. Bye."

"Bye."

11 /TUESDAY, AFGHANISTAN, 7:25 PM

IT WAS NEARLY DUSK when Jarrod donned his party mood. His arriving guests were announced over the communication system. Soon the stairway door opened and into the underground quarters entered Abdullah, a couple of male accomplices, and two young Afghan women. Each woman was youthful and shapely with dark hair and penetrating brown eyes. Fright was carved into their faces, expressing the surprise and terror of a kidnapping. Each was held securely by a muscled Afghan bouncer.

Jarrod rose from his chair. He examined the chattel like a new car buyer examines a Rolls. The captives shifted on their feet, looking at one another with questioning eyes. In vain, each searched for comfort in her sister's face. "Perfect," said Jarrod. "You've done extremely well, Abby. Undress them."

The two thugs ripped the clothes off the two women. They screamed and swung their arms. "What are you doing?" one shrieked, but to no avail. They were overpowered. "Allah be praised!" said the other girl crying. Once their clothes had been thrown about, the two humiliated women cowered and attempted without success to cover their private regions. Both were crying tears of exasperation and trepidation.

"It only gets better," said Jarrod admiring the feminine pulchritude before his eyes. He turned and pressed the admittance button. He reported to the unseen voice in the other room that the refreshments for their party had arrived. The heavy steel door opened. The thugs pushed the two women in. Jarrod followed. The door shut.

12 /TUESDAY, CHICAGO, 6:20 PM

By 6:20 in the evening, the parking lot came alive with the arrival of a dozen African American teenagers. Graham greeted some while filing his way toward the church door and down the stairs into the Fellowship Hall. The U configuration had been replaced by chairs in a circle. A white board stood visibly as part of the circle. Graham said "Hello, Pastor Lee." Leona and a man Graham had not yet met were busy placing things in order.

A young black woman, perhaps seventeen, was engaging Hillar in conversation while adding folding chairs to the circle. She wore a pale pink cashmere sweater, a pearl necklace, black jeans, and fuchsia pumps. Graham could overhear Hillar asking, "Are ya camp?"

"Yeah, I'm camp," she said. They shared a high five. The young woman interrupted her conversation with Hillar and turned to look straight at Graham. Graham noticed that her hair was cropped short, nearly a buzz cut. She had unusually large brown eyes, stretching around her cheek bone to the side of her head.

"Hi, I'm Graham. I'm visiting."

"Hi. I'm Owl."

"Owl?"

"Yeah, my friends call me Owl."

"Now, why Owl?"

She grimaced. In a disturbed tone she said, "Give me a break. My eyes!"

"Oh, yes. Of course." Graham smiled, embarrassed at his own lack of forthrightness.

At 6:30 the remaining teens shuffled down the stairs and entered the Fellowship Hall, noisily slapping one another's hands and giving Leona and the other man, Charlie, affectionate greetings. The buzz was about Spider. Spider had been ejected from the public library. After a few minutes of transition, Leona asked everyone to sit down. She waved a pointed finger at Graham and then Charlie. "Graham, meet Charlie Chadwick. Charlie, this is Graham Washington." They shook hands, and then each found a chair.

Charlie Chadwick took charge. With good humor Charlie facilitated introductions, welcoming everyone to this session of "Trinity Tuesday." He began to speak in a low and almost pedantic voice. Each person leaned forward a bit to concentrate on what Charlie was saying. "I'd like to go around the room and ask each of you what's been happening. We'll select one of your problems. Then we'll do a role play. Okay? Let's start with you, Trayvon. Then Spencer, then..."

"Not me," said Trayvon. "I think we should role play Spider. He got kicked outta the library." Affirmative grunts and "yeahs" echoed around the room.

"Well, Spider?" asked Charlie. "What d'ya think?"

Spider was already into it. "Yeah. I got kicked out of the library. An' I wasn't doin' nuthin."

"Who kicked you out of the library?"

"The cop. A white cop. An' I wasn't doin' nuthin."

"Why were you going to the library?" asked Charlie.

"Ta see my friends. They were writin' term papers. No sooner I'd gotten through the door, an' the cop tol' me to leave. Maybe he don't like black kids."

"Well," announced Charlie. "I think we've got a live one. Who wants to play the cop?" Three hands went up. "Trayvon," said Charlie. "Now, Spider, tell us where to put the cop and you take your position at the door of the library."

After the shuffling of chairs, Trayvon was seated as if behind a desk. At the other side of the circle stood Spider.

"Okay, Spider," said Charlie. "Now, walk into the library. But before you do, think: just how were you walking? What was on your face? What were your gestures? Can you duplicate these for us?"

"Oh, yeah," answered Spider. He reached into his jacket pocket and pulled out a crimson tam. He gingerly placed it on his head, cocked slightly toward the right side. Then, he walked toward Trayvon. His gait was slow. His hands were in his back pockets. His long legs took deliberate steps with a slight angle, so he tipped from side to side.

"Why are you in the library?" queried Trayvon?

"Want to visit my friends," answered Spider.

"You ain't got no notebooks. No pens. No laptop. I don't think yer here to read books. I'm gonna ask you to leave," ordered Trayvon.

"What!?" exclaimed Spider.

Charlie broke in. "Trayvon, what are you observing? Why are you denying Spider entrance?"

"Cause Spider come in here styling. He's not gonna study. He's gonna show off and make trouble. He got no business in the library."

"Okay, Spider and Trayvon," said Charlie, "let's reverse roles." Spider sat down in the chair Trayvon had vacated. Trayvon played Spider's role. He walked into the imaginary library, styling.

"Hey, you ain't here ta study," Spider said to Trayvon. "I'm not gonna let you in this library. Come back when yer ready to read."

"But..."

"You heard me. We don't want no trouble. You look like trouble."

"I ain't givin' nobody no trouble!"

The group whooped with laughter. Trayvon chuckled. Spider covered his face with fingers spread and joined the chuckling. Mission accomplished.

THE FIRST ROLE play had gone quickly. A second dealt with William, nicknamed "The Duke." William complained that he had been thrown out of his house by his stepfather. His stepfather struggled to make ends meet by working at a car wash. Before his arrest, William had netted quite a sum of money from fencing stolen auto parts. Back home, he lavished his new wealth on his mother, paying off her Visa debt and buying her diamond earrings. When he was released from jail and placed on probation, his stepfather said there would be no room for the Duke at his mother's flat. William asked the group: "Wha'd I do wrong?" A role play followed with William playing the role of his own stepfather.

At 8:30 Leona announced that the evening had come to an end. She invited everyone back for the following Trinity Tuesday. She volunteered to email each young person's parole officer regarding tonight's attendance, should they request it. Four hands went up. Leona made a mental note. Then she dismissed everyone.

Leona and Charlie buzzed together for a few moments, comparing notes on the evening's session. Leona thanked Charlie and complimented him on his insights and on how well he had led the role plays. Charlie departed, tipping with a goodbye salute to Graham.

As the Fellowship Hall was released from its din and clamor, Graham sat smiling at Pastor Lee. Leona exhaled, as if to announce things were over. She made her rounds and met Graham outside the front door. Without much conversation they strolled together back toward the parsonage.

13 /TUESDAY, CHICAGO, 8:45 PM

ONCE IN THE HOUSE, Graham opened a paper bag. He pulled out a bottle of red wine. "You hinted that you like California wines," said Graham, handing Leona the bottle. "It's a Field Stone cab. Rich in body. I call it a poor man's Silver Oak."

Leona studied the label. "Oh, I know this one. It's an estate bottled 2008 Staten Family Reserve cab. The *Weinmeister*, John Staten, originally spelled his name Stayten. Scotch-Irish. Now, Graham, I don't know this much about every wine master. I happened to have gone once to a Field Stone blessing of the harvest. John's ordained. Methodist, I think. He invited me to bless the grapes with him. Now, that doesn't really matter. Only a little vintner trivia. Here's what does matter: this is no poor man's Silver Oak, Graham. It's about as expensive and maybe just as good."

Leona looked directly into Graham's eyes. She was impressed that he had listened so attentively the evening before. This was a thoughtful gesture and an expensive gesture, but Leona said nothing about it. She handed the bottle back. Then she officiously walked to the kitchen. She turned to Graham from the kitchen doorway.

"Catch!" she said, tossing a cork screw. By the time Leona had returned with two stemmed glasses and a vinturi, Graham was ready to pour. Once the wine was honored with a ceremonial tasting and a double "Ahh!," the two resumed the seating arrangement from the previous evening. Except this time Graham removed his sport coat unbidden.

"As you can see, I couldn't do without Charlie. He's actually a theoretician. He's doing research at the University of Chicago on what prevents some children from learning in school. Loves kids. He's devoted to helping them succeed here in the inner city. In addition to Trinity Tuesday he leads our Saturday Morning Club."

"So, what's...?" asked Graham.

"The Saturday Morning Club runs from nine to eleven. Saturdays, obviously. It's for younger children in the neighborhood. Crafts and Bible stories. You know the bit."

After a pause, Graham picked up on the previous evening's conversation. "What happened in Tehran?"

"Maybe you didn't hear me. NO!" Leona was less steel-faced than she had been the night before. "You work for the CIA. Just look it up." Leona sipped her wine.

Graham was aware she was baiting him. "But I cannot gain access to this information. You know that. It's classified at a level so far above Top Secret that it's unavailable for any of us in the CIA rank and file. The classification was determined by the White House. Our illustrious president has clamped a lid on this so tight that I can't pry it off. So, I need you as my source."

"If the president's lid is that tight, then what makes you think my lid would be looser?"

Graham paused. "Just what do you owe the president, anyhow?"

"Not a goddamn thing. It's he who owes me. It's he who owes our country, even the world. He's taken a mortgage out on his own everlasting soul, and I fear he'll not be able to pay it off."

A long uncomfortable silence followed. It appeared to Graham that Leona's mouth would remain sealed. Perhaps it was his turn to open things up. He leaned back on the couch, feigning relaxation. "Let me try to tell you what I know. In the battle between good and evil, it's always quite disconcerting to find evil among one's own allies, even one's own trusted friends."

"Or, even within oneself."

"What do you mean?"

"Never mind. Tell me who among your allies is betraying you."

"*Our* allies, Leona. The betrayers belong to both of us." Graham launched into a lengthy description of a deteriorating international situation. He and Leona both knew something that the public did not widely know, namely, the U.S. was already engaged in systematic espionage within Iran. A spy war was well under way. From the point of view of the White House, the American objective was clear: to prevent nuclear weapons proliferation. Once the process of enriching uranium and preparing a delivery system for warheads was eliminated, then Israel, along with Europe, could breathe a sigh of relief. So also could Iran's immediate Arab neighbors who, no less than non-Muslim countries, saw unpredictable Iran as a renegade. With so much at stake, few could criticize America for sending spies to secure the world from this nuclear threat.

"Then, there is Operation CUB," said Graham.

"Operation CUB?"

"CUB is nothing official. It's a nickname for *Contractors Under Budenholzer*. The operation is so secret that we don't even know its name. So, those of us in the CIA simply identify it with Karl Budenholzer, who oversees private military operations."

"I saw contractors at work in the field: protecting VIPs; conducting secret assassinations; guiding drones for the Pakistani government; supervising prisons; executing rendition and interrogating detainees; gathering intelligence through very persuasive means and such. Are the contractors still up to their ol' tricks?"

"I would not use the word 'tricks,' Leona" said Graham. "Yes, their duties are multiple. They perform tasks which our military would not normally do. Many have special forces training and they're led by former Navy SEALs."

"Who supervises them? Anybody?" asked Leona rhetorically.

"Supervise them? As soon as they're given a contract to do a job, Washington's eyes are averted. 'See no evil,' you know. It's surprising how creative contractors get when immune from prosecution. Back in 2004 Order 17 offered immunity to contractors from Iraqi legal action. At that time this immunity applied to about 160,000 private military personnel in Iraq alone. Get that: 160,000 private military personnel, almost a one-for-one match with actual U.S. troops! This set a precedent that holds even today, regardless of the country our contractors are in. Immunity produces creativity, you know."

"I like the way things work out, don't you? We ask our Army recruits to take a base pay of fifteen hundred a month and send them to the war zone. We bring them back shocked, maimed, or dead. And we reward them with glory. We put an American flag on their casket. We pay mercenaries to go to the same zone and return to enjoy spending hundreds of thousands if not millions."

"Leona, you're too cynical. First of all, they don't like to be called *mercenaries*. They prefer the term *private military contractor*, or PMC. Secondly, if it weren't for the PMCs, we wouldn't be a step ahead of the IED makers. We wouldn't have the technology that protects our soldiers."

Leona grunted an acknowledgment combined with skepticism. "My friends call me Lee. Remember?" she enunciated.

Graham sensed the warmth of the gesture and continued. "Here's the problem, Lee. The PMCs have done pretty well, as you say. They've raked in enormous amounts of money since 9/11. Their businesses have grown. But now they want spiraling growth. They abhor downsizing. They have one special cash cow: the U.S. taxpayer. They can't afford peace."

Leona listened. Her face displayed full comprehension of what Graham said. Then she added another of her own sarcastic interpretations. "So, as long as Iran remains a nuclear threat, then the U.S. taxpayer will not object to paying the bill, no matter how big that bill is. It's like hatching a T-Rex egg. We love the cute little tyke as long as it eats the mice and rats in the backyard. But now it's grown so big and hungry that it's about to eat us too."

Graham laughed out loud. "So tragic, and so true."

The conversation continued with Graham sharing details about various contractors at work on various U.S. military fronts. Leona understood clearly the difficulties and dangers he was describing. Among the names Graham mentioned was one Jarrod Grimes.

"Did you say Jarrod Grimes?" asked Leona.

"Yes. He's a real bad ass. For a while he was in charge of unmanned reconnaissance and secret bombing in Pakistan. As you recall, our military was not supposed to be fighting in Pakistan. So, Budenholzer sent in the contractors. Shortly before Osama bin Laden's death, Grimes went after a guy he labeled an Al-Qaeda operative. This alleged operative happened to be attending his brother's wedding. Thirty family members were gathered in a garden for the festival. Grimes ordered a missile shot from an unmanned drone. Everyone was either maimed or killed. Imagine wantonly endangering twenty-nine innocent bystanders in the midst of a celebration just to take out one single operative! Grimes has all the compassion of a crocodile."

Leona paused to think. Graham watched her patiently. She brought to her mind the night SEAL Team 6 took out Bin Laden. Their coded message to the U.S. president was, "For God and Country, Geronimo, EKIA [Enemy Killed in Action]."

Leona interrupted her pause to search her memory out loud. "I met Grimes once. It was in the field, of course," said Leona. "Does he just kill people or is he effective at gaining intelligence?"

"Oh, he's effective all right. In Afghanistan he plays both hands in the game of drug poker. One hand he plays is the contract he won from the Pentagon's Narcoterrorism Technology program. With this U.S. contract he supplies the National Interdiction Unit of the Afghan police with sniffing dogs and narcotics officer training."

Graham sipped his wine, then continued. "And, in order to make himself indispensable to the intelligence community, he plays a second hand. He has recruited a couple dozen cocaine dealers from Juárez, Mexico, right across the Rio Grande from El Paso. He transported them to Afghanistan and put them in contact with the poppy farmers. Opium galore! This provides Grimes with intimate access to the Afghan underworld right along with access to Taliban and other sources. The Mexicans keep the profit in exchange for passing to Grimes what they learn from the farmers and traders."

"Yuck," growled Leona.

"It gets worse. When these Ciudad Juárez druggies settle a big deal and find themselves loaded with profits, they want to celebrate. They celebrate with a ritual they'd practiced at home. They kidnap a young Afghan woman, usually a teenager and a virgin. They rape and murder her. In the process, they bite off the nipple on the left breast. When dried, they put it on a chain they wear around their neck. They collect these like Hurons used to collect scalps."

Leona winced. She sat unmoving, taking in the horror, not knowing exactly how to react. "So, Grimes sponsors this. Does Budenholzer?"

"We don't know what Budenholzer knows or prefers not to know. Still, Grimes could not do what he does without Budenholzer's permission, or at least passive permission."

"I gather that Grimes would like more money for more killing, er, ah, I mean more national security?"

"Yes, it looks that way."

"We should redesign the American flag. Make it simpler. Get rid of the blue and white. Soak it red in the blood our nation sheds around the world. That's the true color of America."

"Oh, come on! I won't stand for that kind of talk, Lee, despite what Grimes does. The blood shedding is not a national policy. It's done by mavericks or renegades, former soldiers who get out of hand."

Leona sat, silent.

"Now, Lee, I need a name. Who is the fifth column in Tehran secretly blocking the nuclear program?"

Leona looked aghast. "Well, for the sake of Atlanta, that's for me to know and you to find out," she said, mimicking a fourth grade girl.

"I'm serious, Lee."

"I'm even more serious, Graham. Officially, I don't even acknowledge that I have such information. Please remember that I've had my come-to-Jesus moment. I quit the CIA. I quit my complicity in such shenanigans. I'm now a pastor, not a spy. In addition, even if I were a spy, I would not divulge such information. Giving you or anybody such information would undoubtedly subject this alleged person to exposure and execution. Such snitching would confront our world with a merciless *nuclear terrorism*, which might last in perpetuity."

Graham stood up with a gasp of frustration. He excused himself to visit the upstairs toilet. Leona, sensing that the conversation was far from over, poured two more glasses of cabernet sauvignon. She was staring out the picture window when Graham returned to his seat on the sofa.

"There's more, you know," he said.

"I guessed there might be."

Graham picked up his glass, allowing light to filter through the cab's translucent ruby color. His eyes shifted from the glass to Leona, then back to the glass. Finally, he set it down without drinking. He thought. He hesitated a moment, then spoke. "CUB is no longer merely a list of competing businesses. CUB has become its own organization. It's almost like a labor union. It's bargaining collectively for higher wages, so to speak. CUB claims to hold the key to America's security. What this means, of course, is that CUB is actually holding America's security hostage. The negotiations look like a ransom demand. Your friend in Tehran is quite possibly a threat to Iran's nuclear success. And more, a threat also to the ability of CUB to negotiate contracts with the CIA."

"I'm starting to get the picture. So, you're here to get the information from me. Then you'll sell it for a high price to CUB. Right?" Leona's sarcasm shot like an arrow.

Graham hesitated, wondering if he should respond like a wounded puppy or with aggressive sarcasm. He did neither. "I can see that I've won over your complete trust."

"Much is at stake. I've got good reason to deny you my trust."

"Much is at stake right here in Chicago, Lee. Not only on the other side of the globe or in Washington. As I said, it would not surprise me that what you thought was a purse snatching was in fact an attempt to kidnap you."

Although Leona seldom found herself confused, she felt she needed some private time to sort out what she was hearing from Graham. She politely asked him to leave. The two bid one another good night, and Graham headed for his car at the front end of the parking lot. Leona retrieved her jump rope. Graham was driving through the lot and turning into the alley when Leona took her first jump. Within seconds the rope was flying at such a speed it was invisible.

14 /TUESDAY, CHICAGO, 10:29 PM

LEONA'S JUMPING was interrupted by the ringing of the parsonage landline. She wrestled with herself momentarily. "Do I stop jumping and answer it or…?"

"Hello. Trinity Church."

Leona could barely hear the panicky and muffled voice of Harriet Bolstad. "Pastor, it's Harriet. I'm in my kitchen. He's got Lars. Someone's got Lars in the living room. He's got a big knife. He's demanding that Lars give him money. He doesn't know I'm here."

"Did you dial 911?"

"Yes, the police are on the way. But what if they come too late? What if…?"

"How many intruders are there?"

"One. I've only seen one."

"Can you leave without being seen?"

"Yes. But I can't leave Lars."

"Harriet, stay right where you are. Don't make a sound. I'm coming."

LEONA'S LEGS carried her up the stairs at three steps in a bound. Right behind her bedroom door her fingers addressed a small numeric console on her wall. She typed in a code, then heard a muted buzz. A large dresser drawer opened automatically. Within the drawer lie an array of firearms, bullet clips, and ammunition. Some were wrapped in carrying bags. One was a small bore target pistol; a single shot .22 caliber. This was her baby. With only a half ounce trigger pull, it had won Leona a trophy in marksmanship. The .22 was lying next to a Magnum .357 double action revolver, both atop a wrapped M5 assault rifle. She grabbed her Kimber Super Match II .45 with a sound suppressor. She pressed an eight bullet clip into the handle. A second loaded clip went into her pocket. The weapons drawer closed and self-sealed.

In a flash the running pastor was out the front door. Left. Into the alley. Right. Then north until she reached 79th Street. She turned left and ran two blocks to South Saginaw. Then right. The Bolstads lived on Marquette, but Leona wanted to approach the house from behind. Her ears picked up the sound of police sirens as she ran.

Leona located the house directly to the rear of the Bolstads'. She ran up the driveway and through the backyard. After scrambling over a fence into the Bolstad yard, she paused. She drew in a deep breath while peering through the Bolstad rear window. She could see Harriet safe but frightened with her ear to the living room door, listening. Leona did not announce herself to Harriet.

As silently as a rabbit, Leona crept around the south side of the house. The megaphoned voice of a male policeman ordered someone to "drop that weapon." At the house's front corner she positioned herself behind an evergreen, an almost perfect Christmas tree. She observed three police cars in the street in position for a stand-off.

On the porch, now lit by spotlights, Leona sized up the situation. Lars was in the grip of a black man: tall, unshaven, and apparently also in a panic. He held a large knife at the front of Lars' throat. Lars stood frozen, fearing a jerk that might end his life.

"I said drop that weapon!" reiterated the spokesman for the police. His voice was electronically magnified, so it boomed in intensity. The spinning and flashing lights created a crisscross of strobes that would intimidate the bravest of attackers.

"I don't want to hurt nobody. But I will," challenged the captor. His face expressed confusion, perhaps panic. "You stay back, or I will."

"If you put down the weapon and put your hands up, you won't get hurt," responded the megaphoned voice. "Step away from the hostage, and you won't get hurt."

The police continued to engage the hostage holder with threats, threats they could not back up because they could not get a clear shot from the street. The would-be robber was temporarily in power. His power over Lars' life gave him the authority to shout orders, or so he thought. The cracking in the captor's voice suggested unpredictability. He might kill his captive in panic, as a last ditch effort to feel a sense of power. The threat was ultimate and immediate.

In her hiding place Leona exacted the self-discipline of her training. Though the adrenalin was raging, she took a few deep breaths to regulate her heart beat. She lowered it. All of her senses and all of her thoughts became utterly focused on one thing and one thing only: the situation. Without actually making a calculated decision, Leona found herself pointing her gun at the assailant's forehead. From her angle the bullet could go right through the man's cranium and out the other side without hitting Lars. Such a shot would be like threading a needle. Much too close to the hostage for anyone with less self-confidence. But lack of confidence in the face of crisis was not Leona's weakness.

Leona walked the target through her gunsights. The Kimber was held in her right hand, with her left supporting the right wrist. Both rested securely on the crotch of a tree limb. She took careful aim. She waited for the split second in which the captor's head would be positioned so that...she squeezed the trigger.

Ordinarily she would fire twice in rapid succession. In this case it was a single shot. Her prey was stunned and stiffened by the impact. Still standing. The knife fell. Then his body slowly crumpled. Lars shrank out of the way. Immediately, the police fired four more rounds, perhaps one from each officer's gun. It happened so quickly, no one could be certain who had fired round number one. Each recruit for the Chicago PD acquires a Glock 17 or 19, but vets select from other options, including Berettas and Smith & Wessons. The variety of bullet holes in the body would not likely raise a question at autopsy.

The body had hardly hit the porch by the time Leona had scooped up her spent shell and was racing to the rear of the house. She tapped rapidly on a window to get Harriet's attention. Harriet unlocked and opened the kitchen door and let Leona in. "Lars is fine, Harriet," she whispered. "Now, listen. Tell everybody that I've been here for half an hour. Got it?"

Harriet nodded, not knowing if she should feel joy or confusion. The two women entered the living room from the rear at the same moment a policeman entered from the front. "Are you all right? Was anybody else hurt?"

"My husband!?" screamed Harriet.

"I survived, my love." Lars stumbled through the front door and grasped Harriet with a hug of relief.

"I was petrified." Harriet said.

Two officers searched the house and pronounced it secure. An ambulance arrived. Other cars arrived. A detective asked Lars, Harriet, and Leona to sit while he wrote up the case. Lars and Harriet held hands. Leona only nodded her head as she listened to the story as told by Mrs. Bolstad. While Harriet [and Pastor Lee] were in the kitchen, they reported, the front doorbell had rung. Lars answered. A man, perhaps thirty or something, asked for bus fare back to his home in Oak Park. Lars turned toward the living room, ostensibly to find some money. The beggar raced through the front door and flashed a large knife, demanding that Lars turn over his wallet and any money he might have stored elsewhere. He asked Lars about other people in the house and Lars wisely told him he was alone.

Harriet had caught a glimpse of the living room activity through the ajar kitchen door, but she wisely stood perfectly still. Pastor Lee, it was said, had not actually seen anything. Lars seemed to be moving too slowly for his captor. After Harriet had telephoned 911 and sirens were heard, the lone bandit took his hostage to the front porch to negotiate his getaway.

The questioning took an hour, interspersed with apologies from Detective David Ragland, a fifty-year-old who combined courtesy with focus. His slightly rumpled brown suit probably fit him at thirty-five, but no longer. "I'm sorry to put you through more stress after what you've just been through," he would say on occasion.

Leona tried to remain obscure, something difficult under the circumstances. When Detective Ragland asked her questions beyond how she was related to the family and happened to be in the kitchen, Leona took the initiative. "Do you know Jaraslov Schmucynski?"

"Doya mean Ol' Shmoo?"

"Yes, Ol' Shmoo. Is he still with the department?"

"No. He's retired. But he couldn't give up. So, Ol' Shmoo now works for night security at Macy's in the Loop.

Ragland and Leona traded a few memories. But Leona declined to say exactly how she and Shmoo had known one another.

Although it seemed an eternity, the interrogation was finally completed and the police officials began departing. Ragland announced that some lab personnel would be gathering evidence from the front porch for a while. But the family could head for bed.

In the quiet that followed, Leona looked the Bolstads squarely in the eyes. "I'm sorry that I pressured you to stay in this neighborhood. It's been selfish of me. I so wanted you to support my ministry at Trinity. But you've paid your dues over the decades. Enough is enough. You can't stay. Lars, find that house in Naperville. Then, get the hell outa here!"

The three hugged. Leona bent her body slightly so the hugging hands could not feel the gun concealed in her back waist.

———

Leona walked home. From one point of view, all had gone well. Her experience as a sharp shooter had been an investment that she could still capitalize on. Lars was safe. Harriet was safe. Even though they were filled with fear, at least they were alive and could greet a better future in the suburbs.

From another perspective, this was a moment of deep grief. She interrogated herself mercilessly. Had Leona's first shot been the one to end that man's life? Or, had she merely stunned him, making it one of the four subsequent shots that did the final job? Did it matter? In her mind, Leona had just taken a person's life. A man was now dead because of her. This was a man she probably had never met. Like the dead squirrel she found on her porch, he was one of God's creatures. The desperate man with the knife carried God's image, the *imago Dei*. And Leona was responsible for the ending of his time on earth. Leona did it. No one else. Or did she? Even if it were her bullet, would the fact that, legally, her act of shooting him was in defense of an innocent life salve her conscience? No. I'm a killer, she said to herself. Was this the first? Would it be the last?

Could the killing be justified? She talked it through with God in a walking prayer. *Suppose I had not answered the phone? Suppose I had kept on jumping rope and simply listened to the phone message after everything was over? Perhaps then, Lars would be dead. No, that won't work.*

Suppose when standing at the tree I had simply refused to fire the gun? Suppose the police would have successfully killed the hostage taker without my help? In that case, I would be innocent. But then one of the cops would be dubbed the killer. No, all of the cops as a group would be responsible. No, actually, the hostage taker himself would be responsible for his own death. This is getting me nowhere. Lars lives, that's what's important. Right? Amen?

So many questions about what might have happened had Leona refused to take action. But Leona had acted. And now history could not be written any other way. Innocence was not an option.

15 /TUESDAY, CHICAGO, 11:58 PM

WALKING the alley from 79th to the Trinity Parking lot was a familiar route for Leona. Nevertheless, not for a moment did she flag in alertness. Once she thought she heard a trash dumpster lid slam down. But when she turned she saw nothing unusual. On another occasion the rustling of leaves drew her attention. But again, no reason for alarm. She did not notice two shining eyes staring at her from the far side of the parking lot. They blinked once, then disappeared.

Leona arrived on her front porch without incident. Even though she'd left the house door unlocked in her hurry to get to the Bolstads, nothing seemed out of place. Crossing her parsonage doorstep, however, she was threatened with a sense of foreboding. Moments ago she was calm, focused. She had retained her composure while struggling with danger and guilt. Now she felt an uncontrollable dread, but not over what had just happened. Rising up in her was an old fear. An old trauma wrestled for a hold on her soul. She tried to muscle her emotions into control through sheer willpower. *Get a hold of yourself. You are home. Here. In Chicago.*

Leona stood upright, took a deep breath, then warily flitted from room to room, turning on lights and checking closets. She returned to the kitchen, filled the electric teapot with water, and found one last bag of chamomile tea. She climbed the stairs and made a nest in her bed.

Before allowing herself to fall asleep, Leona called Graham on the phone. She told him how she had responded to Harriet's phone plea, that the police had shot the suspect, and that the questioning had taken such a long time. No mention of who fired the first bullet. Graham was aghast, but grateful that Leona had survived without injury.

"I think I should stick closer to you," said Graham. "Before you go out tomorrow, please let me know. I want to, well, come along as you go about your day's work. Okay?"

"Yeah. That's okay. Good night."

Leona checked her watch. It was past midnight. Was Leona ready for bed? No. Jitters kept her body restless. Her conscience was in turmoil. Though ordinarily it would be too late for phoning east, she hit the speed dial for Angie and turned on the bedroom LED screen.

Angie's phone rang three times, "Hullo," Angie said with a slow and deeper than normal voice.

"It's Leona. Sorry to wake you. Can we talk?"

"Sure. Just a minute." Angie slid her feet to the floor and walked away from the bed where Harry was snoring. In the next room she switched on her LED. Soon the two were looking at each other on Skype and ready to talk.

"Can anybody else see me?" Angie asked.

"No, of course not. You don't need to brush your hair for me."

"What's up?"

"I think I may have just killed a man."

"What?"

"I shot a man in the head. He died immediately." Leona followed with a recounting of the incident.

"Will you tell the police?"

"No. It would help nothing. At this point the cops think they're responsible for saving the Bolstads. I don't need the complications."

"How do you feel?"

"On the one hand, I think I did the right thing. My CIA training provides me this mechanism: when I click it on, my nerves firm up. I call it my machine mind. Once I flip the 'on' switch, my body and mind synchronize for one and only one thing, my job at the moment. No heart. My heart departs when I click on the *machine mind*. I think clearly. And I'm as invincible as steel. I was able to perform like a professional in a crisis. On the other hand, when I switch off the machine mind and flip on my *human heart*, then the denied feelings come roaring to the surface. Angie, I've shed blood. Not innocent blood, but blood just the same. Who can wash this blood from my hands? It'll be hard for me to sleep tonight."

"Remember, Lee, I saw you when your machine mind broke down. When you returned from Tehran, you were like a Mercedes that had hit a bridge abutment at ninety. Your parts were splattered, irreparable. You were totaled. And your heart was broken too. For months you seemed unfixable. You did not begin to re-integrate until you made the decision to go to seminary. It does not surprise me that you might be double-minded after what happened this evening."

"Angie, I could not have done without you during my recovery. You were so present for me. I treasure all those days when you would read me a poem or a passage from scripture. You helped me put my mind back together with my heart. I owe you my present life, Angie."

"You don't owe me anything, Lee. Remember, girlfriends last a lifetime."

"I won't forget."

"Back to tonight. How secret do I keep this, Lee?"

"Totally secret."

"You probably don't want to let me in on Graham developments, eh."

"Not now. Simply know that I did not and will not tell Graham about what I did tonight."

"Gotcha. Grahams come and go but a girlfriend lasts a lifetime."

"Dare I say, 'killings come and go, but a girlfriend lasts a lifetime?' Sounds terrible, doesn't it." Leona went silent for a few seconds. Angie patiently waited.

"Angie, one more thing before we hang up. Have you seen mom lately? I've not had time to call her."

"I see your mother every evening. On TV of course. I wouldn't miss the *Karen Foxx Spotlight Show*. She interviewed Detroit's mayor tonight, Keith Steinke. She gave him a rough time. She challenged him fiercely for not inviting enough new industry into Detroit. On the other hand, she turned to the viewing audience to tell Detroiters to help their mayor revitalize the Motor City. She's a crusader for Detroit. She closes every show with Detroit's motto in Latin, *Speramus meliori, resurgit cineribus*. It means: 'It will rise from the ashes: we hope for better things.' However, it's not gonna rise. Detroit's hopeless. When everything's finally blown away, she'll still be standing wearing a Tigers' cap and waving a white victory flag."

"That's my mom for you."

"The Germans say, *ein Apfel fällt nicht weit vom Stamm*, which means something like an apple doesn't fall far from its tree trunk. I think that applies to you and your mother."

"You do, eh. I gather you've not seen her in the neighborhood."

"Only on the tube."

"Well, I'll have to bite the bullet and call her. Too late tonight, though. I have to say goodbye now."

"G'night."

"G'night."

After hanging up, Leona sought solace in sleep. But it did not come easily. She offered an audible prayer to God, an anguished prayer in which she told God both sides of her story. "Come on, God, iron out the wrinkles. Why do I have to have such a tortured soul? Why can't you deliver me some internal peace? I've lived up to my side of our bargain. I'm now an ordained pastor. I'm now a shepherd guarding your flock. Why do you call me—literally call me—to blast someone's brains out? Why can't my little church be the city built on a hill, the beacon of light showing the world the path toward godliness and community and peace? For Moses, you led the people of Israel with a mighty arm and an outstretched hand. For me, you're holding your providential hand behind your back. Why? All I can do is give you my 'whys,' God. Amen."

She gained little comfort from this. Her eyes remained wide open. She fell asleep even before those eyes closed.

16 /WEDNESDAY, CHICAGO, 7:15 AM

LEONA'S CELL phone rang at 7:15 the next morning, Wednesday. Leona was in the midst of her morning wake-up ritual, including her meditation on Psalm 32. She found in verse 3: "When I refused to confess my sin, my whole body wasted away, while I groaned in pain all the day long." Then she quizzed herself. *I'm ready to confess my sin. But I still groan in pain all day long. What's wrong with this picture?*

"Hello, Lee. This is Hayim" said the voice on the phone.

"Hi, Hy. How's my favorite rabbi?"

"Are you all right?"

"Yes, of course. Why do you ask?"

"Nancy says you made the morning news. You were a witness to a robbery or something on South Marquette last night. The guy got killed. That's why I'm asking if you're all right."

"Oh, that. Yes, I'm not hurt. The Bolstads are members of my congregation. They didn't get hurt either. Everything's okay, Hy."

"How many miles are you running these days?"

"I've been able to get in ten or even twelve on a good day."

"That's almost far enough to make it to Hyde Park. Make it a good day today. Why don't you come by the apartment for brunch. Nancy's got eggs and toast. No bacon. Sorry."

"That's an invitation an impecunious pastor just can't turn down. Give me an hour and a half. I'll be ready for orange juice when I get there. Ya got kosher orange juice?"

"We've got a gallon. See you shortly."

After dressing in a freshly laundered jogging suit, Leona headed down the stairs to the front door. On the porch she was greeted by another omen. A dead crow. Again, the neck was broken, perhaps from vigorous shaking. The crow found its burial plot in the garden next to the squirrel. With her mind on the crow funeral and the scheduled visit to the Levys' for brunch, Leona forgot about phoning Graham.

Leona's jog took her north, past the South Shore Cultural Center and on toward 55th Street. She could not shut off her mind; so she could not enjoy the beauty of the lakeshore. Like a cinema, her mind kept playing and re-playing the scenes from the evening before. The shock she had experienced after the event was over was superimposed on each scene as she viewed the course of events again. Like Lady Macbeth's cry of forsakenness, "out out damned spot," Leona could not cleanse the blood spot in her conscience.

Despite the unsteadiness of her mind, her body jogged rhythmically on. The tall brick apartment buildings in the neighborhood to her left provided their residents with spectacular views of Lake Michigan. The inhabitants included faculty from the University of Chicago and the Catholic Theological Union, as well as retired couples from Loop businesses.

Leona turned off the lakeside trail and headed inland toward the apartment constellation. In one of the building lobbies she found the familiar names: Hayim and Nancy Levy. She pressed the button next to their name. A voice greeted her and unlocked the elevator.

As soon as the elevator doors closed and Leona had begun her ascent to the twelfth floor, another figure quickly entered the building lobby. It was a young man, a Caucasian, twenty-five, bearded, overweight, yet wearing athletic clothes—a gray and maroon sweatsuit. He bent over to study the list of residents. His face indicated he had found what he was looking for. He took out a cell phone and typed carefully into his calendar, "Hayim and Nancy Levy, Apt. 1220." A moment later he was gone.

17 /WEDNESDAY, CHICAGO, 9:15 AM

As the brunch chatter dissipated and the three were sipping their coffee, Leona turned to Hayim. Hayim and his wife, Nancy, were at that age when they think about retirement, grandchildren, and recreational travel. His hair was turning from gray to white, while the color of Nancy's, aided by a talented stylist, was close to the color it had been decades earlier.

"Now, my favorite rabbi...," Leona paused. "You know how grateful I am to you for helping me through the dark night of my soul back when you were a visiting professor in Berkeley. You provided pastoral care to my other student colleagues as well. We'd make you an honorary Lutheran if you'd eat lutefisk."

"Hey, I eat gefilte fish. Isn't that good enough?"

"No, that's just bad enough."

"Nancy and I listen to *Prairie Home Companion*. Doesn't that qualify us as Lutherans?"

"Why would you find Norwegian Lutherans worth hearing about?"

"It's about small town life. We know what that's about. What happens in Lake Wobegon happens in every small town."

All exchanged warm smiles. Leona continued. "Well, can we lower the iron curtain of confidentiality?"

"This sounds private," said Nancy. "Should I go to the kitchen?"

"Actually, Nancy, your wisdom might be helpful too," said Leona. Nancy settled in.

"What is it, Leona?" asked Hayim. "We've got plenty of hot coffee."

"I'm only a morning two-cupper, but today I'll take a coffee refill whenever it's offered." Leona filled the two in on the events of the week, including Graham's suspicion that she might be subject to kidnapping. She even confessed to the secret shooting of the bandit the night before. She took her time, providing many details. "As you know, Hy, this is not for public sharing. Only you and my friend Angie know the whole truth about me."

"The iron curtain of silence has been drawn, right, Nancy?"

"Right," said the rabbi's wife.

"My soul is aching," said Leona. "I feel like I'm a killer. I'd feel this way whether I pulled the trigger last night or would have let Lars die at knife point or let a Chicago cop pull the trigger or…Oh, I don't know how to make peace with myself."

The rabbi said nothing. He looked into Leona's pained face with compassionate eyes of understanding.

"I keep going over it and over it in my mind," Leona said with her eyes now directed toward the floor. "I'm a killer. But if I had not acted, then Lars would be dead rather than the bandit. I'm the one who made the difference. At least I *think* I'm the one who made the difference. But it doesn't really matter whether it was me or not, does it?"

The look on the rabbi's face revealed that he knew she was not asking for an answer. He waited. Leona continued looking at the floor, thinking. A minute passed. Then, she looked up at Hayim and their eyes connected. He knew it was his time to speak.

"I think you've been thrown into your destiny, Lee. But you also had your freedom. You were free to wait for the police. You didn't need to run to the Bolstad house. You chose to do so. You freely embraced your destiny. This is who you are. This is the Leona I've come to know. This is the Leona I've come to love, I might add." Nancy nodded an agreement and looked directly at Leona's sad face.

Silence reigned, but not for long. "Peace, Hayim. Peace!" she exclaimed with a fist thumping the table.

"Your loss of peace occurred many years ago, Lee. Not just last night. You might think of it this way. You were trained to kill by some of the most professional assassins on our planet. You learned well. Could it be that God was a good steward of your talent last night? Might God have placed you in the line of fire at the right moment to provide, shall we say, salvation for the Bolstad family?"

"Good try, Hy."

"It's more than a try, Leona. It's good theology. Remember, God's got a pretty messy world to work with. A conscience-plagued soul combined with unflinching courage might be one of the tools God uses to clean up part of the mess."

Leona looked at her favorite rabbi with a slight smile, expressing gratitude. Then, she changed the subject. "I live alone, you know. I needed to tell somebody. Thanks. Now I need to think something through. I don't know how these various events are related, if at all. Yet, here's my question."

"Should I fill your coffee cup before you drop the big question?" asked Nancy. Leona shoved her cup across the table and allowed it to be filled. Then she turned toward the rabbi.

"Should I take steps to protect myself? I want to focus my time, my energy, my prayer, my psyche on my ministry and only my ministry. If I give my attention over to these events—and if these events mean nothing in themselves—then I could be wasting valuable resources needed for my parish work. I don't want to cheat my sheep."

"Do you think you can trust this guy, Graham?" asked Hayim.

"No, not yet. Maybe in the future. He's too new and too suspicious to have earned my trust. For all I know, what he's said might be a big ruse to get some information out of me, some information too dangerous for me to have shared even with you. But you didn't need to know the political stuff. I'm rambling here. No. I'm not ready to declare Graham an ally."

"Leona, your safety is important."

"Thanks, Hy. But if all of this is nonsense or coincidence, then my safety is not really at stake."

"The risk is that it might not be nonsense or coincidence. The risk is that someone associated with this CUB, or whatever it is, wants to kidnap you and force you to divulge who the secret anti-nuke guy is in the Iranian government. If contractors kill foreigners on U.S. government whim, they're certainly capable of roughing up, if not murdering, our domestic friends."

Leona could only sit thinking, while her eyes gazed out the Levy picture window at Lake Michigan. "Beneath the surface of the glistening waves," she said, "there's a war going on. Big fish are hunting and killing and eating little fish. The little fish are hunting and killing and eating insects and frog eggs. All a frog egg wants to do is hatch and give to the world the life of a new frog. Yet, its chances of survival are one in a hundred. From the moon, Earth's atmosphere looks like placid Lake Michigan. Yet, what's under the surface is war—relentless and merciless war."

"I'll drink to Lutheran pessimism," said Hayim as he raised his coffee cup.

Leona smiled. "And God loves the whole goddam creation and all of us in it." Her cup met his. Then she clinked with Nancy as well.

"I'll drink to Lutheran grace too," pronounced Hayim. The three clinked cups again.

Shortly before midday Leona was back at street level, walking to let the remainder of the brunch digest. When she reached the lakeshore, she could see that the asphalt trails had increased in human population. A few elderly couples on a stroll. Young mothers in groups of two or three chattering while pushing jogging carriages. Dog walkers. Within ten minutes Leona was up to speed, jogging south.

As Leona passed the Museum of Science and Industry at 59th Street, a fellow jogger approached her from the front. The jogger was a teenager, an African American high school girl—*why is she not in school at this time of day?*—running with such short steps that she was hardly moving. The amateur jogger was wearing the appropriate sweat clothes, but it was clear that this exercise was new to her. *Maybe she's out here on a gym class assignment?* As the two neared one another, the teenager smiled and hollered, "May I ask you a question?"

The two stopped to face one another. Over the girl's shoulder Leona caught sight of a man perhaps two hundred yards distant. He was a heavy-set bearded man in a gray and maroon sweatsuit, walking in their direction. With one eye on the strange man and one on the teenager addressing her, Leona said, "Sure."

"My fingers are all swollen up," the young lady complained. "They're puffy."

"Let me look at them," said Leona. She grasped the girl's hands and tenderly touched random fingers on each hand. "Have you been jogging long?"

"About a half mile. Actually, I run a little and walk a little. Is there something wrong with me?"

"No. When we exercise like this, blood rushes to our extremities. Feel my fingers."

The teenager grabbed a number of Leona's fingers. "Oh. They're puffy too."

Leona kept one eye on the suspicious man in the distance. "When you get home and relax, the puffiness will go down and you'll be normal again. I promise."

"Oh, thank you very much!" exclaimed the girl with a relieved smile. The two parted. Leona jogged southward. As she hit her stride, she saw that the maroon man had begun jogging too, but at such a slow pace that Leona wondered if this would even count as exercise. He was coming toward her. *Is he carrying something in his left hand?*

With each of Leona's long strides, the distance between the two joggers shortened. His eyes fixed on her. Leona noticed two other men sitting on a bench. She anticipated that her path and that of the burly jogger would cross near the bench. Her intuition tapped her on the shoulder. She was alerted, but she did not let on.

Suddenly, a swishing sound behind her. She glanced over her right shoulder. Nothing unusual. Then, to her puzzlement, she saw on her left a large dog falling into rhythm, trotting at her pace. A Siberian husky, perhaps a year or so old. The dog stared business-like straight ahead. As the gap closed, the fur on the husky's neck stood straight up. He snarled at the bearded jogger heading her way.

The two Caucasian men wearing sweat shirts and sunglasses had been sitting stiffly on the bench. They stood up. The bearded jogger panicked at seeing Leona's canine protector, reacting defensively to the husky's snarling. His left hand—carrying what looked like a twelve inch pipe—waved at the two men, who then sat back down on the bench. Leona passed through the now opened blockade. The dog stopped to growl at each of the three men in turn. Then, the husky ran south to catch up with Leona.

Slowing her pace only slightly, Leona looked back. She saw the three departing the lakeshore together, heading toward a parking lot. She turned her gaze back to study the dog. The husky ran with her for another hundred yards. Suddenly, he was gone. Leona finished her run by herself.

18 /WEDNESDAY, CHICAGO, 11:31AM

WHILE PASSING the 24/7 Coffee Shop on 79th Street, Leona noticed a hand vigorously waving at her through the window. It was the hand of Carter Hansen. She interrupted her jog to enter the shop, where Carter, along with Brad Kuhn, was sitting at a table, each enjoying a cup of coffee, both white with cream. "Can I buy you a cup?" asked Carter.

"Heck no," responded Leona. "I've been jogging. Gotta have a gallon of water! I'll get it when I get home."

"Sit down, Pastor," ordered Carter. Then he shouted while waving his hand again. "Waitress, please bring this good woman a large, very large, glass of your vintage water." Carter received a nod from the smiling waitress.

"Carter thinks he can help me grow up right," began Brad. "He's telling me what to do when I become full-time with the Chicago PD. That's tomorrow."

"You look full-time to me already," remarked Leona approvingly. "Your belt's equipped with an entire arsenal. Is that a Glock 17 in the holster? Stand up."

The uniformed man rose to his feet while Leona pretended to study him. "I see a cartridge clip; a pair of handcuffs; mace; a baton, a radio phone; and even a bottle of drinking water. Even a two ounce bottle of Purell. You're ready for battle, my good man. Doesn't all of this mean you're an official cop?"

Kuhn smiled. "You seem more proud of me than ol' Carter is. He's telling me the ropes." Brad sat down and sipped his coffee.

"Yeah, Pastor," added Carter. "I'm lettin' him know what it's like to have a career in law enforcement. Here's the secret advice. Get fat. Don't exercise. Drive around in one of those Victoria squad rolls. Wear your battle rattle even when you're driving. This'll make your back go out. Once your back is sprung and useless, then apply for disability and retire. You'll make more in retirement that you did on patrol."

"Now, Carter, is this what you learn in church?" asked Leona with a motherly expression.

"It's what I learn from watching the lazy bastards in blue. It's a lesson of life."

Brad began laughing. "I've got the picture. Don't worry, Pastor, I'll take charge of my own soul."

"Brad," asked Leona, "why do you carry a bottle of Purell? Do you want to be a cop with clean hands?"

"I wondered that too. It's not standard issue. But some of the veterans at the academy said it's good to carry this. If we suspect someone is intoxicated, we wash our hands in hand sanitizer and then administer the breathalyzer test."

"Brad! Do you know what that does?" gasped Leona.

"Huh. Whatya mean?" Brad looked puzzled.

Leona continued. "Hand sanitizers are typically seventy percent alcohol. If you wash your hand in that stuff and then administer a breathalyzer test, it's sure to test positive. Everyone you test, no matter how sober, will look like a drunk."

"Really?" said Brad, trying to comprehend. "But...'"

"Now, Brad, I just wonder what your mentors are teaching you," said Leona. "What else have you learned in your police academy training?" Leona's disapproving frown forcibly changed to a contrived smile. "Any tips for a pastor?"

"Actually, Pastor Lee, the counter-terrorism training was very interesting. They brought in experts. One was a guy with Special Forces experience. He's a contractor with NSI, the National Security something or other. What he had to say was fascinating."

"What was so fascinating?"

"What he had to say about Muslims. Some people think Islam's a religion of peace. But this guy made it clear that the peace stuff is just a smoke screen. Muslims are out to get us. Make no mistake. We in law enforcement gotta be on the lookout for the signs. We gotta stop 'm before they get us."

Leona sat back in her chair. She sipped her water. "What else, Brad?"

"What if ya see black guys in red tams?" said Brad.

"So, what if I do see 'em?" quizzed Leona.

"That means blood," said Brad, as if teaching a first grade class. "We all know that. Now, if ya see a Muslim with a head band, what does that mean? Well, the color of the band doesn't matter. It means the guy is ready to become a martyr. 'I am ready to be a martyr,' that headband says. He's ready to blow himself up and everybody around him." Brad shook his head as if he had made a dramatic point.

A quizzical expression took over Leona's face. Hanson watched the conversation, directing his vision to whoever was speaking.

Brad continued, confident he had the floor. "Muslims will not rest until the entire world is Muslim. We in America are stupid, because we're politically correct. We want to deny this truth about Islam. But the truth is we gotta defend ourselves."

"But," interjected Leona, "how do you cops on the beat get involved? Islamic terrorism is, well, an international thing. Isn't it?"

"Oh, no, Pastor Lee. It's everywhere, even in the U.S. We were shown pictures of how terrorists cut their beards into V-shapes. We were told to watch DMV registrations for Arab names. We were told that some of these people open up small stores and businesses so they can launder money. When we in local law enforcement spot such suspects, we're supposed to report what we see to Fusion Centers. They pick it up from there."

"Brad, did this guy distinguish between combatants and noncombatants among Muslims?"

"What?"

"Oh, never mind." Leona thought for a moment. "Brad, are the only terrorists we need to fear Muslims?"

"Of course." Brad sipped his whitened coffee.

"Mmmmmm," mumbled Leona. "What if you in your police work found evidence of a terrorist plot? Do you think it might be possible that the terrorists are not Muslim? Maybe they'd be...oh, I don't know...maybe some Americans with...oh, I don't know...some motive?"

"Pastor Lee, I'm not getting at what you're driving at."

"Oh, never mind."

Water finished, it was only a few short blocks to the parsonage.

Once home Leona allowed the steaming hot shower to pour over her long after she had shampooed, soaped and rinsed. This water was soothing, healing, relaxing. The conversation with Hy and Nancy consumed her thoughts, and she offered silent prayers of gratitude for friends who understood her so well. She wondered whether she should worry about Brad Kuhn's worldview. She placed her face fully into the water's force.

After her shower, Leona wrapped her body in a large, white plush bath towel, a luxury that she felt served to prepare her for facing an often demanding day of parish ministry. She vigorously rubbed her hair dry with another towel, as she casually relocated to the bedroom.

She proceeded to ready herself for the day, first slipping into her black clerical shirt and collar, and then her new black suit, this time with the slacks. She stood tall in front of her closet door mirror and examined the outfit with satisfaction. The jacket was custom-designed with an interior zip pocket that allowed her to carry a gun without an obvious protrusion. She slipped her Kimber neatly into the pocket and again examined herself in the mirror, nodding an affirmation to her own reflection. *Just for today. Just in case I need to protect myself.*

The LED on the bedroom wall flashed. It was a text message from

Graham: "Call me." Leona lifted up her mobile phone. She hit Graham's speed dial.

"What's up?" asked Graham. "I've been trying to get hold of you. Do you remember our agreement?"

"Sorry. I forgot. I'm headed out for afternoon calls. Got some people to visit in hospitals."

"What if I would come along?"

"Sure. Pick me up at my gate. We'll go in my car."

19 /WEDNESDAY, CHICAGO, 1:54 PM

GRAHAM SLID into the front passenger seat of Leona's red Ford Escape hybrid. Leona reported the jogging trail incident. "Any sight of the Evanston Cleaners van?" Graham asked.

"No. But then, I wasn't looking for it," she said.

They both puzzled over the curious entrance and exit of the dog during Leona's jog.

"I've just had a thought. Could it be, no, it just couldn't be, that the eyes that glow in the parking lot belong to this guardian?" Graham mused further. "Might angels come in the form of a dog?"

As they drove north on Lakeshore Drive, a black high riding Chevy Tahoe zipped by them in the left lane. "In a hurry, ain't you, sister?" exclaimed Graham, as if directly addressing the speeding driver.

"Graham, control yourself," cajoled Leona.

"Let's catch up and see if we can read what that rod's got printed on its rear window," said Graham. Leona hit the accelerator. In a moment Leona and Graham were tailgating the speedster. Across the large rear window of the Tahoe were two messages for all who would eat its dust. The first read, "NO! This is not my boyfriend's truck!" The other read, "Bad ass girlz drive bad ass toyz." Both Leona and Graham could not help but laugh out loud.

"I sure as hell don't want to tick off the driver of that baby," said Graham, chuckling. "If she only knew just what a *real* bad ass girl I have sitting next to me."

Leona glared at Graham. "No comment, Mr. Washington." Graham thought he perceived a slight coquettishness hidden in Leona's glare.

On the fourth floor of the university hospital Leona and Graham called on Ulla Stigaard. Leona asked the near century-old patient if her new friend, Graham, would be welcome during the pastoral visit.

"Yes, of course," said Ulla in a sweet, yet frail voice.

The two visitors sat down facing Ulla's bedside. Ulla thanked Pastor Lee for coming, reporting how her sight was almost totally gone and that she felt lonely in the blackness. She could hear the voices of her two visitors, but she could at best just make out their shadowy forms.

Leona opened with the expected health questions.

"The doctor tells me that it's terminal, Pastor. There's no turning back from cancer at this stage." Then Leona spoke silently with her hands on Ulla's shoulder, not her voice.

Ulla continued. "I don't expect to leave this hospital. But I've lived for ninety-nine years on God's good green earth. I have nothing to regret. I'm ready to go home. I only wish there could be less suffering on the way."

Graham reached out and placed his hand on Ulla's. Ulla's scraggly skin was marked with brown spots and raised blood vessels. She remarked, "Now, that's a good strong hand. It's comforting." Ulla batted her blind eyes at Graham. "Pastor Lee, is this your new boyfriend?"

"No," Leona responded quickly. "But Graham is a very fine man. Any woman would be glad to have Graham as a boyfriend. You have good taste, Ulla." Leona turned her face to Graham.

Ulla smiled. Graham smiled.

Leona turned back to the blind woman. "Ulla, you say you're lonely in the darkness. How do you pass the time? What do you think about?"

"I recite passages from the Bible. When I was a little girl we spoke

Norwegian in our home. I learned so many passages by heart. After this many years, I can still recall them. I remember them in Norwegian, not in English. It comforts me to say them over and over."

"I bet you know the 23rd Psalm," said Graham.

"Yes, of course."

"Can we hear it? Or, can we at least hear what 'yea though I walk through the valley of the shadow of death" sounds like in Norwegian?"

Ulla composed herself, almost as if she were on stage.

"Herren er min hyrde, mig fattes intet. Han lar mig ligge i grønne enger, han leder mig til hvilens vann. Han vederkveger min sjel, han fører mig på rettferdighets stier for sitt navns skyld. Om jeg enn skulde vandre i dødsskyggens dal, frykter jeg ikke for ondt; for du er med mig, din kjepp og din stav de trøster mig. Du dekker bord for mig like for mine fienders øine, du salver mitt hode med olje; mitt beger flyter over. Bare godt og miskunnhet skal efterjage mig alle mitt livs dager, og jeg skal bo i Herrens hus gjennem lange tider."

A tear migrated down Ulla's cheek, glistening as it reached her chin. She wiped it away with a worn linen handkerchief embossed with the letter 'U'. Leona tenderly touched Ulla's left cheek with her right hand, gently kissing the other cheek.

After exchanging emotional goodbyes, Leona promised to return soon. Graham and the pastor departed Ulla's room. Leona checked her cell phone calendar. "Now, down to the 2nd floor. Got a teenager with a broken leg."

"I'm at your side, Pastor."

Once in the elevator, Leona looked up at Graham. "You possess genuine pastoral skills, my friend the spy."

Graham shrugged with a hint of embarrassment.

"A killer who cares. Mmmmm. Quite a combination." Leona was smiling.

"Who said I was a killer?"

"Well, it goes with the territory, doesn't it? Once you've given your soul to the red, white, and blue, then you're ready to pull the trigger. Right?"

"Lee, sometimes I think you're much too cynical. How can you...?"

The elevator stopped and the doors opened. Graham's left hand reached out and settled in the small of Leona's lower back. Ostensibly this was a gentleman's guiding hand granting the lady's right to go first. Yet, it was more. Graham felt erotic electricity in this touching. He kept this minimal body contact longer than perhaps warranted. Leona accepted the tactile contact without acknowledgement.

The two marched into Room 2210. A thin but husky African American teenager looked up from his bed, "Pastor Lee! How's it goin?" The two shared a vigorous handshake, curling thumbs and gripping wrists. "Who's the new dude?" he asked, nodding in the direction of Graham.

Leona introduced the two to each other. "Hey, Bro," said the young man, who introduced himself as Romeo Davidson. All three could not help but look at Romeo's right leg in a plaster cast and slung a few inches above the other.

"I broke it during football practice," said Romeo. "Got whacked crosswise reachin' fer a pass. The leg's set. It'll take a few more days before they'll let me stand up with a walker or crutches. Caught that pass, by the way."

Unexpectedly, the hospital room door closed on its own. When Graham and Leona looked over their shoulders, they became aware of two others in the room, two African Americans standing behind the closed door.

"I want ya ta meet Gator and Meat Hook," said Romeo.

The two smiled slightly and mumbled, "How's it goin'?"

"They're my bodyguards," Romeo continued.

"What do you need bodyguards for?" Graham queried, somewhat bewildered.

"The Kenwood Apostles are tryin' ta recruit me. Tryin' real hard, if you know what I mean. I want to be independent. I want to play football, not gangbanger." After a pause, Romeo's eyes widened. "Want to sign my cast, Pastor?"

"Absolutely." Leona took out a ball point pen and wrote, "May you always walk with the Lord! P.L." She added a smiley face.

The body guards had little to say. The lively Romeo engaged the visiting pastor and finely dressed black man on various topics for ten minutes. Then, Gator's cell phone rang. Romeo's rang as well. The room was buzzing with conversations as Leona and Graham said their goodbyes.

20 /WEDNESDAY, CHICAGO, 5:01 PM

AFTER THE HOSPITAL VISIT, Leona wheeled onto 60th Street and proceeded toward the lake along the Midway. Her car's Bluetooth speaker signaled an incoming call.

"Hello," she said with strength in her voice sufficient to be picked up by the ceiling microphone.

"Lee? This is Justin Hurley."

"Hello, Good Bishop. To what do I owe the honor?"

"By this time you must've met Graham Washington."

"Yeah. I met your watchdog. Graham is sitting right next to me as we head from Hyde Park toward South Shore."

"Graham, is that you?"

"Yes, Bishop. I'm here with Leona. How are you?"

"The question is: how are you? And more importantly, how are things going between you two?"

"Bishop," interrupted Leona. "I've got some questions for you."

"Let me provide you with some answers before you ask," said the bishop's voice over the speaker. "But first, is anyone else in the car with you?"

"Just the two of us," said Leona.

"Good. Please don't record our conversation. It's just between us and just for this moment. Okay?"

"Okay," sang the duet in the car.

"Here's what I know. I received a phone call from Gerhart Holthusen. Gary's the new CIA director. We're both Oles. Dat's pronounced 'Oh-lees,' doncha know? Sometimes 'Stolies,'" said the Presiding Bishop with a lightness in his voice, which contrasted dramatically with his concern for confidentiality.

"Yes, I know you're both Oles," said Leona. "That St. Olaf bond is pretty darned strong."

"Are you an Ole, Leona?"

"No. I went to Michigan State. I'm not even Norwegian."

"Well, if you went to Michigan State, might you be a Finn from the Upper Peninsula?"

"No. Not Finnish either."

"I'm Creole," interrupted Graham. "Anyone care about that?"

"Creole?" The bishop sounded excited. "That's African, French, and indigenous, isn't it? Did you trace your roots, Graham?"

Leona interrupted. "Now, Bishop, is this what you do at Higgins Road, spend your time taking an ethnic census? I've got some urgent questions that need answering."

"Right, Lee. Back to my story. Gary phoned about a matter he considered very secret. He warned me that one of my pastors might be in danger. *You.*"

Leona winced.

The bishop continued. "Gary told me he wanted to provide you with protection, but he needed a cover. This operation could not look like a CIA activity. So, we worked out the details for Graham to take a newly created position here at Churchwide headquarters. Gary did not tell me exactly why you are in danger nor anything about the politics involved. He asked me to trust him. An Ole can trust an Ole. Lee, this is what I know."

"Are you asking me to trust Graham like you trust Gary?" Turning to Graham she asked, "Graham, I want to be sure you're trustworthy. Are you an Ole too?"

"Not only am I an Ole, I sang baritone in the St. Olaf Choir," said Graham beaming.

"Listening to your choir sing 'Beautiful Savior' runs shivers up my spine," said Leona. Then she smirked briefly and enunciated loudly: "Okay, Bishop, that's what you know. Now, what is it you don't know?"

"If I were Socrates I'd ask you: how could I possibly tell you what I don't know? If I could tell you, then I'd know it. So, by definition...."

"You told us you'd tell us what you don't know. This is not the time for a philosophy lesson," barked Leona.

"Graham, that Leona's a real sassy tiger, isn't she?"

"More like a tiger cub, I think. More like a docile lap cat who stretches her claws once in a while."

"A lap cat and a tiger cub are about the same size, but they have very different futures," added the bishop.

"Thanks for patronizing me, you two. Here's the point: you guys are the ones saying my life is in danger. I have to make some decisions here about whether I'm going to protect myself or not. If you've got something relevant to say, then say it!"

"Here's what I don't know, Leona," said the bishop. "I don't know how to measure the degree of danger you're in. Nor do I know its source. Nor do I know how long you might remain vulnerable. All I can say is that Gary sent Graham to us. It would be prudent if we took full advantage of Graham's skills as a...whatever you are, Graham. Don't go it alone, Leona."

"Are you speaking *ex cathedra*?"

"It's that other guy, the one in Rome, who's infallible. I'm simply telling you to be a good steward of God's grace and let Graham do his work. I don't want to wait until heaven to see you again. Do you get my drift?"

"Yes, good Bishop."

THEY SIGNED off and disconnected as Leona's Escape entered the South Shore neighborhoods. "Graham, I still don't know who you are," said Leona.

"Well, what do you want to know?" asked Graham.

"Start anywhere," Leona prodded.

"Let's see. I was born in New Orleans. Creole, as I said. Grew up with Mardi Gras, crawfish barbeques, red beans 'n' rice, and beignets with chicory coffee. Although most of the kids in my neighborhood went to Catholic parochial schools, somehow I ended up in a Lutheran grade school and then high school. As a senior, I won an academic scholarship—a full ride—to St. Olaf College."

"How did you survive the Minnesota winters?"

"By placing this bayou boy in the path of a Great Plains winter wind, I got to see what hell looks like when it freezes over. Even the devil departs Minnesota before Christmas."

"Probably goes to New Orleans in time for Mardi Gras. At least, that's what I hear." Leona smirked. "So, why the CIA?"

"I got recruited while studying. I was in my second year at Princeton Seminary when I was approached. The recruiter said they needed analysts for NRMs. You know, New Religious Movements."

"Domestic or abroad?"

"Abroad. Falun Gong in China, for example."

Leona slowed the car as they approached an intersection with a red traffic signal. In her rearview mirror she spotted a flash of green and realized that the driver behind her—a driver holding a cell phone to her ear—was approaching too fast to stop. Leona reacted. She hit the accelerator and swerved abruptly to the right. The screeching green Chrysler swerved to the left. It skidded to a stop in the middle of the road with its front fender just to the left of Leona's driver door. No collision. Leona took a deep breath.

"You dumb ass!" screamed Graham at the unknown driver of the wayward vehicle.

In a calm yet insulting voice, Leona spoke. "Graham, you've got to get a hold of your road rage."

"Road rage? Hell, Miss Goody Goody. The problem is not my road rage. The problem is that each car on the highway is driven by a fuckin' nincompoop. Now, that's an objective fact of life."

"Oh, is that true?" quizzed Leona with feigned naiveté.

"Yes, it's true. And you've got to stop being so goddamn nice. I want to see you give her the finger!"

"I'm sitting here wearing my clerical collar. Need I say more?" Leona turned and rolled down her window. The driver of the Chrysler had dropped her cell phone and was sitting still, shaken and temporarily catatonic. Seeing that Leona wanted to communicate, she lowered her window.

"Are you okay?" asked Leona.

"Yes, now I am," said the shaken woman.

"Close call, eh! But now it's over." Leona spoke in a loud yet comforting voice. "Maybe you'd like to leave your cell phone on the floor while you finish today's drive."

"That's for sure!" The woman's voice communicated gratitude. She slowly regained her composure. The phone remained where it had fallen.

Leona took a deep calming breath for her own benefit. Shortly, the two cars went their separate ways. Graham rolled his eyes and shook his head in mock disapproval.

Leona initiated the next verbal exchange. "So, you studied Falun Gong, eh. Are the gongers still embarrassing the Chinese government? Oh! That reminds me. I'm hungry. Chinese?

Graham paid for an order of Moo Goo Gai Pan and one of sweet 'n' sour pork plus brown rice take-away. They headed back to the parsonage and spread out their dinner on Leona's dining room table. They chuckled together when acknowledging that both preferred chopsticks over a fork.

"Does the presiding bishop have any clout with you, Lee?" asked Graham. "Or, do I have to hit you with the infallible pope? What happened to you in Tehran?

"I do my best not to lie, or even tell partial truths," Leona began. "I've promised not to speak of this. I'd like to keep that promise."

"I understand, Lee. But as you can see, it might help us analyze the situation, a situation that could mean life or death."

"I've seen enough of life or death situations. They no longer scare me. But I rail against them. I protest. I protest to God. But well, I'm digressing. You want my story, don't you?"

Graham nodded.

After a pause, Leona asked, "are you wired?"

"Of course not."

"Then, please place your cell phone on the table. I don't want to see the speaker switch on."

Graham complied. Graham would have acceded to any of Leona's wishes, so ready was he to learn about Tehran.

21 /THURSDAY, AFGHANISTAN, 7:01 AM

"Oh, I see you've got my Bible on your desk," said Jarrod as he entered the room, carrying a cup full of morning coffee. The heavy metal door closed behind him. Jarrod took a seat and crossed his legs.

The eyes of the man seated behind the large desk searched quizzically among the items strewn on his desk surface. He did not seem to find the alleged Bible. So, he sipped his espresso, holding the cup in his right hand while he turned his left palm up as if to ask, "What?"

"Right there," said Jarrod, pointing to a medium sized book from the U.S. Government Printing Office, *FY2009-2034: Unmanned Systems Integrated Roadmap*.

A large grin appeared on the face of the one enjoying a short whirl in his desk chair. "No doubt you've got it memorized. You probably can cite me chapter and verse."

"Just about," said Jarrod.

"Then, I don't have to read it myself. I can simply ask you: does it have the word of eternal life for us?"

"You could say that. If not eternal life, then certainly abundant life. It points us to the narrow way of the profit, that's f-i-t, not p-h-e-t. We're gonna make a killing."

"Killing, literally or figuratively?" he said with a laugh at his own cleverness.

"Probably both," continued Jarrod, responding with a self-satisfied smile. "It's clear from this bible that Uncle Sam is prophetic about the future. Our military's Combat Commanders or COCOMs will want more and more unmanned systems for such things as—and here's what they say—surveillance; signals intelligence or SIGINT; precision target designation; mine detection; plus chemical, biological, radiological, and nuclear reconnaissance. We've had our day with Predators, Reapers and Global Hawks in the air and PackBots and Talons on the ground. Note how it says that the future will need drones for 'Expeditionary Runway Evaluation, Nuclear Forensics, and Special Forces Beach Reconnaissance'."

"Maybe we won't need grunts anymore."

"Grunts will use drones to avoid soiling their uniforms with blood stains. They can use drones to kill accurately at a distance and remain antiseptically clean. Actually, it's not merely a question of avoiding risk to personnel. Unmanned systems are proving to be superior to troops in all three domains: unmanned aircraft systems or UAS, unmanned ground vehicles or UGVs, and unmanned maritime vehicles or UMVs. The Warfighter demand is going to grow, and our profits will grow if we're ingenious enough to cash in."

"So, just how will we divert the cash flow so that it fills up our bank accounts?"

"Here's the plan. Two businesses. The first will be Unmanned Security Systems Incorporated. We'll set up the factory in South Haven, Michigan. We can test the UMVs in Lake Michigan and both the UGVs as well as the UAS on the Sleeping Bear Sand Dunes in the northern Lower Peninsula. We've got our engineers working now on a design for aerial reconnaissance vehicles the size of a model airplane. We'll call it the *AirEye*. An AirEye could look like a bird, a crow or something harmless to those on the ground who spot it coming."

"A crow? Why not a hummingbird?"

"Bigger. AirEyes will be equipped with visual and audio surveillance capacity, which just might fit into a hummingbird-sized drone. However, we want to add low caliber single shot firing. Can you imagine an infantry soldier on patrol in an Afghan village or in the countryside? He walks. He doesn't know exactly what to expect. He launches his AirEye. It flies about twenty-five feet overhead and perhaps a hundred feet in front. By looking at a screen the size of a cell phone, he can see what's on the other side of the fence. He can see what's around the next corner. With the AirEye gun he could even take out someone lying in ambush."

"Why only one shot? Why not a magazine?

"The recoil will blow the AirEye out of position for a second shot. One's all we can handle. But if the shot is carefully aimed, it'll be enough."

"Gotcha. Any domestic application?"

"Can you imagine the following? Along the U.S. and Mexican border we'll demonstrate by directing our AirEyes to scout out drug traffickers. We'll make a big kill. Lots of publicity. Then police departments all around the country will line up to buy not only our technology but our training programs. Again, imagine: a police car with an operator sending our aerial drone through neighborhoods at ten miles per hour transmitting back visual and audio reports. When the cops see action, they go into action."

"Can we corner the cop market? Cops are already using drones."

"Here's our edge. Cops who are now using drones do so while on patrol. Once we've convinced the patrols that our AirEye is superior, then we can offer our complete Drone Center to a city. The Drone Center will be like a mini-airport. A small cadre of desk pilots will send AirEyes all over the area, gathering intelligence and watching what they see on monitors. When they spot a neighborhood needing attention, they will notify the closest squad car to look into it. So many of our municipalities are in a budget crunch. With AirEyes, cities can reduce their patrol personnel by fifty percent or more. They'll love our products, because they appear to save money."

The man behind the desk grinned.

Jarrod continued. "We've got a second plan too. Our second factory and business headquarters will be located in Tehran. We'll call the company Remote Intelligence Incorporated. Here we will design and build UAS drones for rogue forces. Recall what I said about adding firing capacity? Now, imagine this: an aerial drone the size of a model airplane guided from the ground that flies above buildings looking for snipers. Once a sniper appears on the monitor, the controller guides the drone around the sniper, sneaks up on the sniper, and fires a single deadly shot at close range. This is defense. The armed AirEye could equally be useful for offense. With our armed AirEyes, no politician in any country will be safe from assassination. Oil rich terrorists will line up to buy our products."

"What about jamming?" The man behind the desk held his chin in his hands. "Suppose an enemy finds our frequency and jams our remote control?

"We'll overcome that with the Lamarr principle," announced Grimes.

"Huh?"

"Ever heard of Hedy Lamarr?"

"Do you mean the movie actress?"

"That's the one."

"How does she fit in here?"

"Hedy Lamarr was born into a Jewish family in Vienna. Her name then was Hedwig Kiesler. When she became a glamorous beauty and starred bare-breasted in a 1933 Czech film, she was invited to the kind of parties where she got to know weapons developers for the German military. She overheard many discussions about torpedoes and how they worked. After she moved to Hollywood and changed her name to Hedy Lamarr, she led a second life as an inventor. During the Second World War, she developed a device to prevent the jamming of remote controlled torpedoes, hoping to sell it to the U.S. Navy. She synchronized the transmitter *and* the receiver in a radio control mechanism to change frequency simultaneously. She called it frequency 'hopping'. The Navy never actually used it. But she, along with a guy named Antheil, actually patented the proof of principle. In short, we'll just do a little frequency hopping. The jammers won't be able to catch up. No problem."

"Now, Jarrod, I see another problem. You equip the terrorists to outflank and outmaneuver the police and security forces. Great. But what if we make enemies and these enemies decide to use your technology against us?"

"Did I mention our third company?"

The two started to laugh at the same time.

"It'll be located in Fiji. That's where we both will be."

The dual laughter only increased.

"I like this talk of profit and cash," said the man behind the desk. "But I wonder if we should get our asses in gear."

"Okay," said Jarrod. He stood up and left through the office door. In the anteroom he addressed one of the men who served as office secretary. "Call Bagram Air Field. Tell our maintenance crew to ready the Cessna Ten to fly. We'll arrive in an hour and a half. We'll want to take off immediately. We'll refuel in London, not Dubai."

"Yes, sir."

Turning to Louie, who was sitting on the other side of the room, Jarrod said, "I'd like you to drive us to Bagram Field. Can you be ready to go in ten minutes?"

"Certainly," said Louie. "I'll gas up the Hilux." Louie disappeared up the stairway.

"The base will want to know what flight plan to file," interrupted the secretary. "Where are you going?"

"Tell them we're going to Midway. That's Chicago," said Jarrod

22 /WEDNESDAY, CHICAGO, 7:05 PM

GRAHAM HAD ASKED for Leona's story. She was finally willing to tell it. "This is going to be very difficult for me, Graham. If I decide in the middle to stop, will you respect that?"

"Yes indeed, Lee."

Leona opened by explaining how she had graduated Michigan State University with a B.S.. Then she added, "When I was a little girl I was fascinated with the question: is there life on other planets? So, I took the opportunity at MSU to go on for a doctorate in astrobiology. My thesis had to do with the need for all spacefaring nations to cooperate on planetary protection. I loved East Lansing. While I was there I was approached by a CIA recruiter. He encouraged me to use my biology to become an analyst. Only later did the idea of becoming an operative enter the picture."

Graham had seated himself comfortably on the couch, welcoming a lengthy monologue. Leona's shapely crossed legs set up a competition within Graham between what his eyes were seeing and what his ears were hearing. He had to work hard to remain focused.

"Why would you even consider service in the CIA?" asked Graham.

"I was young."

"You're still young!"

"As I was saying, I was young and had taken a real interest in foreign policy at MSU. I had patriotic feelings like most of us, and 9/11 reminded us how fragile peace can be."

"The fall of the twin towers shocked all of us. But not enough to prepare us for what would follow 9/11: two wars lasting for decades. How did this affect *you*?" Graham was trying to keep Leona talking.

"I wanted to make a difference. And to make a difference with the skills I had developed in natural science seemed to provide just the right opportunity. My work, I thought, could play a small but important part in America's service to the world, to establishing peace and justice everywhere on the globe. Making the world safe for democracy, you know. And especially protecting all of us from the proliferation of nuclear weaponry."

"You really thought that?" pressed Graham.

"Yes, I did. In addition, of course, the CIA recruiters introduced me to important people in the military and in Washington. I was impressed. They treated me like somebody with a significant future. I wanted to live up to their expectations. Did this happen to you too?"

"Precisely. The agency recruiters have a way of making an ordinary citizen feel important," commented Graham.

Leona went on to explain how she was recruited into the CIA initially as a lab researcher but later re-recruited for field operations. "I studied Arabic and Farsi during my intensive training. I learned hand-to-hand combat, electronic surveillance, and mind control. Among other accomplishments I became a marksman, a crack shot."

She looked him squarely in the eyes. "Now, Graham, I'm not bragging. I'm simply trying to inform you."

"Oh, yes. I get that. And, it's okay with me if you brag a little."

"I'll try to stick to the facts. I was told that with my feminine beauty on the outside and hardened skills on the inside I could become the perfect bait in a *honey trap*, a sexual arrangement to gain intelligence. Well, I had the cunning and courage to spring such a trap."

"How often did you spring the honey trap? What did you catch?"

"I'll not answer that. What's important, as we all know, is that the

9/11 attack in 2001, along with the wars in Afghanistan and Iraq, contributed to the construction of a new worldview, to a new way of understanding reality. According to this worldview, the American way of life is under attack from Islamic *jihad*. I read the Qur'an and the history of Islamic theology, focusing on those elements that seemed to foster violence in the service of Allah."

"So, you're both a biologist and an Islamacist, eh?"

"Sort of. Cram courses do not in themselves make one an expert in Islam. Immersion helped. But even so, I can still be sophomoric about what I think I know."

"Where did the CIA send you?

"After brief tours of only a month each in northern Africa and the Malay peninsula, I was assigned to The Islamic Republic of Iran."

For a momentary distraction, the two opened their fortune cookies. Both contained the word "happy" but neither of the fortunes left an impression.

"Back to Iran," said Graham.

Leona continued. "Before doing anything practical, I studied Iran's history. For five millennia this region was known as Persia. Persia made it into the Bible, with special mention of Cyrus the Great. Cyrus liberated the Jews from their Babylonian captors. The Persian Empire lasted from the sixth century before Christ until conquered by the Greeks in 330 BC. During the third century after Christ, Christianity spread like wildfire from the Middle East to Mesopotamia and up the Royal Persian Road to central Asia. Not many people know this little fact of history," said Leona reaching for her drink.

After a sip she continued. "During the Sassanian dynasty—which had replaced Greek rule with native Persian rule—many Persian leaders joined Christian churches. But then in the fourth century, Constantine took over Rome. He established Christianity as the state religion. Fears ran rampant in the non-Roman world. Persian leaders tried to distance themselves from Christianity. They engaged in massive persecution and marginalization of the religion of Jesus. Even before Muhammad's century, Christian growth in Asia had been contained. Muslims then conquered Persia in 651 AD. By the sixteenth century the land became a Shia stronghold. Although we in the West simply write off Persia as a Muslim country, the history is much more complicated and nuanced. Unless we get this straight, we'll never understand."

"That's Persia. Where does Iran come in?"

"With the Nazis. The Nazis persuaded Persian leadership to change their nation's name to Iran in 1935. The modern Persian term *Iran*, recalls the ancient pre-Persian term Aryānā, now a name given to many Persian girls. The word Iran is a cognate of Aryan. The country's name today, then, means 'Land of the Aryans.' *Fars* is the original Persian name for Persia. I learned to speak some *Farsi*."

"So, that's what you read. That's ancient history. Let's get to your history."

"Please be patient, Graham."

"Okay." Graham sat back and relaxed the muscles in his face.

Leona looked about the room. Then, she turned again to make eye contact with her visitor. "Once I arrived in Iran, the CIA Station Chief set me up with a post-doc slot at Sharif University of Technology in Tehran. I was strategically placed among an international group of laboratory faculty studying the effects of radiation on the human body. We learned that acute exposure is far less deleterious than chronic exposure, meaning that workers in a typical power plant are not likely to suffer permanent damage should they experience a brief nuclear accident. But this study was a cover. My unannounced goal was to gain intelligence on nuclear weapons development in that country. It was my task to make contact with the mystery person you would love to identify."

"Did you wear a burqa?"

"I dressed very conservatively. In fact, I liked the burqa and full body covering. This meant I could travel about in public without being recognized as a Westerner. I was seldom acknowledged as a foreigner."

"I'm glad you're not covering up now that you're back in Chicago," remarked Graham, looking up at the ceiling as if he were expressing secret and embarrassing thoughts.

Leona smiled, keeping her eyes aimed squarely at Graham. "I'll take that as a compliment. Thank you. Now, back to business."

Leona adjusted herself in the chair. Her voice dropped to a near whisper. Graham found it necessary to lean forward to hear clearly.

"When I was in Iran, it was difficult to measure the degree of threat. More recently, CIA fears regarding Iran's capability to develop a nuclear weapon have been exacerbated by progress in rocketry. In 2009, Iran launched its first satellite on a Safir-2 rocket. In 2011, its second satellite, Rasad-1, went into orbit. And, as you may know, Iran's also got the Shahab-3 missile, the one most likely to carry a warhead."

"Do any of these missiles constitute a threat to us?" interrupted Graham.

"No, not in themselves. None of these launch vehicles would be capable of sending a warhead to North America. Nevertheless, these events mean we have to watch both weapons development and delivery development."

"Is that what you did?"

"In my situation, I could not look into the missile matter. I had to zero in on uranium enrichment and weapons development. The lab work on rad exposure put me into contact with those connected to enrichment at Malek-Ashtar University of Technology, also in Tehran. The Iranian plan is to enrich the uranium 235 isotope. Out of the ground, natural uranium includes about one percent of the isotope. When enriched in centrifuges to 3.5% or even to 5%, you get fuel for a power plant. You need 90% or above to make a bomb."

"Why don't they just use plutonium 239? It's much more explosive."

"Because plutonium processing takes a big facility. Easy to spot by air reconnaissance. Uranium 235 facilities are smaller, easier to disguise. Here's what's interesting, Graham. They plan to detonate the bomb with an implosion. In the core of the warhead on top of the missile they'll put uranium 235. They'll surround it with a uranium tamper and an evenly distributed explosive. When it first goes bang, it implodes, compressing the 235 to critical mass. Then, boom! A really big bang."

"But with the 2016 stoppage of Iran's nuclear weapons development program, the world is now safe, right?"

Leona glared.

"Did you connect with our mole?" asked Graham.

"He's not a mole. He's not engaged in intelligence transfer to the U.S. or to any other international interest. Rather, he's a Muslim committed to world peace. And he believes his own nation is a threat to that peace. So, from within he tries to retard Iran's progress toward weapon development. You've probably heard of Stuxnet."

"Stuxnet? Who hasn't?"

"Here's what's important. Stuxnet is a computer worm, a weapon in the cyberwar. It appears that Israeli intelligence at Dimona in the Negev successfully placed this worm into Iran's computers at Nantanz, discombobulating the centrifuges used to enrich uranium for use as nuclear fuel in reactors. The speed of the Nantanz centrifuges must be modulated perfectly, because slight vibrations make the machines break down. Stuxnet was carefully designed solely for the Iranian system, to make these centrifuges run erratically. The vibrations caused them to break down. It wreaked havoc. This set back Tehran's ability to make its first nuclear arms for at least two years. Let me say that the person about whom you're speaking does this kind of work, but on his own."

"That doesn't answer my question. Did you connect?"

Leona ignored Graham's question. "Here's another interesting facet. The Nantanz computers are not connected to the Internet. So, how was the Stuxnet worm introduced? It must have been someone on site who used a USB thumb drive. Cool, eh."

"Would this person on site with the thumb drive be a spy for Israel? Is your mole friend connected with Israel's Mossad?"

Leona stood up. Then sat down again. She seemed to look over Graham's shoulder and out the window. In a voice that was obviously controlling an underlying impatience, she mumbled calmly, "What do you think of Mossad's euphemisms, Graham? I especially like the phrase 'better world' to refer to killing an enemy agent. Or, 'measles' for an assassination that appears to be a death by natural causes."

"Damn it, Lee! You're frustrating. I asked you if your mole friend works with Mossad."

"I will ignore the 'mole friend' remark." She returned to her sitting position, crossing her legs. She spoke with emphasis. "No. He's not connected with Israel. I tell you he is an Iranian and not an international stooge. Here's the problem. The CIA wanted me to offer our mysterious peacenik resources so he could more effectively carry out his sabotage. But I thought then, and still think now, that this could be the worst thing for us to do."

"Why?"

"Because he's been very effective in his anti-nuclear work to date. And, he's gone undetected largely because he has no international connections. Should we in the CIA establish such a connection, we might inadvertently render him more vulnerable to detection."

"Damn it again, Lee!" Graham raised his voice. "You're really good at not answering my questions!"

"By agreeing to tell you about my experience in Tehran, I did not agree to tell you absolutely everything."

"But knowing who this person is could be important. It could be important to protect him. Scientists in Iran associated with the nuclear program are subject to assassination. Perhaps you recall how in 2010 Majid Shahriari, the nuclear physicist, was driving on Artesh Street in Tehran. A motorcycle pulled up next to him. The guy on the cycle attached a magnetized bomb to Shahriari's Peugeot and then sped away. Boom. The bomb killed the scientist and wounded his wife and bodyguard. That could happen to your mole friend too."

"I remember the incident well. So, let's ask: who killed Shahriari and why? Two possibilities. It could've been Mossad trying to slow down arms development. Or, it just as well could have been the Tehran government itself, taking out one of its own. Scientists such as Shahriari have international connections. That's the nature of big science today. Perhaps Shahriari's loyalty was suspect. Perhaps Tehran thought it could get rid of this threat and blame the Zionists. Things can get pretty crazy in Iran."

"Regardless of whether it was Mossad or Tehran, your mole friend might be subject to the same treatment. I think you should tell me his name. Perhaps I could arrange for some protection."

"Graham, I've said passively, No! Now I'll say actively, NO! What is there about the word 'no' that needs further explanation? Shall we move on, or do you want to just end it right here?"

"Okay. Let's move on."

23 /WEDNESDAY, CHICAGO, 8:14PM

"The day came when everything went wrong." Leona sighed. She stopped talking and stood up. Her hands clasped each other behind her neck, pressing her own tense flesh. After a silent moment, she dropped back down into the La-Z-Boy. Her posture was erect.

"I was working in the lab, enjoying myself with a colleague and new friend, Mehdi Rashed. The lab doors flung open with a bang and in marched a half dozen police, perhaps the Ayatollah's guards. Everyone's head jerked to see what was happening. The officials came straight for me. They cuffed my hands behind my back and put a hood over my head. A thick darkness overwhelmed me. My heart raced. I became nauseated and sweaty. I was terrified. No amount of advanced training can eliminate that feeling of terror."

"Oh, my God, Lee!" said Graham shaking his head. He paused. "What happened then?"

"They escorted me out and shoved me into a van. I was thrown into the back. No seats. I was sprawled on the floor. They drove for an hour. Maybe longer. I lost sense of time and direction. I was delivered to a prison. To this day, I actually do not know which prison I was taken to."

"Could it have been Evan prison?" Graham bent his torso a bit forward, revealing a touch of urgency to his question.

"Probably was. But I simply don't know because of the blindfold."

"Did they harm you?"

"No, there was no physical abuse, if that's what you're asking. Just some bruises from the manhandling."

"Then what?" Graham laid back, resuming his more relaxed posture.

"When my hood was ripped off I found myself amidst a crowd of people in a room the size of a classroom. Undecorated institutional green walls. No windows. Cement floor. More than half of these bewildered people looked American. The others looked to be of different nationalities, some Iranian. Mostly men, but a few women. I'd never seen any of them before. A soldier climbed a low speaker's platform and addressed us in Farsi, and I know enough Farsi to have understood what he was saying. He said that all thirty of us were spies for the United States."

"Spies!" Graham exclaimed. "That's the excuse Iran uses when kidnapping foreigners and demanding ransom in the form of bail."

"No bail would help in my case. The guy went on to tell us that the foreigners among us were in the country illegally. He claimed that all of us were guilty of crimes against the Islamic Republic of Iran. He added that his government would be asking the American government to publicly acknowledge its responsibility for this reprehensible violation of international law. Once this public acknowledgement had taken place, then we would be freed and deported back to our home countries. I took this to mean that the Iranians among us would be sent to the United States, but I could not be certain how to interpret this."

"What did you learn? Did all thirty of you come from the same place?"

"No. From the murmuring I heard that day, these alleged spies were rounded up from all over Iran and brought to this particular place. I guess my name had been on the bottom of the list and was the newest in the arrested group."

"Then what happened?"

"The guy in charge stepped down to talk on his cell phone.

Perhaps an hour or so passed. We could talk with one another. Those I spoke to were clearly CIA. Then, Mr. Man-in-Charge stood up again. He reiterated in Farsi that we would be held in individual cells until the White House would personally confess to the world its mistreatment of Iran. Further...."

Leona's cheeks glistened with rolling tears.

"He said that President Akbar Golshani had already placed a telephone request to the White House and was awaiting an answer. We should hope President Andrew Dodge had better honor the Iranian request soon. Why? Because each day one of us would be executed until this request would be honored. Each of us in our cells would not know when we went to bed at night who would be the next one to be executed. We, who survived, would be told each morning which among us had been sacrificed."

24 /WEDNESDAY, CHICAGO, 8:34 PM

GRAHAM BEGAN to writhe on the sofa. But he did not interrupt.

Leona broke the silence. "It's going to get worse, Graham. Before we go on, maybe I should get us something to drink. If you need a bio-break, go ahead."

While Graham headed for the bathroom, Leona went to the kitchen to pour some wine, two glasses of cab. She placed some Italian crackers in a small bowl. After her turn in the lav, the two returned to the living room.

Leona leaned back in the La-Z-Boy. Then, she leaned forward once again and spoke with a deliberate cadence. "I was taken to my cell. Very small. Maybe six by eight. Only a low three-legged stool to sit on and a rusty bucket for urine and feces. The floor was wooden planks. Old. Musty. Dank. I slept on the floor with one thin blanket. Sometimes unidentifiable insects kept me company."

"What about food?"

"We were given an adequate supply of bottled water. Food once a day. Usually yogurt with some wedges of cucumber. The yogurt was nearly or already spoiled. I tried to eat it before it went rancid. I was successful only occasionally."

"What could you see?"

"Through the barred window in my wooden door I could see a few bare light bulbs hanging from the ceiling. Some were burned out. Those that worked were off most of the time. I had to endure the dark. The wall boards had a few separations, so I could see through the cracks enough to determine when it was night and when it was day. I had my watch, but my mobile was taken away."

"Did they interrogate you?"

"Almost daily. I would be taken to a small room. Two or three interrogators would question me."

"In English? Or Farsi?"

"English."

"Did you tell them what they wanted?"

"Yes. They threatened harm to the max. So, I thought, why not give them what they might already know. I told them about my background and my assignment."

"Did you disclose the, what shall we call him, saboteur?"

"No. It appears they were unaware of him. That was a relief. They never asked me. It was easy to avoid divulging anything about it."

"So, what else happened?" Graham asked.

"Our cells were lined up in a row with a single hallway leading to each door. We could not see the other prisoners. When the guards left us alone, I tried to engage in conversation with the occupants of the cell on my right and the one on my left."

"Did you get to know anything about them?"

"Yes. On my right was a woman, Aryānā Golshani. Her family name is the same as Iran's president. She was probably in her early twenties. She had grown up near Mosha, northeast of Tehran. When she was only nine, her father gave her as a bride to a neighbor, a deliveryman twenty years her senior. Part of the deal was that the husband would honor her virginity until at least one year into her puberty. He did not wait. She was raped. When she begged to go back home, she was beaten and held hostage in her new house. Because the community supported these arrangements, she had no oasis to flee to." Leona sighed. "Oh, Graham, I'm digressing, I think."

"No, Leona. Take your time. Any detail may be important."

"Well, as you can guess, I came to like Aryānā, *really* like her. Even though I could not see her when we were secretly talking through our cell walls, I remembered what she looked liked from the earlier gathering."

Leona picked up a tissue and dabbed her eyes. She placed a cracker in her mouth, but seemed unaware of the crackling noise it made during her chewing. Graham waited patiently until Leona spoke again.

"Here's Aryānā's story. When she was twelve, her husband was accidently killed in a truck accident. She was told about the death, of course. While the family was grieving, Aryānā escaped and ran to a courthouse. She asked to speak to a judge. She told the judge her story and pleaded to be returned to her natal family. The judge made this possible and, so, Aryānā went home."

Graham listened intently, filtering through his mind the precious personal qualities of this amazing creature sitting before him telling such a gut-wrenching story.

Leona continued. "Aryānā told her father how she had been mistreated. Then she demanded better treatment from her father. She told him she wanted to go to school. The father took pity on her. Maybe the father felt some guilt as well. Anyway, he made arrangements for Aryānā to attend school, an elite private academy. She excelled. She was eventually admitted to Sharif University where she studied linguistics with a major in English language and literature. It was there that she met a CIA agent—someone who had preceded me —and was recruited. Aryānā was angry enough at her own experience and feminist enough to rebel against her culture and against the political regime that supported it with police power."

"Her name is Golshani. Is Aryānā a member of the president's family?"

"Yes, but distantly. Too distantly for it to have made a difference. As you may know, Iran's president is only second in command. The Suprene Leader, the Ayatollah, uses the president and the executive branch to police Sharia, you know."

"Yes, I know."

"Well, as you can imagine, Aryānā was ripe for CIA recruitment. She had not been working long undercover when she, like me, was rounded up and imprisoned."

"So, who was on the other side of your cell?"

"In the cell to my left was Bruce Belk. At first, Bruce tried to tell me all this was an unfortunate mistake. He said he was in Tehran on a tourist visa, on vacation. He claimed he had nothing to do with the CIA and that his arrest was a miscarriage of justice. After the executions began, Bruce confessed to me that this had been a lie. He had been planted in Iran by the Station Chief, just as I had been.

"Executions? Did they...?"

"Yes, they did. But let me finish. Bruce was forty-eight. A wife and three daughters. He was working as a nuclear engineer at the Seabrook Nuclear Power Station south of Portsmouth, New Hampsire. He had previously served a stint at Los Alamos. His specialty was uranium enrichment. He had been invited by the Golshani government as a consultant on the Bushehr One reactor. This opportunity was too good for the CIA to pass up. Belk became a temporary agent. I think he underestimated the risk."

Leona paused, unceremoniously sipped her wine, and reached for another cracker.

"Go on," said Graham following suit.

"Now, to the executions. On the morning of the third day, the guards walked past each cell. They were wheeling a gurney. On it was a body. It was one of the men I'd seen but not talked to at the opening meeting. His eyes were open, staring upward. His shirt was ripped and he was bleeding from the chest and head in multiple places. I surmised he had been executed by firing squad. Maybe three bullets total. The guards made certain each of us knew that this man was dead because our president, the U.S. president, had not agreed to acknowledge us as spies in their country."

Leona looked down. She wiped her eyes with the back of her index finger. Then she continued. "It was a dreadful moment. This man was dead. Never again would he see his wife or children, if he had any. I adopted the logic of my captors: he died because our president in Washington was willing to lie to Iran and lie to the world about us. All he would've needed to do was acknowledge that we belonged to him; and then we could've gone home. Evidently, our president was willing for us to die rather than confess what was true about the CIA in Iran."

25 /WEDNESDAY, CHICAGO, 9:03PM

LEONA STOOD UP. She walked around in a small circle, then reached for a straight back dining room chair. She banged the legs on the floor, placing it with the back directly in front of Graham, who was still on the couch. She straddled the chair and looked her new confidant in the eye.

"Graham, I have a machine mind. I bet you have one too. It's a pattern of thinking and acting that is impervious to feeling. I switch it on when I've got a job to do. But when there is no job, I switch back to my human heart. Sitting twenty-four hours a day, day after day, in a dark and dank cell is not the right time for a machine mind. I was in my heart. And my heart was sinking, sinking into a black hole of unfathomable depth. I had no influence, let alone control over the needless deaths of these operatives who thought they were serving our country. Nor would I have any control whatsoever regarding my own fate. It's a form of excruciating mental torture, Graham."

"Yes, I know." Graham lifted his chin slightly, indicating he wanted Leona to continue.

"The next morning," Leona went on, "it happened again. The guards showed up shortly after dawn with another body. This time the executed man had been beheaded. His head was sitting next to his feet to dramatize the point. Again, we were told that this execution was unnecessary. It was due to our president in the White House."

"Ugh," muttered Graham.

"This became the daily routine. Each evening we would wonder: 'Will it be me they're coming for tonight?' Then, in the morning, we would see who turned up dead. Most were executed by firing squad. A few were beheaded. One was drowned. I began putting hash marks on my cell wall. Later, I discovered that others had done this too. On the morning of what would be the fourteenth execution, I tapped on Aryānā's wall. No answer. I began to fear what this meant. I tapped again, and again. No answer."

Leona began to cry out loud. Graham waited patiently.

"When the guards walked by with the gurney, it was Aryānā. Her head had been severed. She was naked. I could see some bloody wounds in her lower pelvis. I can only imagine what perverted cruelty they must have exacted on that poor girl." Leona began sobbing. Graham leaned forward and grasped her right hand in both of his. He waited.

"I can see why Ulla was so thrilled to have you hold her hand," she remarked.

Leona removed her hand from Graham's and pounded the coffee table. "This went on for twenty-seven goddamned mornings!" She pounded the coffee table repeatedly, harder with each pound. "Twenty-seven! Twenty-seven executions! Bruce Belk died on execution day twenty-three. By that time he was petrified. I could hear him crying on the night they came to take him. Twenty-seven!"

"Who survived?"

"Me, obviously. The other two I came to know only on the trip back to the U.S. Whatever Washington and Tehran had agreed on, I simply didn't know then or even now. It came as a shock. Late on the evening of day twenty-eight, I heard the key slip into my lock. 'Oh, God!' I thought. 'I'm next'."

Graham winced again.

"My cell door banged open. At first the hall lights blinded me. This was it. I knew it. Two guards aggressively grabbed me and pulled a black hood over my head so I could not see. This had to be the procedure leading to torture and then execution, I thought.

"What then?"

"No handcuffs. Their strong hands clenched my arms, and they escorted me out. No one spoke to me. We walked the length of the corridor, and I thought of myself as dead woman walking. We exited through a door and I could feel the fresh outside air. I was thrust into the backseat of some kind of vehicle, perhaps another SUV. When the car stopped and I was pulled out, I found myself boarding a helicopter. Still only blackness under my hood, but I could feel the wind and hear the roar of the rotor. No one spoke a word. I remained mute."

Leona's two hands formed a single fist on the chair top. Graham reached forward and placed his left hand on hers.

"My hood was only removed minutes before we landed at an airfield, Mehrabad International Airport. Then I realized that there were three of us prisoners. Within moments we were rushed aboard an Emirates plane to Riyad, Saudi Arabia. From there a U.S. Air Force transport took us to Langley Air Force Base in Virginia. After a cursory debriefing, we were simply sent on our way. Simply sent on our way! Imagine that, Graham!" Leona paused. "I resigned from the CIA on my way out. My resignation was willingly accepted. The divorce was mutual. Uncontested."

"How did you feel?"

"At first it was a moment of grace. Exactly why I was spared has never been explained to me, at least not fully. But to have stared into the black hole of death and then to see the sun shine again, well, I don't have the words. It was the gift of life, the ultimate gift."

Graham slipped his hand away from hers, but their eyes remained locked on one another. "What a gift you are, Lee. God knew what he was doing when he spared you. Although I've only known you for a couple of days, I'm feeling grateful. Now, is that too schmalzy?"

"Yes, much too schmalzy and much too quick. But thank you, anyhow. You see, gratitude is not all I feel. I've also got some anger, anger big time. Although it was a moment of grace for me, I don't know what to think about the others: the twenty-seven who suffered such horrible deaths in that prison. It's so unjust. So unfair. So cruel. I feel as much anger as I do gratitude." And even more despair."

"It sounds like you're suffering from moral injury."

"Injury! More like moral obliteration! Before I went to Iran my moral metaphysic was as tight as the gears in a Grandfather clock. Everything worked together. It chimed precisely when scheduled. Then a demon on top of the John Hancock Building threw it off. I watched it go down and down and down, until I lost sight of it. But I know that when it hit bottom, it splattered across the pavement. It will never get put back together again. When my universe broke, my soul broke with it."

Leona looked away before reengaging. "Actually, Graham, it was the catalyst in me for a crisis of faith. How could I believe any more in America if my country—even in the name of global peace—would stand by and needlessly watch the shedding of innocent blood. And, what about God? God is bigger than America. I know that. But these persons suffered such cruelty and terror. I can't comprehend it. Where the hell was God?"

Graham was empathetic with the emotional Leona but felt he needed to press his business. "Who were the other two survivors?"

"I will not mention their names. I will tell you, however, that shortly after our release one committed suicide. He hanged himself. When President Dodge found out about the suicide, he summoned me to the White House. I was escorted by plane from Berkeley—actually Oakland—to Washington. That's how I first met the bastard of the Oval Office. We talked alone. I thrashed him over this outrage, this tragedy, this wanton sacrifice of twenty-seven human beings who were serving him and this nation. The blood of twenty-seven persons —actually twenty-eight by then—was on his hands. We did not see eye to eye, as you can imagine. He sent me home, actually back to seminary, with my sworn promise not to tell this story to anybody. Anybody! I have kept that word—almost but not quite totally—until this moment. Two others know. But I'm not going to tell you who either is."

Graham was shaking his head, eyes glassy. "Oh, Leona, what you've gone through. This is so painful."

"It's worse than painful, Graham. It's like falling into a pit, a pit with no bottom. Think of Aryānā. She was robbed of her childhood. Then, just when she made it to the university and had a glimmer of hope—some larger purpose in life—she was dismembered and left to die in ignominy. And this applies to all twenty-seven, twenty-eight counting the suicide. What does this mean, Graham? Does it mean we can't trust our president? No, something worse. Does it mean that the good ol' red, white 'n' blue is not worth shedding blood for? No, something worse. What does it mean? It means *nothing*. And this nothing doesn't just sit there doing nothing. No, this nothing is aggressive and vicious. It rises up and grips my soul and drags me down and down toward the abyss of meaninglessness. I think I now know what hell is."

The two sat quietly, neither looking at the other. A minute passed.

Leona spoke first. "Dirty, that's how I feel. Covered with scum."

"Lee, you did not pull any triggers. You did not perpetrate any violence. Others did the dirty work, not you. You were a victim."

"Victim or no victim, I feel contaminated by evil. You know how a woman feels after she's been abused or raped? She feels violated. But there's more. She feels polluted. Her innocence has been taken away by force. It doesn't matter that she's a victim, that somebody else has done the crime. I feel like I've been raped. Not literally, but figuratively. And I'll have to trudge through the rest of my life feeling filthy."

Graham listened. Fidgeting, he picked up the pillow with the Luther seal and placed it on his lap. He kneaded it, as if he were baking bread.

It was Leona who broke the silence. "When I returned from Langley to my family's home in Michigan, I fell into depression like a stone falling off a cliff. I was unable to talk about this. Couldn't sleep at night. Couldn't avoid a shadowy fear all day. Couldn't get the picture of Aryānā's severed head out of my mind. Sometimes I could hardly even pray about this."

"I can't even imagine what that was like, Lee."

"My road to recovery was long, rocky and filled with potholes. I was not alone on this journey; my mother and my best friend, Angie, steered me. When I finally turned a corner, I changed gods. I shed that idol, my country. I went to California to study in a divinity school. I apprenticed myself to the gospel and I prepared myself for ministry and for a higher calling. Even in seminary I had my doubts, of course. There I met Rabbi Hayim Levy who cradled my soul while I was spiritually twisted and rung out like a wash rag. Eventually I emerged a different person. Well, not completely different."

"I thought you went to a Lutheran seminary?"

"It was Lutheran. It was also ecumenical, because it was part of the Graduate Theological Union. Rabbi Levy was a guest professor, visiting one semester per year from Chicago."

"Oh. How are you different now, Lee?"

"I became a pastor, obviously. The work of a pastor is small, fragmentary at best. I no longer work out of a grand vision of collecting food to prevent starvation, or peace on earth, or universal justice, or saving the planet from climate change, or whatever. Rather, I work day by day to share just one little crumb of grace—just one eye-blink of love—with people whose lives are painful, brutish, and short. I have to leave the rest up to God, if there can be a God with this kind of world. I can't lift a single brick to build even a step on the porch of God's kingdom."

"Are you suffering from survivor's guilt?"

"You betcha. In spades."

"Do you believe that by quitting the CIA you're completely disconnected from what it did, or does? Are you innocent now as a pastor, whereas guys like me still in the service are marching under orders from Satan?"

"No. I don't believe that I'm innocent. Nor are cvic. Looking back, I think I now know what evil, even radical evil is. I've formulated Leona's Law of Evil: *You know it's the voice of Satan when you hear the call to shed innocent blood.*"

My point here is different. There's no way I can become disconnected from someone else's sin. I'm connected, whether I like it or not. I'm connected like every citizen of this nation or of any nation in this world. We all share in the violence at home as well as abroad. When I try to extend a helping hand, I'm fully aware that I have blood on that hand. It may be invisible blood, but it's blood all the same. Pontius Pilate fooled himself into thinking he could wash the blood off his hands. I try not to fool myself. I hope you don't try to fool yourself, Graham. I'm a killer, whether I pull the trigger or not."

"You pulled no triggers, Lee. That's clear."

"You're not reading reality, Graham. Sin isn't just my free action, just my trigger pulling. It's more than that. It's like lava flowing from a volcano that engulfs us. It engulfs the victims and the victors alike. What being connected means is that I share in the guilt of the killers in Iran and those at home who set up the circumstances for these twenty-seven, twenty-eight, deaths. Responsibility is like a virus—and I'm infected."

26 /WEDNESDAY, CHICAGO, 9:48PM

"Does Budenholzer know that you're in contact with me?" Leona asked.

"No," said Graham. "This operation has been planned solely by Holthusen. Even though Budenholzer is director of the Special Activities Division or SAD, he knows nothing. At least we think he knows nothing. Until he has more intelligence regarding who's involved, Holthusen will wait to bring Budenholzer in on this. No need to sound an alarm too soon. What we want is for CUB to show its hand before we slap it."

"Could Budenholzer himself be siding with CUB? Or, could he even be masterminding CUB?"

"As of right now, it appears he's innocent. *We* use the abbreviation, CUB. Budenholzer doesn't. Even though this acronym bears his name, it doesn't necessarily mean he's even involved. CUB appears independent. More than likely the bad guy is Jarrod Grimes. He knows how to assassinate without leaving a clue to trace anything back to the CIA. Maybe he knows how to organize without leaving a trace as well."

Leona thought for a minute. "If I get into a scrape and I cannot get hold of you, whom should I contact at CIA?"

"I'm afraid you'll have to go straight to the top. Ask for Holthusen himself. I'll give you the code if you're ready to memorize it?"

"Shoot."

"*Cyrus Twelve.*"

Leona repeated it to herself. "Cyrus of Persia, eh."

Leona escorted Graham to the parking lot. Graham took a risk. He held out his arms, offering a hug of solace. Leona collapsed into his arms, her head nestling on his coat lapel. Slowly she wrapped her arms around so that her hands could feel his shoulder blades. The embrace was relaxed. It lasted longer than ordinary departure courtesy would warrant. Graham kissed her lightly on the top of her head.

As Graham turned to walk toward his car, he remarked: "Do you see those eyes? There, watching you again. If it's a demon, then you're in for trouble. If it's an angel, then this might be a moment of grace."

Leona stared into the dark. She could barely perceive the flickering of two blue-white jewels in the garage's shadows. "Maybe we're being watched by a CUB spy. Does CUB hire four-legged spies?"

Graham saluted and departed. Although it looked like the end of the evening to Graham, it would not be for Leona.

27 /THURSDAY, PAKISTAN, 11:02 AM

INSIDE THE HOUSE Leona locked the front door. She turned around. Her back fell against the door and she closed her eyes momentarily, placing her mind in a dark silence, allowing a moment of mental refreshment after her emotional thrashing.

She drew the drapes on the windows and turned off all of the lights except one living room table lamp. En route to the kitchen she clicked the remote to turn on the large LED screen above the La-Z-Boy. "One more night cap," she said to herself as she poured the few remaining drops of leftover cab into her glass. She switched off the kitchen light and returned to make herself comfortable on the living room couch, her left elbow on the Luther pillow. She picked up her iPhone. 10:02 pm. "It must be 11:02 am in Lahore," she muttered. Then, she dialed a long series of numbers in Skype, thought by most to be an untraceable method of communication.

Leona heard a click on the other end, but no voice. Clearing her throat she spoke distinctly: "In the name of God, the Most Compassionate, the Most Merciful."

"Leona, is that you?"

"Yes, Muzaffar. Can you turn on your camera? I've got mine on."

The large LED screen flickered. The face of a man appeared: a fifty-year-old Pakistani man dressed with a snug white cap, white brocade shirt, and graying beard with glasses covering his face. "Oh, Leona, I can see you. Allah is good. I want to know how you've been?"

Leona Foxx and Muzaffar Haq exchanged family news and provided each other with respective health reports. Leona told her friend on the other side of the world about her parish work. They compared the weather in Chicago and Lahore.

Leona lifted her wine glass so Muzaffar could plainly see it. "I toast you, my friend." Then she laughed.

"If Noman were here, he would toast you. I'm the strict Muslim, you know."

"Yes, I know. I'm teasing you with my degraded Western values."

"To what do I owe the honor of this call?"

"I would like to say that I want to talk about theology. But alas, it's politics. Sorry. What can you tell me about Islamic fundamentalism in Pakistan? Is there any growth in sympathy for Iran's nuclear program? Official or unofficial? I know this is a complicated question, but I need to get a feel for the situation in your part of the world."

Muzaffar thought for a moment. "As you're probably aware, Leona, what you call 'Islamic fundamentalism' is undeniably growing in influence. For those of us here in the university, it is disruptive. We try to teach with critical consciousness, but our students voice rigidity and dogmatism. I don't know if they actually believe all they say, but they're encouraged to protest by their local imams. We Muslims have never gone through a version of the Enlightenment or Reformation like you have. We're stuck in the pre-modern world. So this kind of popular religiosity risks losing what academic substance we can offer. In my biology lab, I'm now challenged by creationists just as you are in America."

"Muzaffar, what do you attribute this to? Heightened spirituality? Is it healthy?"

"I wish I could say that, but it does not appear that way to me. It appears driven by cultural anxiety and power politics. For three centuries we've suffered from a sense of cultural inferiority in relationship to the West. Today, some of our leaders think that if we are faithful to Allah, then Allah will raise up his holy wrath against you and all your kind. The flames of this religious rhetoric are fueled and fanned by those who think they can gain political power through it."

"How does this cash out between Pakistan and Iran? Pakistan has the bomb. Iran does not. Do you—I mean do the rising Islamic rightists—want another nuclear power as your neighbor, even if it's an Islamic state?"

"This is a delicate one. On the one hand, Pakistani leadership wants to prevent nuclear arms proliferation. Any country, not only India, could use WMDs against Pakistan. On the other hand, some of my passionate Muslim friends believe that it is Islam—international Islam not divided by national boundaries—that makes up the people of God. For these devotees, a nuclear Iran would strengthen the people of Allah globe wide. I simply cannot predict how it will all shake out."

"Muzaffar, you're such a man of peace. This tense situation must keep you up late at night."

"I can only ask Allah to bring peace. And I do."

"Muzaffar, perhaps you can help me. I've lost some of my contacts in Iran. Might you know Qudrat Al-Damad? Do you know how to get hold of him?"

"No, I don't recognize the name. These days I'm not communicating much with our friends in Tehran. The email addresses keep changing, as do the phone numbers. No more Tweet chats. I don't actually recall meeting someone with that name. You might try going through the office of the Grand Mufti in Cairo."

"Well, I'm trying to be discreet. I'd like to make contact quietly, with no noise around it. Thanks anyway."

"Sorry to interrupt, Leona, but I have a student appointment shortly here in my office."

"May God be with you, Muzaffar."

"May God be with you, Leona."

Leona clicked off. She took a long slow sip of her wine, emptying the glass.

28 /THURSDAY, CHICAGO, 2:01 AM

LEONA HAD ENJOYED LITTLE MORE than two hours of deep sleep. Her parsonage phone rang. "This is National Security Officer Norman Hastings. Did I awaken you, Reverend Foxx?"

"Yes. What's this about?"

"Cyrus Twelve. Please put on your clothes and come downstairs. You'll receive further instructions."

"Wait! Who's...?"

The connection was broken.

She had heard the code "Cyrus Twelve." *Could this be a CUB trap? Shouldn't this code be private for only herself and Holthusen?* After puzzling about this for a few seconds, Leona stood up and threw on her jeans and sweatshirt. Almost unconsciously, she slid her pistol into her waistband. She simultaneously brushed her hair and teeth, then wrapped her hair in her signature pony tail while racing down the stairway toward the front door.

Loud thunder-like rhythmic sounds assaulted her ears. The house shook. The noise grew louder. She thrust the front door open. The roar became deafening. To her left she spotted a black SUV blocking her parking lot exit to the alley. Turning her head she saw another blocking the street exit. Men on both ends of the parking lot were communicating on radios or cell phones. Suddenly, she and her surroundings were bathed in an intense blue white light. Her right arm rose to her forehead to protect her from both the light and a blast of wind. Descending from above was a helicopter, landing in the almost empty parking lot.

One of the men on the ground approached her and shouted, "Are you Reverend Foxx?"

"Yes, I am. What's this all about?"

"Just a moment, ma'am."

ONCE ON THE GROUND, Leona identified a Bell 206B-3 Long Ranger IV. Norman Hastings, a tall man about Leona's age wearing a gray suit, escorted her by the arm to the open helicopter door. She pulled herself up and into the empty front seat and fastened the belt. After she boarded she noted that the pilot was a U.S. Marine. He nodded to her with a friendly salute. Behind her sat two men in suits, each with a radio wire running from one ear. The Long Ranger IV lifted off.

Through the windows Leona surveyed the scene below: neighbors exiting their houses and rushing to the helicopter landing site. *The noise must've awakened them*, she thought. *Maybe they think this is a police action?* She observed the plain-clothed occupants of the SUVs guarding the parking lot entrances talking with the neighbors. *Probably explaining the commotion. I wonder what lies they're telling.*

After only a minute, the black SUVs left their positions at each end of her shrinking parking lot. The floodlight turned off. Only the city lights of Chicago remained to offset the darkness of the night. It all happened in a matter of seconds.

What the hell is going on? Leona asked herself.

"Did Graham send you?" she asked turning to the two seated behind her.

"No," said the apparent security officer behind the pilot. "I don't know anybody named Graham. We were sent by someone else. You are completely safe in our care," he assured her. "It will only be a few minutes to our destination."

Climbing to a thousand feet the pilot shifted their direction to the east, over Lake Michigan. Leona took in the beauty of the city lights receding as the sky became darker. They turned north. Below and west Leona recognized the Adler Planetarium and, to its right, Buckingham Fountain. She felt the craft descending. *What?! Are we going to land on the water?*

Within minutes, Leona sighted the probable target: a Great Lakes freighter at anchor in the bay. It seemed to have very few lights compared to other freighters within view. Yet, as the descent progressed, it became clear that this would be the landing site.

The helicopter spun and rocked for a brief period, then went still. The engine cut off. All four passengers disembarked onto the ship's deck. Leona stretched, feeling the cool breeze of the water off Lake Michigan on her neck. Another security agent, perhaps fifty wearing a tie and a dark-colored windbreaker, approached.

"Reverend Foxx?"

"Yes."

"You have an appointment. Please follow me."

The two walked briskly on the starboard side toward the ship's bow, toward the cabin complex. Passing by two guards with machine guns, her unnamed escort stopped briefly. "I know you're pack'n heat. Would you please give it to me? I'll return it."

Leona complied. He knocked on a weathered and rusted steel door. The door opened a crack. He announced, "Reverend Foxx has arrived."

The door closed. Sixty seconds passed. Leona stood motionless. Her escort looked at her with an expressionless face. Finally, the door opened again, this time wider. A rather large plain-clothed security guard said, "The president will see you now, Reverend Foxx."

29 /THURSDAY, CHICAGO, 2:29 AM

ONCE INSIDE LEONA viewed a cozy but elegantly appointed office, complete with comfortable chairs, multiple LED screens and computers, plus a wet bar. Behind the desk sat President Andrew Dodge. On her side of the desk two other individuals stood up to greet her. She recognized the sixtyish woman on her left as Leslie Richardson, the Vice President. The man to her right she also recognized. It was CIA Director, Gerhart Holthusen.

"Welcome, Pastor Lee," said the president, now also on his feet. Perhaps you know Vice President Richardson and Director Holthusen?"

"A pleasure to meet you, Madam Vice President," said Leona. She turned right. "Nice to see you again, Mr. Holthusen."

"My pleasure," he responded. All took their chairs, Leona sitting center and facing the president. "Had I known I would spend the middle of my night with such an august gathering, I would have worn my new black suit. I bought it for this kind of an occasion. Now, I don't get to show it off. You'll have to accept me in my jeans and sweatshirt."

Grins appeared on all four faces.

"Why do I get the feeling that this is an important meeting?" queried Leona taking the initiative. The vice president seemed a tad surprised at how relaxed the new arrival appeared and how impertinent, perhaps? Holthusen's knowing smile only grew.

The president took the floor. He offered a perfunctory apology for disturbing Leona's sleep and for whisking her to an unknown destination and for any other inconvenience this might have caused her. Leona waited with growing impatience for the formalities to subside. The president went on to describe the Great Lakes freighter as an ideal secret rendezvous spot. No one in Chicago knew that the president was visiting his hometown. Well, not yet of course. He sought a few private hours for doing business before his official reception at City Hall, scheduled for Friday noon.

"How is your ministry at Trinity Church?" asked the president.

"With all due respect, Mr. President, I doubt if that is the reason you brought me here. Even my bishop wouldn't go to this much effort to find out about my ministry." Leona's body language was becoming increasingly icy. The vice president mirrored Leona with a corresponding iciness. She said nothing.

After an uncomfortable pause, the president looked at Holthusen, "Gary, would you please show our guest the file?"

"Certainly." Holthusen opened a manila folder and placed it on the desk in front of Leona. He opened it. The first item was an eight-by-ten inch photo of a man dressed in a pin-striped suit, salt and pepper hair, perhaps sixty. "Do you know this person?" asked the vice president.

"Of course I do," responded Leona. "This is Karl Budenholzer. I've seen him many times at CIA headquarters. I took orders directly from him on my first assignments. Why do you ask?"

"Just to be certain we're on the same page," answered Holthusen. "Take a look at the second picture."

Leona flipped Budenholzer's photo over to the left and studied the second one, that of a rugged soldier of fortune, dressed in a safari jacket. "This is Jarrod Grimes, of course."

"How well do you know Mr. Grimes?" asked the Vice President.

"Not well. I saw him once or maybe twice in the field, in Iran. That's all."

"Have you ever seen Mr. Budenholzer and Mr. Grimes together?" asked Leslie Richardson.

"No. Although it should not be all that unusual. Grimes works on contracts for Budenholzer."

"The next picture shows the two together," Holthusen offered. He sifted through the file and placed in front of her a photo of Budenholzer and Grimes standing next to one another. They were standing in front of a business jet, a Cessna Ten, sporting white shorts, turquoise polo shirts, sunglasses, and straw hats. "This shot was taken at London Gatwick. Probably a refueling stop."

Leona studied the photo. "I see each is wearing a light chain around the neck. What is that hanging from the chain?"

"Don't know," said Holthusen. "We amplified the photo to see. Looks like a piece of jerky, huh? Curious, eh?"

Leona's hands began to tremble. *Oh, I wish I did not know what I know. Her heart rate doubled. I've got to switch on my machine mind.* Seconds passed.

"Is there anything wrong, Lee?" asked Holthusen.

Everyone remained still. Holthusen bent to look compassionately into Leona's face. She turned slowly toward Holthusen and simply thanked him with her eyes. Then, she closed the file, straightened up in her chair, and faced the president. She said nothing.

"Frankly, Lee, we need your help," said President Dodge. "The situation in Tehran continues to be difficult. We cannot discern for certain whether Iran will soon be in a position to launch and detonate a nuclear weapon. Our intelligence remains ambiguous. On the one hand, video surveillance and other information suggest that Iran has not pursued bomb building since 2003. On the other hand, Tehran defied the 2006 United Nations resolution calling on Iran to suspend its nuclear enrichment program. Even with the 2016 announcement that Iran had dismantled its nuclear development program to make way for ending sanctions, we have good reason to think that weapons research continues. Somehow Iran has found a location we don't know about. Even though we cannot accurately assess the threat, we believe a threat exists. Despite the many years we have lived with this, the course of events is now beyond our control and even beyond our prediction. We need your help. That's why we've brought you here tonight."

"I gave you my help once. Remember?" The president nodded his head affirmatively. She continued. "I gave you my help and twenty-eight loyal spies, including Iranian assets working for America, needlessly died. They died at the hands of executioners, executioners who would not have shot or drowned or beheaded them if you would have intervened on their behalf. These were people who offered to help you. These were people who were willing to take risks because they thought they were working for a world free from the threat of nuclear terrorism. And you sacrificed them. For what? You're no further ahead now than you were when you were draining the blood out of your agents like an auto mechanic drains oil from a crank case."

"Leona, I tried to explain to you..."

"No explanations can justify what you did. And still today you think your shit doesn't stink. Well, let me tell you it stinks all the way to high heaven!"

At this the vice president stood up. "Young lady, do not talk to our president in this way! When we're in this office, we show respect. We need respect if we are to deliberate and move forward."

"Actually, Madam Vice President, I have a great deal more respect for our president than it may sound at the moment," Leona responded looking directly at Leslie Richardson. "I can't say the same for you, however. While you're spending four years in Washington as vice president, you've temporarily suspended your participation on the board of Texarab Oil Company. But you haven't suspended your company's profiteering, not only at the gas pump but profiteering from depletion allowances and outright government contracts. With your husband, General 'Bull' Richardson, in the Pentagon, you have a nice cozy push-me-pull-you."

"Just what do you mean?"

"Here's what I mean. The Pentagon pushes for increased military action wherever possible, and the procurement office buys more petroleum to support the troops. The president pushes for reconstruction of what we blow up in Afghanistan, Iraq, and whichever country comes next on the hit list. Who gets the re-construction contracts? Doberman Construction, a subsidiary of Texarab, that's who. In Congress you push our reps and senators for tax exemptions for large corporations so you can suck the life out of the tax-paying middle class and spend their hard-earned money on yourselves. All these *pushes* amount to a cash *pull* for you and your cronies."

"I don't like the sound of what you're saying, Reverend Foxx," interjected the Vice President.

"Nor do the citizens of Bagdad like the sound of 'shock "n" awe' or the families dying of starvation in sub-Saharan Africa like the sound of international silence. With all your wealth and influence, you could have considered investing in peace instead of war. Imagine how much better our world would be if the resources invested in bombs that explode only once were diverted into food aid for Africa's starving, aid that could have a lifetime of impact on those who survive? Instead of burning gasoline to move military trucks up the roads of Afghanistan, suppose you send these trucks to deliver food and medicine in Africa to those who need it?"

"Private enterprise exists solely to make profit," said Leslie, now fully engaged in the debate. "The free market simply responds to people's needs in an openly competitive way. It cannot on its own take up responsibility for charity, for giving to those unproductives who do not earn their place in the global economy. That is the responsibility of governments, or even churches." She grinned, showing satisfaction that she'd thrown in the word, "churches."

"But," replied Leona, rising to her feet but not rising to the bait about churches. "What if a government is motivated to be charitable but does not have the resources to spend on aid to the needy because its tax revenue has been turned over to special interests?"

"What are you talking about?" demanded the vice president.

Leona went on. "Please recall: shortly before the end of a previous presidency, our nation's leader decided to fill up American oil reserves. He paid $140 per barrel, the highest price at that time in history. When the reserves were full, the price dropped to a fair market value of $40. This was a form of pillaging our own nation on behalf of Texarab and other petroleum investors with their hands out for government welfare. Because of joint contracts between Houston and Riyadh, a torrent of cash flowed from the other forty-nine states through Washington to the Middle East and then back into Texas. The amount of profiteering has been obscene by any count. And now you, Madam Vice President, are in Washington to blow up the taxation and regulation dams that could slow the torrential cash flow."

"If what you say were to be true, Reverend Foxx, then I would be guilty of criminal manipulation of my office. Certainly you must be mistaken. This cannot be the case. I believe you are voicing your political opinion, not something factual. You belong to that effete group of losing liberals who blame international business for all the world's woes. Maybe you're even green. It's hard for me to take you seriously."

"What you call political opinion I deem to be a matter of grave moral concern," Leona exclaimed. "Last week a Chinook helicopter was shot down in the mountains bordering Pakistan and Afghanistan. Two dozen casualties: six Afghan regulars and eighteen Navy Seals. The bodies of the Seals were brought back to America, and our president here met the caskets at the airfield. He announced to the Seals' families and to the nation that they died as heroes. They died defending freedom from its enemies. They shed their blood so that we might live in freedom. Their blood is salvation for our nation. What he did not say is that some of our finest young men and women must be sacrificed for the profits of Texarab."

"How dare you!"

Leona would not be thwarted. "Technically, we as a nation are scapegoating these physically fit and courageous young people. We hallow them in their death so that no one will speak the truth, namely that they died to keep the price of Texarab stock from falling. What you do, Madam Vice President, is use America as a cash cow and then have your spineless president here call it *sacred* when you butcher it. Tennessee Williams called this 'mendacity'. Jesus called it 'hypocrisy'."

The CIA director reacted with disguised surprise when he glanced at the president. The president was not dismayed or angry. He was actually grinning.

Astonished at Leona's frankness and extremism, Leslie Richardson turned to Andrew Dodge. "I think this conversation is not going the direction we'd hoped, Andrew."

Andrew Dodge remained glued to his chair. He spoke in a calm voice, yet with a slight hint of agitation. "Madam Vice President. Mr. Director. I believe I can handle things from this point. It's very late. I believe I can excuse the two of you. Go get some sleep."

The two executives bade the president and Leona good night. The president stood up and followed them to the door. Once they had departed he stuck his head out the door and whispered to the guards. Then he double locked the door from the inside.

Leona was still on her feet. The president turned to gaze at her. He paused. His eyes skipped around the room, awkwardly. Then, he stared again at Leona. He walked slowly toward her.

Once close enough, she threw her arms around him and nestled her head into the curve of his neck. His arms moved around her body. He gently hugged her, gripping her waist from behind.

"Oh, Andy," she sighed.

"Lee, I've missed you."

30 /THURSDAY, CHICAGO, 3:24 AM

THE MUTUAL CARESS turned time into eternity. Or, strictly a fragment of eternity. The president arched backward to say in a sing-song voice, "Spineless? Is that what you think I am?"

"Oh, Andy. I'm sorry. I think I got carried away," lamented Leona. "Of course, you're not spineless. I'm just troubled. I hope you can forget that remark."

"No problem, Pastor."

"Maybe I shoot my mouth off when I don't have the right ammunition," Leona went on. "Next time you see Leslie Richardson, would you apologize for me?"

"No, I won't," said the president sharply. "You're like a prophet in ancient Israel: you speak truth to power. May I fix you a glass of sherry?"

"I'd rather have port, if you've got it."

"Port for the lady!" he exclaimed as he waltzed to the wet bar. "I'll take the single malt Scotch."

The two found chairs at right angles to one another. They each drank their first sips in silence. Then Andrew spoke. "I can't tell you how refreshing you are to me. I'm surrounded all day long, every day, by sycophants. 'Yes, Mr. President.' and 'No, Mr. President.' If I would bend over, they'd push and shove in line to kiss my ass. But you, lady pastor, thunder down on me the wrath of God. You make me feel like shit."

Leona's smile indicated understanding. "I'm really glad to be here, Andy."

Andrew lifted his glass and the two toasted.

"May I try this one more time, Lee? You don't seem to get it, no matter how often I repeat it." Andrew halted. "When you were incarcerated in that Iranian dungeon, I had only been in office a few weeks. I was still trying to wrap my mind around all the briefings. Karl Budenholzer was at that time CIA Director. He's since been demoted and replaced by Holthusen. I asked Budenholzer what to say to Golshani. He dictated my actions. I trusted him. On each communication with Tehran I repeated, 'We don't negotiate with terrorists'. Golshani, as you can imagine, retorted that he's not a terrorist. He reminded me that he is the president of a sovereign state. And sovereign states have the authority to execute, to take human lives."

"You simply let Budenholzer lead you like a cow with a ring in its nose?"

"I was slow on the uptake, Lee. When the gravity of the situation finally sank in, I took control from Budenholzer. Golshani and I agreed that he could make public that America had hired spies to gain intelligence in Iran; and he could say what he wanted once the three of you were safely in Saudi Arabia. As it turns out, this did not become big news. The tsunami that hit Japan swallowed up the media's attention, and this little Irangate was hardly noticed. Much to Golshani's chagrin, virtually nobody cared about three spies. If I could do it over again, I would..."

Leona interrupted. "This idea that a sovereign state, whether Iran or the U.S., has the right to snuff out human lives: where does that come from? Each of us in that prison was a human person. You're a human person. Doesn't that trump state sovereignty?"

"This is no time for political philosophy, Lee. I'm telling you that sitting here with you right now isn't..."

"Yes, I know." Leona grabbed Andrew's hand and gave it a tender squeeze.

THURSDAY, CHICAGO, 3:24 AM

THE PRESIDENT STOOD UP. He grabbed the glass from Leona's hand and sauntered toward the wet bar to pour refills. Over his shoulder he began a discourse, possibly rehearsed silently in his mind. "Whenever I feel stressed or discouraged, I think back to the first year when you'd come stateside. Once every month or so we'd spend a day or two, alone with the secret service."

"The *very secret* service," Lee interjected.

Andrew walked toward her. "Those were good days, Lee. After making love we would simply lie in one another's arms. We'd talk until sunrise. What we shared came from the depth of our being, from the emptiness and fullness of our souls. Yes, you were still angry at me. I was still angry with myself. Our private time was filled with *Sturm und Drang*. But it was also filled with the most profound joy I've ever experienced."

Leona's face glowed with her recollection of the same shared joy.

"Lee," he said, "you taught me the difference between just sex and making love. I can't thank you enough for that."

"Our love was beautiful, Andy. But it couldn't continue could it?"

"No, it had to stop."

"But Lee, I needed you then. I need you now."

"You've got Mildred. I've got my ordination. You don't need me."

"Did you have to shut off your hormones just to get ordained?"

"By no means! And that's a crude remark, Andy. My feelings did not change. I believe you know that. You are simply not available to me. And such a secret has impeachment written all over it. Divorce too. I will contribute nothing to either. You know this."

"Yes, I do." The President thought for a moment. "I'm trying to remember, Lee, since you began your second year of seminary, how often have we had a chance like this to talk. Has it been twice a year?"

"That's about right," she responded. "Twice a year or so. I never know when a secret service agent might show up at my door and whisk me to the White House for a confidential rendezvous. Tonight was the first time via helicopter. It was kinda fun, actually."

"I have to know how you're doing, Lee."

"I appreciate the fact that you're concerned about my well-being. But I don't see how I contribute anything to your work as the head of state."

"It's not my work as head of state. I bring you to see me because my psyche needs your visits. You're like a pill—a reality pill. When my head aches after listening day in and day out to one bullshitter after another bullshitter, I need relief. Everyone who talks to me walks on eggshells, trying to say what they think I want them to say. I feel like a babysitter for three hundred million people. And the media! Ouch! Every contact with a reporter is like walking into a bear trap. I get prodded with jabs, accusations, provocations. I'm prodded to say something I will eventually regret. Sooner or later, I do say something I regret. And then I get to watch it on news program after news program. So, you see, Lee, you give me two things a sick person needs. You heal me with your uncompromising realism. And, more importantly, you accept me for who I am. Even though I'm responsible for the worst thing that ever happened to you in your life, the way you treat me makes me feel forgiven. If I don't see you every so often, I'll drown in a whirlpool of distortions and criticisms."

31 /THURSDAY, CHICAGO, 3:48 AM

"So, where do we stand?" Leona asked the president.

"With you and me? Or, with the geopolitical situation?"

"Let's do the second. The first is settled."

"The contractors are getting together. They're becoming what OPEC was in the 1970s. For many years we had diversity. The larger businesses hired mercenaries, usually hardened and combat experienced special forces personnel. Some of our best soldiers found themselves at a loss after discharge. They became addicted to the head rush of the risk, danger, and excitement of combat. By shuttling these thrill addicts into mercenary forces, it keeps them under a semblance of discipline and off our streets at home. The U.S. hires them to protect VIPs and other sorts of assignments. Everything is legal. Mercenaries are subject to the same laws as our troops."

"Do *they* know this?" asked Leona with a sarcastic tone.

The president smiled knowingly. "A second group is made up of private companies who develop battlefield technology. The evolution of Improvised Explosive Devices goes faster than a bullet train. Each six months the IEDs become more sophisticated. We need our techies to keep up, to move even faster. We find a way to override the IED trigger mechanisms. Then they override our override. Then we come up with the next generation of overrides. The insurgents adapt. And so on."

"These are nerds, not soldiers. Right?"

"Right. Finally, there are a number of very small outfits. Budenholzer hires them for the dirtiest of the dirty work. Knowledge of what they do—or even knowledge of who they are—is a no-no. I don't ask. Nobody tells me. That's the way it is."

Leona's grimace communicated a humorous recognition of irony: the chief executive could not be told what his underlings were actually doing.

"What I think has been happening is this," the president continued. "As these contractors hire and fire, the personnel move around. They circulate. They communicate. They've begun to organize. As an organization, they can demand more money for their services and divide up the market. Among other things, they see profit in keeping tensions with Iran alive. A peaceful end to the debate over nuclear terrorism would be bad for their business, so to speak."

"Which contractors are in and who's out?"

"We don't know which of the smaller ones are in. All of the larger ones send representatives to strategy meetings. We know, because we've got a mole. When spies meet, some are spying on the spies."

"Do you have any evidence of conspiracy?"

"No hard evidence of any wrongdoing. Organizing is not illegal, as long as price fixing and such are avoided. Yet, we have our suspicions. What we suspect is that someone in CUB wants to ensure that the cold war between the West and Iran continues."

"*Cold* war?"

"A hotter war would be better for CUB. If Iran were to announce it was on the brink of deploying a deliverable WMD, then the Israelis would demand we act or they would take the matter into their own hands. Any Israeli action would precipitate such an overwhelming Arab reaction that it could lead to international chaos. So, we would probably preempt Israel in taking military action in order to protect Israel from close range retaliation. At least this is how Holthusen and I think the logic works."

"Where does Budenholzer fit? Is he pissed off that you demoted him? Is he CUB's dupe or its mastermind?"

"We don't know at this point. No evidence of wrongdoing yet. So, what we're doing with you comes straight from Holthusen, bypassing Budenholzer."

"When Budenholzer finds out, won't he be even more ticked off?"

"Probably. We'll have to take that chance. But he might be grateful if we prevent the worst from happening and protect him from his own contractors. As I said, we have a mole. CUB's leaders have met twice that we know of, both times in resorts. Once in Morocco and once on Cyprus. In neither case was Budenholzer present."

"Someone's gotta lead these leaders. Who?"

"If there is a leader, then that would be Jarrod Grimes. Grimes is president of one of the larger companies that hire mercenaries—Grimes Security Company. It's possible that Grimes also runs a second company, a small operation that specializes in top secret operations, the kind of operations nobody finds out about. Grimes could be the key man, but the mole cannot confirm this beyond a shadow of a doubt."

"Does Grimes have a mole in the CIA?" asked Leona.

"Good question. I don't know. If so, then the intelligence could get confusing. Our mole might be getting deliberately misleading information."

Leona said nothing.

"Here is what all this means for you, Lee," the president continued. "We have good reason to believe that someone in CUB believes you hold the key to CUB success. What your key will unlock is the individual in Tehran who has, to date, thwarted the production of the first deliverable nuclear weapon. Whoever this person is, he's a hero, an unsung hero. If CUB could eliminate him, then the international tensions would dramatically increase. With increased tensions, our government would be willing to enlarge our contracts for undercover work in Iran and elsewhere. You know this person, and CUB wants to know what you know. This is why you're in danger—imminent danger."

Leona grimaced.

"Lee, it gets worse," the president added, showing desperation on his face. "We also have reason to believe that CUB has a Plan B. If they fail to uncover and expose Tehran's saboteur, CUB may perpetrate an act of terrorism and blame the Iranians. It might be modeled after 9/11. This would arouse such an outraged call for revenge here in America that our government would have to take some action against Iran just to appease the enraged mob."

"This is not looking good, Andy. Are you confident about your intelligence?"

"Yes, we're confident in what we know. But we're sorely aware of what we do not know. And, in light of your question about a reverse mole, perhaps what we think we know is askew."

"Do you know the terrorist target?"

"No. But we're trying desperately to find out, as you can imagine. Lee, you've never actually told me the name of our Tehran undercover guy."

"Two things, Mister President."

"Lee, I'm Andy."

"Okay, Andy, two things. First, he's not *our* undercover guy. He's not our guy at all. Please don't forget this. Secondly, I have not told you his name. Nor have I told Holthusen. Neither of you need to know. You yourself are better off not knowing. More importantly, our unsung hero in Iran has a family. He loves his country. He's not a traitor. His motive is simply to prevent proliferation. Should he be exposed, he'd be vulnerable to the most heinous of punishments. No one would gain. And the world might lose. The stakes are so high that I plan to go to my grave with this secret, if need be."

"You're as brave as you are spirited, Lee. But I fear that if CUB gets hold of you that you might become a victim of harsh measures. Such measures were successful at breaking Al-Quaeda suspects during Rendition. They could break you too."

"I'm not comfortable with your logic. On the one hand, if I supply the name of the Tehran insider, then we prevent a terrorist attack, right? On the other hand, if I do not divulge the name, then we'll suffer a terrorist disaster, perhaps a copy of 9/11. If we sacrifice one person in Tehran we can save the lives of countless Americans. Is this the logic?"

"Yes, Leona, that is the logic of our situation."

"So, why don't you sacrifice me? You're used to sacrificing..." Leona stopped. "Oh, Andy, I'm sorry."

"Lee, I know. You're still so traumatized by what happened. Scarred for the rest of your life. And I'm part of that scar. Your anger toward me is seared into the sinews of your soul. I so, so, regret that. Believe me, Lee, I do not want to place you in any more danger. Not this time."

"So, you're not going to sacrifice me or our unnamed Tehran comrade. Right?"

"Right."

"Still, all this is well worth worrying about. I gather this means I need to take steps to protect myself."

"Holthusen wants to help."

"Oh, yes, I know. He's already started."

Leona thought for a moment. "We need to head off CUB before they light the fuse on their terrorist dynamite. Right?"

"Right."

"How are we going to do that?"

"I'm only the president. How should I know?"

Leona sat quietly, with a pensive look on her face.

THE PRESIDENT LOOKED into Leona's eyes, waiting until they met. "No matter how difficult this moment is, and no matter how grave the danger to you, I still treasure this time we have together. When you walked in a few minutes ago, my heart leapt like a gazelle. How I've longed to see you. And, now, here you are! Right here! I can see you. I can touch you. You're real. How I wish I could put you under house arrest—White House arrest."

Both laughed. They clasped hands while staring at one another.

Andrew leaned over and kissed Leona on the right cheek. She responded with a brief kiss on his lips. Then she sat back in her chair.

"How are things with the First Lady?"

The president turned his gaze to the side. "The same."

Leona said nothing.

Andrew continued. "It's not working. I'm trapped."

"Is she on board this ship?"

"No. Tomorrow, Friday, Mildred will arrive at O'Hare on Air Force One. Prior to her arrival, I will have been secretly taken to O'Hare. We'll be connected before we're seen by the public. It'll appear that I'm arriving with her. When the state visit is done, this freighter will sail north through the straights, turn south again, finally docking in the Detroit River."

"After you meet your wife at O'Hare, what then?"

"Mildred and I will be taken to the John Hancock Building. We've got an apartment set up on the 85th floor. Once we're settled, then we're off to a reception at Buckingham Fountain. I'll get a key to Chicago, a key so big it could not possibly fit into any locks."

Leona was silent. She leaned back and crossed her legs. "Should I get used to these late night pick-ups and clandestine meetings with our head of state? Or, is this the last one?"

"Well, Lee, how else could I possibly see you?"

They smiled at one another. "Have you told anyone about us?" he asked.

"No, except for my best friend, Angie. Not to worry. She's trustworthy. I'll never talk to the news or write a memoir. Even though I'm pissed off at you, you can still trust me."

"I wish you had not told anybody, even your closest friend."

"Presidents come and go, but a girlfriend lasts a life time."

"I know you like baseball. Who's your favorite player?" asked the president, clearly wanting to change the subject..

"Hank Greer."

"We've arranged to take in Saturday's game between the Cubs and the Cards. The mayor and some other dignitaries will sit with us right behind the home plate screen. How I wish I could have you sitting next to me. But of course, that's impossible."

"Will Mildred be there?"

"Yes. She'll sit on one side. Mayor Daley will sit on the other."

"Mmmmm." Leona frowned. "What about security?"

"It'll be quite a job in an open space such as Wrigley Field. However, sometimes when I'm surrounded by security I hardly even notice it. I'll root for Hank Greer and think of you."

32 /THURSDAY, CHICAGO, 4:23 AM

AFTER A PARTING EMBRACE, Leona was turned over to security for her trip back home. The man in the tie and wind breaker led her toward the helipad at the center of the ship. He returned her weapon without saying a word. Leona took it and packed it in her waistband.

"I'm Leona," she said.

"Hi. My name is Allen, Rex Allen."

"Will you be with the president on Saturday at the Cubs game?"

"I reckon I will."

They arrived at the helipad and the whirling blade noise made saying any further goodbyes impossible. Leona boarded. Soon the chopper was up and she was looking over the City of the Big Shoulders once more.

AS THE HELICOPTER CLIMBED HIGHER, Leona's mind traveled back to another such ride, one that took her from the depths of hell to the warm, embracing arms of home. Her memories were watery, blurry, distorted. *Perhaps God protects us,* she thought, *by allowing us not to remember every detail.*

Nevertheless, what Leona will always remember from those days and months after returning to Michigan from Iran is the love that brought her back to life, back to her self. Leona's self had been broken, shattered. But the unconditional love of her mother and the patience of her best friend put the broken Humpty Dumpty back together again. The broken self was the one that cared so deeply about the world, about justice, about intimate caring, about making life better. This self was smashed, crushed, demolished, destroyed. The new self which emerged lost none of its previous passion, but now trust would be tempered by circumspection and high ideals by more modest expectations.

Leona called to mind those Michigan moments when she awoke from a nearly catatonic sleep to warm, tender strokes on her arms, back, legs, and temples by her mother and Angie. They instinctively knew that touch was the greatest healer. And it was. Presence, not words or drugs or sleeping pills, became the healing therapy.

Could she ever thank them for not giving up on her? Leona knew that no thanks were needed. Angie and her mother understood her when she didn't understand herself. She especially recalled how Angie came every day, sometimes twice a day, to visit, always bringing something to read or share. One was a poem by Mary Oliver. "Mend my life," pleaded Oliver in "The Journey." She repeated the title to herself, *mend my life*, in many of her prayers.

For a moment Leona's attention was drawn to the horizon. *Is it night or dawn?*

Her mind drifted back to Angie's visits. They discussed Buddhist aphorisms, especially analyzing one on selfless loving: "Selflessness unites people. It is a healing herb that unifies strangers and brings families together. It is the love for others that is higher than self-love. It is our only hope." They asked about what St. Paul could mean in Romans 1:17 by emphasizing that just shall live by faith. Leona's mind had turned from the disease of torture and death in Iran to the healing of love and grace in her own home.

Leona's Aunt Kathryn, her mother's younger sister, made her the needlepoint pillow adorned with the Luther Seal, the pillow that garnishes the leather couch in her parsonage. Leona came to identify the crest's black cross with her own experience in the Tehran prison. More. She could also identify the large red heart of God as inclusive, as incorporating without sugar coating all the dark tragedy within the more comprehensive reality of divine love. *But can I believe this without doubting?* The petals of the white rose symbolize joy, consolation, and peace. *Can I be cheerful?*

"Excuse me? What did you say?" asked the pilot, as he turned around to stare at Leona. Startled, Leona realized she was so deep in thought she forgot where she was. She had not noticed that some of her thoughts were voiced.

Leona smiled for a moment, "I was just thinking out loud."

She looked out the window to see the yellowish glow of streetlights that outlined her own neighborhood.

When the craft landed in her church parking lot, Leona noticed the SUVs were back, blocking both gates. She exited as she had entered. In seconds the Long Ranger IV was up and out of sight. The SUVs disappeared. All was quiet once again. Had any neighbors heard the landing noises, everything would be back to normal by the time they lifted their window shades to see what was happening.

The sun was not yet up. The dimness of the gray was punctuated with streetlights blinking out, one at a time. Leona walked slowly toward the parsonage porch. Movement on the porch startled her. It was the head of a large dog popping up from a body stretched out at the foot of her screen door. When the dog saw Leona, he sprang to his feet and ran around the house to the right. Leona raced after him. She realized that she was chasing a Siberian husky. The husky scrambled up a scrub of vines and over the fence. Leona watched as he raced down the alley and turned west on 80th Street. He was gone. Or, so she thought.

Slowly, Leona meandered back toward her front door. As she opened the screen door, she heard a faint peep. She paused. At her feet she found a small kitten. She scooped up the little creature in her hands, precipitating a litany of crying meows. Unimpressed with the protests, Leona turned the delicate animal around in her hands. She reckoned the mewing beast at ten to twelve weeks old. The fur was black everywhere. Everywhere except for a few white hairs arranged in a moon shape on the underside of the kitten's neck. Over the protestations voiced in the squeaky mewing, Leona pressed the soft fur against her cheek. Then she packed the kitten under her arm and unlocked the wooden front door.

In the kitchen she spread out some newspaper to protect the floor. Into a small saucer she poured a couple ounces of milk. She searched her inventory of refrigerator leftovers and pulled out a clear baggie containing shrimp. The pastor-turned-cat-chef chopped the shrimp into fine pieces. She placed the seafood into another small saucer. After only a few exploratory sniffs the kitten became busy with eating.

Leona picked up her iPhone to write a text to Hillar. "H, w/time do u go 2 school today? I make bfast 4 u if u stop by."

Leona closed up the kitchen, incarcerating the foundling inside. She took her coffee, juice and gingerbread man upstairs. She read Psalm 33. Verse 5 stood out for Leona: "The Lord promotes equity and justice; the Lord's faithfulness extends throughout the whole earth." After a coffee sip, she read on more intently. Verse 10: "The Lord frustrates the decisions of the nations; he nullifies the plans of the peoples." She devoured her gingerbread like she devoured what she was reading. Verse 16: "No king is delivered by his vast army; a warrior is not saved by his great might." *How transient and ephemeral are the powers of this earth! she thought. How vain and short-sighted to put trust in our nation's military might! Yet, how difficul,t if not impossible, it is for me to avoid devoting my life to an idol.*

By the time she'd turned on CNN and parked the remaining refreshments on the lamp stand, her phone sounded. The text read: "7 am. Yum. Pancakes. H." Leona reset her phone alarm to 6:30 and then slumbered.

33 /THURSDAY, CHICAGO, 7:00 AM

AT 7:00 AM LEONA, with her kitten kitchen helper, was busy with pancakes on the stove. The doorbell rang. *Why isn't Hillar walking in?* Oh, I must've left the door locked, she thought as she hastened through the dining room and the living room. She unlocked the wooden door and swung it open. Hillar had already opened the screen door and was about to step in.

Suddenly a commotion broke out. Hillar was knocked to the side. Through both partially opened doors swished a large gray animal. The husky. He ran through the doors, passed the pastor, and into the kitchen. By the time Hillar and Leona arrived in the kitchen the dog was sitting erect with the kitten at its feet. The kitten acknowledged the presence of the new visitor and sat down between the dog's front legs. Four animal eyes were now looking up at four human eyes.

The two humans were at first amazed. Then they laughed. "Well, Quaz," said Leona, "do you think introductions are called for?"

"Are they only visiting, or are they looking for a new home?" asked Hillar.

"Do you feel like we're the gold and they've just filed a claim?" Leona laughed loudly.

Leona and Hiller went about their business. They placed the pancakes and accoutrements on the dining room table. The dog was served a pancake, which disappeared immediately. Then, a second pancake. The kitten lapped up a second dish of milk.

"I believe I've seen the dog before," the pastor told Hillar. She told him about the strange incident at lakeside, where a dog, sensing danger, had protected her. "I thought that might have been a moment of grace," Leona declared. "If it's the same dog, does this mean another moment of grace is about to happen?"

"Could be."

Leona tried mentally to put some puzzle pieces together: *two eyes in the dark; a dead squirrel; a dead crow; a living kitten. Are these all connected to this one dog?* Then she spoke to Hillar. "Do you think you could help me today?"

"What ya need, Pastor Lee?"

"This morning I'll look around the neighborhood to find a mother cat with a litter. If I find none, I suppose the parsonage will become a hotel. I'll leave you a text. I think we'll need a cat box, kitty litter, a dog collar, and a leash. What else? What do you think? Animal food? The dried kind that comes in bags?"

"After school I'll stop by Target and Jewel to see what I can pick up."

"Here's a few twenties. I hope this'll cover it. You've got a house key, right?"

"Right. But it's at home. I can get it though."

"If I'm not here, come directly in and prepare for our guests."

Leona put on her sweats and headed for the neighborhood to combine her jog with a search. She read posters and paper fragments tacked to telephone poles announcing lost pets or found pets. None reported missing either a husky or black kitten. She returned, showered, dressed, and headed out for pastoral calling. Graham joined her. Ulla and the Bolstads were on her visitation list. Leona provided

Graham with a brief account of her meeting with the president, but she left out selected details.

Graham was shocked. "Did you discuss my assignment with Holthusen?"

"No. There was no time for me to talk with him."

"To think all of this happened on my watch, and I was not here on duty. Ouch."

"What're you gonna do, sleep in your car?"

"I wonder if I should stick closer to you."

"Look, nothing's gone wrong yet. I think I can take care of myself."

"CUB will make its move soon. The storm is coming. And, if CUB fails to get from you what it wants, these guys may resort to Plan B. This is not looking good either way, Leona."

34 /THURSDAY, CHICAGO, 4:00 PM

BY LUNCH TIME Hillar had received his text from Leona. No strays or ferals giving birth in the alley. No signs on telephone poles looking for a missing Siberian husky or a black kitten. The die was cast. As his shopping cart filled with merchandise, Hillar sent a text. "2 heavy 2 carry. Target pick up @ 4pm?" Moments later a reply: "Yes."

GRAHAM AND LEONA pulled into the Target loading zone to pick up Hillar and the purchases for the new family members. Back at the parsonage, Graham helped unload, asking himself how this physical labor made it into his job description. Graham then plopped into a comfortable chair and began phoning and texting. The pastor and Quasimodo assembled the pet paraphernalia, positioning the covered litter box with its top in the far corner of the dining room. The kitchen was too small for both a cook and a cat; and the basement was too far away. The dog's bed was situated near the litter box, but not too near. Dogs rarely sleep in their beds but a pet bed makes a dog home look official. Food dishes were set on the side door landing, at the top of the basement stairway.

"Now, if only the animals think like we do," said Leona.

"What should we name them?" asked Hillar.

"I've got a suggestion for the cat: Midnight. She's all black with a moon sliver on the neck. Just like midnight."

"But don't cats need to be named something ending in 'itty'? It will never come if you call it Midnight."

"Don't they call cats 'Puss' in England?" protested Leona.

"No self-respecting cat is gonna come to 'Puss'. Gotta call it 'Kitty, Kitty, Kitty' in a high voice."

"I like the name Midnight. If the cat doesn't come, then we'll try Kitty. Okay?"

"Gotcha, Pastor. How about the dog?"

"It's your turn to name it."

"Well, only one name fits: 'Buck'. I had to read Jack London's *Call of the Wild* in school. It's about a dog that grows up in San Francisco. It gets taken to Alaska during the gold rush and made to work as a sled dog. Little by little the dog becomes more like a wolf. Finally, at the end of the book, it is a wolf! His name is Buck. As a dog, Buck is loyal to the people he loves. But as a wolf, Buck is a vicious fighter, even a killer. This dog looks to me like I would imagine Buck."

"Then Buck it is. It'll be up to you to teach Buck his name. May I call him Buckie now and then?"

Hillar glared.

Leona continued. "I'll take care of Kitty, I mean Midnight."

Hillar called, "Buck." The dog's eyes met Hillar's. "Buck! Buck!" The dog walked over to the kneeling teenager. Hillar talked to Buck in a soft and soothing voice while he petted his coarse thick fur and scratched his ears. If a dog could purr, Buck would have.

Suddenly and without warning, Hillar jumped on the dog. Buck resisted; he had been caught by surprise. Hillar wrestled the dog to the carpet and laid his full weight on the animal's torso. Buck's head volleyed to and fro, whining. He did not bite. He did not even growl.

"What are you doing?" flashed Leona. "Get off that dog!"

Hillar appeared not to hear the order. He continued to wrestle and kept the four-legged creature pinned to the floor. An astonished

Leona grabbed Hillar's shirt and pulled him toward her. Hillar eventually loosened his grip on this incarnation of *canis familiaris* and stood up. Buck rolled over and stood up as well.

"Ya gotta let the dog know who's boss," said Hillar. "Dogs evolved from wolves. Wolves run in packs. Each pack has an alpha male. The other males are subordinate. The alpha male fights with his rivals to show he's in charge. The others submit. I've got to show Buck that I'm the alpha male. Now, it's your turn to be the alpha male, Pastor Lee."

"I think I'll skip my turn, Quaz. Thanks all the same."

WITH PETS UNDER CONTROL, Hillar turned to Graham, who had just arrived. "Wanna see what I got?"

"Sure."

Hillar reached into the large Target bag. Glancing toward Leona he said, "I bought this with my own money." He proceeded to pull out a small box. He nodded toward the front door. Soon, Graham and Hillar were sitting on the front porch. Buck was wandering the yard, keeping the two within sight.

Hillar unwrapped his U Control Silver Bullet RC Helicopter and a packet of batteries. He and Graham assembled it. In minutes the five-inch helicopter was flying about the yard, out into the parking lot and back. After a pair of crashes, Hillar remarked: "I've got to get the hang of it. Do you wanna try it, Graham?"

Buck watched intently. From time to time Buck squirmed on his haunches. He did not bark. He whined. When Graham took the controls, he directed the helicopter to fly west on the grass parallel to the asphalt. Buck chased it. Buck leapt up and snapped, trying to catch it. Once Graham had gained finesse as a remote pilot, he would lower the helicopter to tempt the jumping hound. When Buck would leap and snap at it, Graham would raise it up out of Buck's reach. The frustration energized Buck into more leaping and more snapping. By this time Leona was at the door, all were laughing—except Buck.

Hillar declared he would have to try the same thing. He took over and taunted this canine's passion. It was difficult to know whether Buck was playing or deadly serious.

Eventually, Hillar headed for home. Graham and Leona talked over strategies and schedules. They agreed that Graham would sleep on the living room couch, a hide-a-bed. Later that evening he would return to Hyde Park, check out of his hotel, and return to the parsonage with his small suitcase.

In the meantime, Leona assembled a salad and prepared grilled cheese sandwiches for their light dinner. Graham's phone vibrated. He read the text while chewing a bite of his sandwich. Then he turned to Leona. "Our mole reports that CUB is on to something. They're investigating a guy in Tehran named Qudrat Al-Damad. Do you know him? Is he the peacenik?"

Leona began to chuckle. "Well, that tells me a lot. Qudrat Al-Damad is a decoy. Last night I Skyped a close friend in Lahore and dropped Qudrat's name. That was a test. I was fishing. It appears that we've caught something. No, Qudrat is not the target. But now I know that my communications are being monitored. We've bought a little time while CUB chases a wild goose."

"Might you have accidentally put your friend Qudrat in danger? What if CUB simply takes him out without investigating?"

"I'm not worried. Qudrat doesn't even exist. I made him up."

"Made him up? Wow," exclaimed Graham. "That reminds me, I have a present for you." From his pocket he pulled out a Droid and placed it on the table. Compliments of the CIA. Exclusive non-traceable line. It connects directly with a satellite. No one will monitor you on this one."

"No one?"

"Well, no one other than the CIA, of course. Let me mention a couple special features of this phone. As I said, you have an exclusive non-traceable number. It also has a beacon, a GPS tracker. We can find you—that is if you keep this phone with you. We can find you anywhere. Now, note this tiny extra button on the bottom. If you press it in, the phone automatically dials me on another independent line. The screen remains blank. I'll be able to hear whatever is going on, but I won't be able to talk to you. You'd have to call me on the first line if you want to hear from me. So, what do you think?"

"I get the feeling that I'm back to work."

35 /THURSDAY, CHICAGO, 6:20 PM

THE GREEN JEEP Cherokee was waiting with engine running when Jarrod Grimes and his traveling companion exited the terminal at Midway Airport. Grimes' companion looked like he might be sixty, physically fit with signs of gray in his previously brown hair. They were greeted by Walter Gross, Chicago division chief of Grimes Security Company. Wearing a gray sweatsuit with silver and black Nike Free Runs on his feet, the six-foot Gross looked casual yet somehow also in uniform. He held open the rear door for what little luggage the two arrivals were carrying. He also loaded a box, an aluminum box weighing enough to require two hands to lift.

As if foreordained, the two travelers let themselves into the back seat. Gross took charge of the right front seat.

"Hello, Lanny," said Grimes to the waiting driver. Lanny's face was unusually broad, too broad for his undersized Chicago White Sox cap. His pinkish crater-pocked nose looked like it had once been bombarded by a mini meteor shower.

"Lanny, greetings," grunted the other man while fastening his seat belt behind the driver. Lanny waved his right hand with two fingers up and two folded as if to say, "Gotcha! Now, forward." Lanny put the Cherokee in gear and the party of four exited the airport.

"What've ya got for us, Walt?" said the man in the back seat with the assumption of authority.

"With regard to Reverend Foxx," Gross began in reportorial style, "we are monitoring her every activity. We have a plan in place to kidnap and interrogate her. We'll ask her questions with extreme prejudice."

"Better be soon. Time's running out," emphasized one of the back seat voices.

"The Foxx kidnapping is imminent. We also have prepared the alternative plan, the one that'll make the big impression. We know where the president will be staying: the 85th floor of the Hancock. The chopper is ready. You know, the right amount of gas 'n' oil and explosives and such. We have removed the two Golshani boys from their mother's care, and we're babysitting them while they wait for their helicopter ride to heaven."

"Good work, Walt."

Grimes spoke to Gross. "In the silver box you loaded is the radio equipment. We've modified our drone guidance system. The control panel is now ready for installation in a Bell 206B-3 Long Ranger IV. I suggest you place it in the very front. And when it hits, we want that sucker destroyed beyond recognition."

"Gotcha," said Gross.

36 /THURSDAY, CHICAGO, 7:44 PM

Dusk had passed and night was falling when Graham excused himself. He drove off toward Hyde Park. Leona watched while Buck wandered the yard, doing his business. He did not seem to be at risk for running away. He returned directly. It was clear that, in this dog's mind, he was home.

Leona returned to the kitchen, tidying up, using the time to formulate a schedule that would enable her to balance her pastoral responsibilities with this new set of obligations that had seeped into the present from a past she had hoped to forget. She made a mental run through Friday. Then Saturday. Then Sunday. *When will I have time to ready the sanctuary for Sunday? Sermon prep? Maybe the best I can do is my Thursday evening routine: taking care of the sanctuary.*

Leona grabbed her keys, and after she double-checked that the parsonage door was locked tight, she walked with a brisk gait to the front door of the church. She let herself into the sanctuary and turned on the simulated candle lights lining the walls. She stood for a moment in the dim quiet, reminding herself of how precious these quiet moments could be. Leona headed to the chancel to position the candles at the edges of the altar. She placed the Liturgy on a bookstand, then carefully set the communion chalice and paten on the retable. She did this slowly and respectfully, as if it were a rite unto itself.

Her eyes scanned the nave. The pews seemed neat and in order. She was pleased.

The bulletins should be done. Today's Thursday. Pauline, her volunteer secretary, routinely printed bulletins on Thursday. *I bet Pauline put one on my desk in the sacristy.* Leona checked the sanctuary one more time and flipped off the lights. Despite the darkness, Leona could easily feel the familiar way up the steep stairway leading to the pastor's office and sacristy.

In one elongated automatic motion, Leona slipped the key into the lock, stepped in, and reached for the light switch. She let out an uncharacteristic gasp: her hand had made contact with another hand. The door slammed shut behind her.

Through the dark she heard a deep, youthful voice: "We're not going to hurt you, Pastor Lee. Please sit down."

Shocked but still with her composure intact, Leona stood motionless for a second. Strong hands on her shoulders guided her slightly to the left and pressed her down into a chair.

"You're tricky. And dangerous," said the voice. "We want to make sure you just sit there."

As Leona's eyes adjusted to the darkness in the room, she could make out the shadowy figures. The voice was coming from behind her desk. One figure stood to her left. A second to the right. She sensed someone else in another chair to her right. Leona's mind was calculating her next move.

"We wanna talk with you. Don't want any violence. Git my drift?" The figure behind the desk spoke with authority. *Is this a try by CUB to kidnap me?* she asked herself.

"Now, if you sit still, we'll turn the lights on and you can see us. Okay?"

"I'm sitting," Leona said.

"I asked: *Okay?*"

"Yes, Okay."

Leona heard the fumbling for the light switch. The ceiling light went on. Then saw three male visitors in their early twenties, each African American, each wearing a red tam. To her right in a chair was Hillar, obviously a captive. He fidgeted nervously, fearing what would happen next.

"Recognize me?" asked the young man behind the desk. Leona stared at him. "Recognize what I have around my neck?"

Suddenly it came to her. This was the purse-snatcher on the train platform. "I pulled your chain," she said defiantly, "if you'll excuse the expression."

"Did you get a good look at this?" He held up the medallion. Leona leaned forward to examine it close up. It could've been the one she grabbed to gain control over her assailant. She nodded.

"It's a scorpion. They call me Scorp. Do you know what a scorpion is?"

"Yes, it's a crayfish with an attitude."

This drew a round of chortles, including one from Scorp. "This means that if you mess with me you get stung."

"Is this kind of like an alpha male, Hillar?" she said turning her eyes to meet Hillar's. Hillar could only grin sheepishly. He relaxed a bit.

It was obvious that Scorp had missed the point. Leona took the floor. "Nice to meet you, Scorp. Who are your friends? Black Widow and Tarantula? Did I meet them at Cheltenham as well?"

"Yeah," said the one standing to her left. "I'm Quint. You downed me with an axe kick before I could take a breath." Quint was shaking his head sideways, emphasizing the drama.

Leona turned to the lanky one on the right, the van driver. "I'm Everett."

"It would be nice to see you three boys in church on Sunday. Ten thirty. But to what do I owe the pleasure of this particular meeting? And why have you scared the shit out of Hillar?"

"You ain't afraid, are you, Pastor Lee?" said Scorp.

"Fear is not one of my vices," she said.

"Good. Usually not ours, either. We'd like to lose our fear of you too. Can we just have a friendly talk?"

A mood of tentative relaxation filled the small room. Scorp continued to lead. "By this time, Pastor Lee, you must've figured out that our little incident Monday at the train station was not a street mugging,"

Leona nodded affirmatively.

"Some guy promised us bucks if we would deliver you to him. Big bucks. A lot more than would be in your purse. But we didn't know two things. We didn't know that you was, like…a tiger on speed. And, we didn't know you was, well, a pastor."

"Are you here to kidnap me tonight? I suppose that by taking Hillar captive you think you can persuade me to not fight back."

"No such thing," Scorp went on. "Neither you or Hillar are gonna get damaged by us. We just wanna talk. Maybe we can come to an understandin'."

Scorp proceeded to explain to Leona and Hillar how his gang, the Woodlawn Stoners, had been approached by some white guy with a job to do. The job seemed simple enough and the money would be good. The Stoners Council of Twenty-One appointed Scorp, Quint, and Everett to do the deed. The white guy loaned them the van, the Evanston Cleaner's van. Had they been successful at kidnapping Leona, she would have been delivered to the white guy at the Wrigley Field parking lot on West Grace Street.

"So, why don't you simply kidnap me now and cash in?" asked Leona.

The three in control looked at each other. "Because of Spider," said Everett.

"Spider?"

Scorp took over again. "Yep. Spider tells us what you been doin' fer him, and for others on probation. Didya know that yesterday Spider went back to the library? He apologized to the cop. He 'n' the cop got ta talk'n,' and they shaked hands. We think Spider's got a new friend in blue."

"I figured Spider was one of yours. He's got a red tam. How about Spence? What about Trayvon?"

"No, Spencer and Trayvon are independents."

"What about the Duke?"

"Duke's one of ours. He's tak'n his stepfather to the Cubs game Saturday. He's pay'n fer it. See what good yer doin,' Pastor Lee? Spider and Duke say you respect them. They's mighty grateful."

"Don't thank me. Thank Mr. Chadwick."

"It's all the same. Mr. Chadwick's here because you're here. You're the pastor to the neighborhood. Ya might not see us in church Sundays, but you're *our* pastor, Pastor Lee."

"I'm your pastor?" Leona paused to grasp what was being said. "Then, why'd you rough me up?"

Quint interjected, "Cause we didn't know then. We didn't know who you was until after Monday, until Tuesday. Spider done tol' us ta back off when he found out it was you we were roughin' up. Now, we're see'n' things better."

Leona did not respond immediately. The room was quiet. Leona spoke. "Scorp, did you pull me to safety so the train wouldn't cut my head off?"

Scorp nodded affirmatively. Leona was momentarily stunned. After the significance of this interchange sank in, Scorp spoke again. "I may be a gangbanger, Pastor Lee; but I ain't no killer. Neither is Quint nor Everett."

"I thought you Stoners put dead bodies in trash cans for the fun of it," said Leona with an ambiguous facial expression. "Just how did you spend your largess from the Neighborhood Recovery Initiative?"

The three Stoners looked at each other with puzzlement on their faces. After a moment of silence, Quint spoke. "Woodlawn got money from the NRI, all right. We got temporary jobs. I stood up on 63rd passing out flyers to our friends, flyers say'n we gotta stop crime. We got paid $8.75 an hour. It was worth it."

"Yeah, I got paid for marching in a parade with the governor," added Everett. Then with a grin, he added, "which kinda crime should we be stopping, ours or the governor's?"

A warm smile crossed Leona's face. Her entire body smiled, even if it was not obvious to those looking at her. Scorp looked into Leona's eyes. "Putt'n it plain, Pastor Lee, we're ready to change sides. We wanna protect you. We don't know who these guys are, but they're not gonna harm you as long as we're here."

Leona and Hillar looked at one another. Leona was obviously running something through her mind. "You want to change sides?"

"All three captors nodded affirmatively. "Yeah, that's right."

Leona continued to think, then spoke. "How did you know my schedule? You planned your attack. How did you know my whereabouts?"

"Remember, Pastor Lee. You were in the Loop. Did you talk or text with anyone?"

Leona thought for another moment. "Only Hillar. I gave him a heads up on my return to South Shore. I expected to connect with him at the Church Council meeting."

"Hillar, what did you do then?" asked Scorp.

Hillar, thought for a moment. "Nuth'n."

"Nuth'n? No mobile phone calls? No texting? No tweeting?"

"Oh, yeah," said Hillar. "I texted Owl and then finished my homework so I could go to the council."

"Is it coming together yet?" Scorp asked Leona. "You've got a mole."

"Owl?" exclaimed Leona and Hillar in unison.

"Hillar," asked Leona, "what do you have going on with Owl?"

"Well," Hillar said choppily, "Owl and I text or talk a few times a day. To think of it, she asks me what the pastor's doing. I didn't think..."

"The white guy," interrupted Scorp, "told us to connect with Owl. She set us up with where'd you be at what time. We had tried to ambush you before Monday, but we couldn't catch you by surprise. Monday was our best chance."

"May I stand up?" asked Leona.

"Sure," said Scorp.

Leona rose to her feet, held her head in her hands, and began to pace the small room. The heads of the four moved back and forth in unison as they studied her movements, not quite knowing what she was up to.

Leona asked more precise questions about their conversations with the white guy, what else he wanted to know about her, whether he had an accent or not. She incorporated each answer into her thought process.

She took her seat again. "Where's the Evanston Cleaner's van?"

"Parked in Woodlawn," answered Everett.

"Does the white guy know yet that you plan to change sides?"

"No," all three said in near unison.

"Good," exclaimed Leona. "I think I want you to kidnap me. I think I want you to deliver me to the white guy."

The others looked confused, even aghast. Leona instructed Hillar to text Owl that evening, including in his message a report that Pastor Lee would be home alone the next day, Friday, at 11:00 am. Scorp should wait for a message from Owl. He would then call the white guy and also alert the sitting duck at the parsonage. Leona would alert Graham, who would be ready to follow the van to Wrigley Field. Once the white guy showed himself in the parking lot, Graham would take care of the rest.

"Do you gangbangers have heat?" Leona asked.

The three tams looked at each other quizzically. Then, Scorp addressed the pastor, "we can get it."

Leona requested the three of them bring firearms. Just in case. No, Hillar could not come. He would have to stay in school. He would hear later what had happened.

At Leona's suggestion, each punched everyone else's cell numbers into their mobiles. Leona inaugurated her Droid. The group circled and put their hands together in the middle, almost as if it were a basketball team cheer. Leona prayed aloud. Then they departed.

37 /THURSDAY, CHICAGO, 10:17 PM

LEONA RETURNED to the parsonage as Graham was arriving. Graham parked his car at the yard front walk. Leona asked him to restart the engine. "Head for the Loop," she ordered. En route she recounted the events of the evening and the plan for Friday. It would be Graham's job to follow the van in his own car. At the opportune moment, Graham would then take out the unnamed white guy. Exactly what "take out" would mean in this circumstance remained undefined. But it would include extracting from the white guy the terror target of Plan B.

"This could erupt into gunfire," said Graham. "Also, I don't have the authority to arrest. Should we get some backup?"

"I don't want any arrests," answered Leona. "As for backup, that's what we're gonna work on now."

The two drove north on Lake Shore Drive, on to Michigan Avenue, and into the Loop. "Turn left and then left again onto Wabash," Leona told Graham.

Once on Wabash, Leona spoke again. "Now, stop here and park with your flashers on." The car was stopped next to Macy's. An elevated train rumbled by with near deafening sound on the tracks above their head.

"Early in my CIA training I was loaned for six months to Macy's," said Leona. "It was a sort of internship as a store detective. No one knew I was from the CIA, of course. I appeared to be the dumb chick who needed guidance from my seniors. I got to know the security staff. It was wonderful. We became like family."

Although it was approaching 11:00 pm and the store had long been closed, Leona rang a bell. "Security," they heard over the small speaker.'

"Is Shmoo working tonight? Tell him it's Leona Foxx."

"Leona! This is Ahmed. Come in."

Security buzzers buzzed. Doors opened. Graham and Leona entered the building and were greeted by Ahmed, a middle eastern man in his early fifties, whom Graham surmised must be an old workmate. "I'll call Shmoo," announced their host. "He's making rounds on the sixth floor."

When Schmucynski rounded the corner into the aisle, Leona raised her voice, "Shmoo, are you Pōlish?"

"No," he retorted. "The word is 'pahlish'!"

Shmoo hugged Leona, picked her up off the floor, and tossed her left and right, like a father greeting a daughter. "Oh, Leona, it's sooooo good to see ya."

Graham watched the greeting ritual at a respectful distance. Then Leona offered introductions all around, including Ahmed. Shmoo invited the group to join him in the staff snack room with its formica tables and vending machines. Once the coffee was poured, Leona got down to business. She focused solely on what would happen the next day.

"Somebody thinks they'll be kidnapping me. I'm not gonna tell you why. Just know that it's a fake. It's a sting. We want Graham to nab the napper. Then Graham will question him, so to speak, about an important matter. Have you got a couple off-duty cops you could make available tomorrow? No, wait a minute. Do you have a couple privates?"

"No cops will be off duty at that time tomorrow. The president's making a speech at Buckingham Fountain during lunch hour. Every cop with the day off wants to be on duty, because the pay gets doubled. You'll need ta go private. Yes, I know a couple who could be available. Rent-a-cops who like private security better."

"Sounds good."

"Are you certain there'll be only one kidnapper?"

"No. That's why I'd like some backup. We need to be ready."

"I'll call around tonight. Who'll pay for it?"

"Graham's got a budget. He'll pay whatever their rate is."

Graham's face showed surprise. Then, he nodded affirmatively.

"Should I ask them to show up at the Wrigley parking lot?" asked Shmoo. "What time?"

"By 11:30 or earlier," said Graham. "And we need a way for them to recognize us."

"No problem," said Shmoo. "I'm coming too. Gotta protect my little Lee. We won't get anything mixed up."

"Everyone says they want to protect me. Thanks, but I do a pretty good job of protecting myself, I'll have you know," trumpeted Leona. "One more thing, Shmoo. In the van with me will be three red tams."

"Ya mean Stoners?"

"Yes. They're with us. They're on our side. Remember that."

"Gotcha."

ONCE IN THE car heading back to South Shore, Graham turned toward his passenger and smirked. "Little Lee, eh!"

38 /FRIDAY, CHICAGO, 1:08 AM

LEONA HAD JUST FLOPPED onto her bed when a spray of color flashed across her forty-inch bedroom LED and she could hear the opening bars of Beethoven's "Joyful, Joyful." With dispatch she opened the top drawer of her dresser and removed a book-sized computer-like object. After opening the flap, the screen lit up immediately with multi-colored fragments. Looking like an unruly pile of broken cut glass, no form was discernible. Leona waited, patiently.

The disarray danced across her screen. Gradually, something came into focus. It was dark, and remained dark. Leona returned momentarily to the drawer and removed a black veil. She threw the veil over her head, draping it down to cover her face. Then, she reassumed her comfortable position on the bed and stared into the camera on top of her screen.

The convulsing color on the screen gave way to a figure, the face of a person similarly veiled in black. The background walls were also black. A light shone backward toward the wall, leaving the veiled figure in the darkness of the foreground. Leona waited. Eventually, the greeting came. First in Farsi, then in English. A resonant male voice spoke with Cambridge enunciation, "Khadijah, are you there?"

"Yes, Abu Talib," responded Leona.

"God is good," exclaimed the male voice with a note of cheer.

"Indeed, God is good," added Leona.

As the shadow on the screen turned nervously from side to side, Leona could make out a silhouetted profile indicating glasses and a lengthy beard. "I would enjoy exchanging niceties, Khadijah, but I have an urgent matter to discuss with you."

"I have some urgent matters to report to you as well, Abu."

"Perhaps you should go first," he said.

"Agreed." Leona proceeded to tell the man called Abu Talib how the CIA had come back into her life, about Graham, about CUB, and how she was being interrogated about the secret person in Iran countering nuclear enrichment. Although his identity was still protected, the raging political waters seemed to be eroding his dam of secrecy. Even with the shadowy images, the listener's nervous body language spoke of anxiety.

"Despite our encryption and other cautions, Khadijah, can we still be sure this conversation is not being monitored?"

Leona chuckled briefly. "Yes, we can be sure. At least for tonight. My wireless signals leaving the house are in fact being intercepted. I've learned that. I even sent a bogus message, and now CUB is racing around Tehran trying to find someone who doesn't exist." She laughed again. "My hardwire is mounted on a telephone line that stretches to 79th Street and then linked directly to a satellite. A month ago the city brought a crew to replace a burned out alley light. I watched. No one discovered my cable. So, we're safe for the time being." Abu could not see Khadijah's triumphant smile, but he sensed it. His smile was similarly hidden in the shadows.

"Now, let me tell you about my situation," he began. "I have been asked to devise a new technology for uranium enrichment. We will use lasers. When finely tuned, lasers can ionize uranium-235 and the material can be easily collected on a negatively charged plate. As you know, our current use of centrifuges requires large facilities, easy to spot by satellite reconnaissance and easy targets for Israeli bombs. But lasers are small, cheap, and discreet. This is a game-changing technology, Leona. I mean, Khadijah."

"How quickly does Tehran expect you to be up and operating?"

"Immediately. Well, you know what that means. Soon. They are now procuring the laser technology and identifying a facility site. I don't know its location yet."

"What are your plans, Abu?"

"This puts me in a difficult situation. By putting me in charge, I will be placed exactly where I need to be to keep slowing the progress toward weapons grade material. But with everyone looking over my shoulder, they will be demanding that I produce positive results within a short period of time. Because of the simplicity of the new technology, I don't know how to sabotage it without discovery."

"The situation is growing dire," mumbled Leona. "You've been working alone for so long, Abu. How much longer can you continue to stall and prevent a crisis?"

"I fear my time is running out."

Silence took over. Each looked at one another, watching the minimal movement of the other's black form.

"Maybe there's something you can do, Khadijah. You know Charles Elliott, don't you?"

"Yes. I met him while studying in Berkeley. He's in the physics department at Cal."

"Are you in personal contact?"

"No regular contact. Still, if I were to make an appointment..."

"Please make an appointment. As the inventor of this laser process, he knows more than anybody just what the details are. Perhaps he can supply me with the information on how to make the lasers appear to function yet fail to ionize the U-235. We could install the lasers, make them work, and fall short of producing the enriched material."

"But even if you would be successful, it would buy only a little time. The crisis is coming, sooner or later."

"This has been the case all along, Khadijah. We've got to get Dodge and Golshani to cut out this saber rattling before it's too late. In the meantime, I still need to stall. Do you think you could get this information for me from Professor Elliott?"

"This means you'd no longer be a Lone Ranger."

"Well, what am I to do?"

"Here's a problem, Abu. If Elliott agrees to provide me with this information and I successfully transmit it to you, he would in effect become a traitor to the U.S. He's not likely to agree to play this role."

"Well, Leona, I ask again: what am I to do? Ask Elliott if he's a citizen of the world or only of his own country. This could be our only hope."

Silence intervened again.

"I'll ask him," interrupted Leona. "But I can't simply phone him or send him an email. I'll have to go to California and talk to him in private. Then I'll send what I get over our encrypted wireless."

"How soon can you do this, Khadijah?"

"Next Monday at the very earliest. In the meantime I've got a mess here in Chicago to clean up."

"Monday it must be," said Abu. "I thank you, Khadijah."

"It's me who should thank you, Abu. Actually, it's our planet who owes you thanks."

39 /FRIDAY, CHICAGO, 5:58 AM

SHORTLY BEFORE 6:00 am Leona's iPhone rang. The kitten on her quilt looked up. Buck, sleeping on the floor, rose to his feet. When Leona answered she heard Hayim Levy talking rapidly. "Sorry to wake you, Lee, but I'm concerned. I needed to call somebody who'd know what to do in an emergency. There's a man in our parking lot with a gun, a rather large pistol."

"Did you call 911?

"Yes, first thing." The rabbi stuttered but spoke again. "The police are on the way. Let me tell you. Our apartment intercom sounded a few minutes ago. A man's voice said that my car had been broken into during the night. He said he was a maintenance man. He asked if I would come down the elevator and look at the damage with him. I agreed."

"Something's fishy, Hy. More."

"Then I walked over to the picture window, the one that overlooks the lot. I looked down. A van pulled up. The driver got out, and from the seat he drew a large pistol. Then he put it under his sweatshirt to hide it. Another guy came out of our building and is now in the driver's seat."

"The man with the gun, what does he look like?"

"I can see him right now. Maybe twenty-five. Caucasian. Bearded.

Overweight. Wearing a sweatsuit. Sneakers."

"What color is the sweatsuit?"

"Gray and maroon."

"The van. What kind is it?"

"A cleaner's van."

"Can you see what it says on the side?"

"I think so. Let me...yes. It says Evanston Cleaners."

"Hy, I'm coming over. Is Nancy there?"

"Yes."

"Listen to me. Please lock the door to your apartment. Don't go down. Stay where you are until I contact you. Remind me: how many flats on your floor?"

"Only two. Doctor Max Samuelson lives next door. He's your doctor, right?"

"Yes. He's my gynecologist. Do as I say. Stay inside. I'll get there in minutes. Bye."

"Bye."

LEONA THREW on her sweats and running shoes. She punched the code into her wall console. The weapons drawer popped out. Leona grabbed a Browning Buck Mark Lite and stuck it in the rear of her reinforced waistband. She flew two steps at a time down the stairs, with Buck running after her.

Graham was sleeping soundly in the living room on the hide-a-bed. "Graham, wake up! You're driving. Get those pants on!"

Buck had taken a seat on the floor to watch the action. Leona opened the front door and Buck raced out, banging both Leona and the door. Holding the doors open, she called urgently into the living room: "Get going Graham. It's an emergency." Then turning to the dog who was lifting a leg against the fence post, she called, "Here Buck." The husky loped up to the porch and back into the house, as if he'd been obeying this command for years. Leona slammed the house door and the two humans piled into Graham's car. "Drive. I'll tell you where. We're going north on Lake Shore to Hyde Park, to 55th."

On her Droid Leona hit the speed dial. A groggy Everett answered. "Everett, this is Pastor Lee. Quickly. Where is the Evanston Cleaner's van?"

"Ah, it's right here. In my backyard."

"Please be sure. Go and take a look."

"Okay." Everett walked to his window. "Yep. It's right where I left it."

"Thanks. Bye."

LEONA DIALED Hayim on her iPhone. "Hy, what's happening?"

"Oh, Lee, something's not right. Max Samuelson is walking out of the building toward the parking lot. He goes to the hospital early to make rounds. I'm watching while I'm talking." There was a pause. Leona could hear his breathing. Hayim continued, "The guy with the gun is tracking Max. He's following Max. Why is he following Max?" Hayim's voice was growing louder. "Oh, no!"

"Hy, what's going on?"

"He's approaching Max with the gun. Max doesn't see him yet."

"Hy...?"

"He's firing. Max is down. Oh, God! Max has been shot."

"Graham, faster."

Graham grimaced.

Leona turned again to the phone. "Those bullets were meant for you, Hy. What's happening now?"

"The gunman is in the van. He's pulling away. Oh, God, I can't believe this. The police aren't here yet. Max is helpless on the pavement."

"They'll be there soon," said Leona.

"Oh, now I see a squad roll coming from the other direction. It's stopping in the parking lot. The police don't see Max yet. They don't know what happened."

"Stay where you are, Hy. I'll call you in a few minutes."

As Graham's tires screeched to a halt in the apartment parking lot, they were assaulted by a cacophony of sirens. Rhythmic red and blue lights flashed. Detective Ragland was kneeling over the still warm body of a doctor who would never again make his morning rounds.

"Hello, David," greeted Leona. "Is he dead?"

Ragland looked up. "Yes, unfortunately. Remind me, how do I know you?"

"I'm Pastor Leona Foxx. You met me after the hostage situation on Marquette."

"Oh, yes. You're the one who.... I shouldn't have forgotten this soon." His eyes surveyed her figure like a tourist gawking at the Taj Mahal.

"Should I turn around so you can see my ass too, Detective Ragland?"

He coughed into his hand. "What brings you here?"

"This hit was on my doctor, Max Samuelson. He was such a dear man. He loved me, as he loved all of his patients. But we've got a murder here that demands immediate attention."

"You seem to be unusually knowledgeable about a murder so soon after it was committed. Did you pull the trigger?'

"No, of course not. But I can give you the name of an eyewitness. I want you to be discreet, however. By interrogating him you could put him in danger. Promise?"

"Promise. Who is the witness?"

"His name is Hayim Levy, Apartment 1220 in that building over there. I'll call him and tell him you're on the way up. Again, please do not expose his name to the public, because this might bring the killer back for a second shooting. Got me?"

Ragland nodded. Leona dialed the Levy number and alerted the rabbi that the detective would soon be calling on him.

"One more thing," the pastor said to the detective; "where will you be midday today?"

"How would I know? I simply go from felony to felony, from murder to murder."

"Can I call you if I need you?"

"Sweetie, you can call me any time. Here's my card with my cell on it."

Leona turned, "Come on, Graham. We've gotta go."

"Oh, one more thing," said Ragland. "I can see a slight bulge in your sweat pants. Just above your derrier. Now, you're not a pistol pack'n pastor, are you?"

"Want to search me? Or, do you want to interview a murder witness?"

Ragland grinned. "Bye, Pastor."

40 /FRIDAY, CHICAGO, 7:36 AM

BACK AT THE parsonage they found Hillar sitting on the front porch. The forlorn expression on his face was intentional.

"Why aren't you in school, Hillar?" scolded Leona.

"I want to spend the day with you guys," pleaded Hillar.

"No. Absolutely not. Get to school," demanded Leona. "We'll tell you what happened when we see you later."

Hillar complied, but with a sulk. Inside the parsonage, Midnight and Buck were waiting for their breakfast. Leona obliged, each receiving dried food in their bowls.

"Graham, would you please clean the litter box?"

"What? Clean the litter box? This is an outrageous example of chauvinism—female chauvinism!" Graham could hardly control his laughter.

"Look, I'm going to make you some breakfast. If I'm going to cook for a male chauvinist, then I'm practicing co-dependent chauvinism." Leona chuckled. Then she turned toward the kitchen, speaking over her shoulder. "The pooper scooper is behind the litter box. Get to work or you'll starve."

Leona prepared bacon and eggs and served breakfast. "We'll need protein when the big action begins later."

Following breakfast both registered a need for their morning routine. "You can take the first shower, Graham," said Leona.

"Oh, no. Ladies first!"

"Okay, I'll holler when I'm done and you can have the bathroom."

Graham had read fourteen emails and responded to three on his Droid by the time he heard a voice from upstairs, "The bathroom's free now, Graham."

"Got towels?" Graham hollered up the stairwell.

The upstairs voice responded. "I don't like hollering, Graham. If you've got something to say, then come and say it in a normal voice."

"But you hollered at me," he screamed.

"That doesn't matter. I still don't like it."

Graham trudged up the stairs. At the top he found Leona in her vanilla colored fleece robe with her hair wrapped in a large white bath towel. "Here's your towel and washcloth," she said, handing him an armful. Graham grabbed the gift, winked, and closed the bathroom door behind him. The latch failed to secure the door, so unobserved it popped ajar.

Leona waltzed down the hall to her bedroom, leaving the bedroom door half open. She dropped her fleece robe on the floor and flung her head towel across the room. She stood naked in front of her closet door mirror. She combed her wet hair back to facilitate drying. She was in no hurry. She brushed slowly.

Is that Graham singing in the shower? She walked to her own door. *Yes. It's Graham singing to himself. She listened."*

"Night time..."

Andrew Lloyd Webber? Phantom of the Opera?

"Silently the senses abandon their defenses, helpless to resist the notes I write; for I compose the music of the night."

Yes, it's Phantom! It sounds like Graham's baritone voice is pushing tenor. Actually, he adds resonance and strength to what could be weak if sung by a lonely tenor. Leona slipped into her fleece robe and crept silently like a Winnebago in moccasins to the bathroom door. She opened the door to a twelve-inch margin, just glimpsing a human form behind the steamy glass shower panel. She listened while she watched.

Graham transitioned into another Phantom strain, the duet between Raoul and Christine. "No more talk of darkness...I'm here, nothing can harm you...Love me. That's all I ask of you." He sang with such compelling resonance that Leona found herself dramatically moved. The male solo was nearing the point where the female solo would join. Leona entered the bathroom proper and approached the shower door. She readied herself. At the precise moment, when Graham paused for a breath, she interjected at three-quarters volume. "Say you love me every waking moment...Promise me that all you say is true. That's all I ask of you."

Graham was startled. He was startled that Leona's voice was so close. He was startled also because this lyric soprano hit the high notes. As if he were Raoul, he responded, "Let me be your shelter. Let me be your light.."

Leona responded: "All I want is freedom, a world with no more night; and you, always beside me, to hold me and to hide me..."

Graham: "Then say you'll share with me one love, one lifetime...that's all I ask of you..."

Leona: "Say you'll share with me one love, one lifetime...say the word and I will follow you..."

At this point both Graham and Leona sang in unison. "Share each day with me, each night, each morning..."

Leona's fleece robe dropped to the bathroom floor. She stood for a moment next to the shower. Both were silent. Graham opened the shower door, and his eyes just caught Leona's naked backside departing. The bathroom door closed behind her. It latched.

41 /FRIDAY, CHICAGO, 10:45 AM

EARLIER GRAHAM HAD PARKED his silver Honda CR-V over on 80th, so it would not be visible during the departure. This was a precaution, in case the parsonage was under surveillance. By 10:45 am the Evanston Cleaner's van was parked at the parsonage gate. Scorp and Quint rang the doorbell. Leona opened the door. All stood around for a few moments to greet Buck and pet Midnight. "What are your instructions from the white guy?" Leona asked.

Scorp responded. "We're supposed to tie your hands and remove all your identification. Then, we deliver you to somebody at Wrigley at 11:45. We're supposed to park and then our guy will make contact."

"OK. I'll empty my pockets and leave my ID at home," Leona said. "I'll keep my Droid. It's my link to Graham. You can tie my hands with plastic cord. I've got some in the kitchen, but we'll make it easy for me to break loose. Are you carrying heat?"

"Each of us has a rod," said Scorp.

"I pray that the three of you will not have to use them. If you're not killers now, I don't want to be the one who starts you down that road. The heat is just in case something goes wrong. Use bullets only if you need to defend yourselves. Got it?"

"Sure."

"Here's my Kimber," said Leona. The eyes of Scorp and Quint

opened wide at the site of the gun. Leona proceeded as if all this was usual. "Please leave it in the van. I just might have use for it. Now, I want you guys to understand something. Your job is to put me in the hands of the white guy. Nothing else. Use the heat only if something goes wrong. As soon as I'm dropped off, I want you guys to leave. Graham and I will take it from that point. If any trouble breaks out, I want you gone. If the police get involved they'll only blame you gangbangers. Are we clear?"

All nodded.

"Graham, you can leave by the side door to get your car. We should go to the north side on the Kennedy Expressway and take Halstad further north. Downtown might be jammed because of the president's lunch speech at Buckingham. Got gas?"

"Yeah. We got enough gas," said Quint. Graham nodded a yes.

"Let's roll," said Leona leaning down to hug the two animals goodbye.

The two Stoners exited the parsonage with Leona, whose hands were bound in plastic clothesline. All climbed into the van. Everett drove out of the parking lot onto South Burnham. Graham followed. The dashboard of Graham's car included a modified GPS, tuned to Leona's Droid. Graham could watch both the van and the GPS arrow.

In the van, Leona provided her three Woodlawn accomplices with more detail; and they to her. Had Hillar communicated with Owl? Yes. Had Owl passed on the information to Scorp?

Yes. Was the white guy on board with the plan? Yes. Graham heard every word.

At a quarter before noon the van passed the Wrigley field parking lot. The gates would not open until the night game scheduled for 7:05 pm. Everett pulled into the designated driveway and parked in front of a closed gate. He shut off the engine. Shmoo and the cops-for-hire were nowhere in sight. Nor was Graham anywhere to be seen. Leona hoped they were invisibly present. The waiting began.

Noon came. No action. Leona asked Quint to check his iPad to see if he could get a livestream of the Buckingham Fountain festivities. They could. They watched as the mayor and president with his first lady stepped up to the platform. A band was playing "Hail to the Chief."

Their concentration was interrupted by a vehicle pulling into the driveway alongside their van. It had backed in so its right side paralleled their right side. The arriving vehicle was another Evanston Cleaner's van, identical to the one they were in. With the engine still running, a man threw open the sliding door and stepped out. He looked familiar to Leona. *Did I see him while jogging home from the Levys'? Does he fit the description Hy gave me of this morning's murderer?*

"Is this the white guy?" she asked Scorp.

"Yeah. That's him." Scorp opened the panel door. Leona stepped out with her hands tied in front. The white guy said nothing. He gripped Leona's upper arm and forcefully shoved her into the adjacent van. Scorp spoke. "What now?" He received no reply. The van door slammed shut. The white guy ran around and got in the rear seat next to Leona. The kidnappers' van immediately raced out into the street and drove off north on Halstad.

Scorp and his two friends were dazed. Everything had happened so quickly. They frantically discussed what they should do.

"Pastor Lee told us to do nuth'n," exclaimed Quint with a tremor in his voice.

"But maybe they're gonna hurt her," said Everett.

"They shoved her," said Scorp. "I don't see Graham or anybody else. No cops. No backup. Maybe there's more danger here than the pastor thought there'd be."

"What should we do?" asked Quint.

Everett said, "Close the doors!" He rammed the van into drive and sped up Halstad in the same direction as the first van. Scorp and Quint were thrust back into their seats as Everett accelerated.

In the kidnapper's van, Leona was belted into a back seat. She found herself in the company of three men. The so-called "white guy" sat in the back next to her. In the front were two others, both in their thirties, Caucasian, and dressed in athletic clothes. The driver sported a White Sox cap, much too small for his wide head. This was just the situation she had hoped would develop. Now it was her turn to get some information.

"Ms. Foxx, do you know who we are?" asked the one riding shotgun, the right front seat.

"No. But I hope you'll tell me."

"We don't plan to. What we would like from you is a name. A simple name. If you give us this name, we will let you out and drive away. You'll never see us again."

"You want a name?"

"Yes."

"Here's a name for you: Max Samuelson."

"Who's Max Samuelson?"

"Max Samuelson is the man murdered this morning by the guy sitting to my left."

"What?!" said the so-called white guy?

"You heard me."

The shotgun rider looked at the white guy. "I thought his name was..."

"Levy, Walt," interrupted the one to Leona's left. "That's it. Levy. Who's Samuelson, you fox?"

Leona had now learned at least one name, Walt, riding shotgun. "He's the guy you killed. Actually, he was my doctor. You'll hear about it on the news, I'm sure. You guys seem to know how to misfire. So, why did you want to rub out Rabbi Levy?"

The three tried to look one another in the eye. They were obviously confused, astonished at what their captive seemed to know. "I thought you said you don't know who we are," said Walt.

"I did say that. I don't know who you are. Inform me. Who are you and why did you want to shoot my favorite rabbi?"

"Because he's your favorite rabbi, I guess," said Walt. "We had thought you knew more about us than you apparently do. We thought you had confided in Mr. Levy and that he could expose us, especially if you would turn up missing for a period of time. Let me ask about the other name. Here's what we really want. Who is the Iranian in Tehran slowing nuclear weapons development?"

Leona said nothing. No one pressed the question, at least not immediately. The Evanston Cleaners van droned on northward. Leona entered into her own thought world, a world where she was undergoing a conflict between the machine and heart. The word "martyr" came to mind. *Might this be the day I will die? Might I be executed by this American triumvirate of CIA contractors? If so, would the word "martyr" apply?*

This word confused Leona. When she had first begun her theological studies, she learned how a martyr was a person who died confessing faith in Jesus. Justin Martyr, one of the great theologians of the second century, was burned at the stake because he would not compromise on his religious commitment. While Leona was in seminary, something odd happened. One of its recent graduates, a man of about thirty serving as a missionary in Ethiopia, had died in an auto accident. One of the seminary chapel services was dedicated to his memorial. During the sermon, the seminary president described the dead missionary as a martyr. This was confusing to Leona. An auto accident? Why a martyr? An auto accident is nothing like being burned at the stake. Is the term "martyr" simply honorific for people we like?

What made this more disconcerting for Leona was the recent use of the label "martyr" in the world of Islamic terrorism. To die killing enemies of Allah meant that suicide bombers would become martyrs; and upon their death they would be given an immediate free passage to heaven. The same word could be used for a terrorist as was used for the saint Leona admired: Justin Martyr.

Again, she pondered: *What if I die today, executed by these thugs for keeping an international secret? I would not be dying for my Lord. I would rather be dying to keep an obscure Muslim from suffering this fate. It would be a trade, his life for mine. Where does this fit in the world of martyrdom?* Leona clicked on her machine mind.

42 /FRIDAY, EVANSTON, 12:31 PM

THE KIDNAPPERS' van turned right on Wilson and left onto North Sheridan, driving north. Within a few minutes they were viewing Lake Michigan to their right. A voice broke in through the Bluetooth. "Is that you, Lanny?"

The driver spoke, "Yeah, it's me." Leona learned a second name.

"Is Walt with you?" the radio voice continued.

"Yeah, I'm here in the passenger's seat. Whatya want?"

"I need ta doublecheck. Did you say the 85th floor?"

"Yeah, that's right."

"Did you pick up your package?"

"You bet. The package is in the back seat, ready for delivery."

"Good. We're tracking you from above. Seeya on the ground."

"Okay."

Overhearing this conversation was fortuitous for Leona. Like basketball players, this team was telegraphing its passes. Walt, looking at his watch, mumbled deliberately and gleefully, "Less than thirty-two more hours." Heads nodded. Leona scrubbed her memory. She reminded herself that Andy had said he and Mildred would be overnighting on the 85th floor of the John Hancock. *Might this close the loop? Might the Plan B event take place about eight Saturday evening?*

"You're not listening to me," said Walt, turning his attention back to Leona. "The name!"

"I gave you a name. And, now, you want another name. Isn't one name enough?"

"You don't seem afraid of us."

"I'm not."

"You should be. You might not live to deliver your sermon Sunday."

Leona continued to study the body language of her companions inside the van. She wondered whether or not Graham could hear this conversation and when he would take action. Graham could not hear her inner thoughts, to be sure; but he certainly would know when to rescue her. Her task at the moment was to learn what kind of terrorist act is being planned, most likely, at 8:00 pm on Saturday evening at the John Hancock. What could they be planning? How could she find out?

A half football field behind them Graham drove in his CR-V, listening to the conversation between Leona and her kidnappers on his Bluetooth. Directly behind Graham was the second Evanston Cleaner's van. Following the van was a SUV carrying Shmoo and two colleagues. All were keeping pace. These trackers would keep the prey in sight but not overtake the rabbit they were chasing.

The van radio signaled again. "Are you there, Lanny?"

"Yeah."

"We'll drop down between the highway and the lake. We'll hover until we see you hit the beach."

Leona surmised that momentarily she would be passed off. Perhaps that voice was coming from a chopper. If so, once in the air, then Graham and the rent-a-cops would be no help. She needed to act with haste.

"So, again, where are we going?"

"Do you like to swim?" asked Walt.

"I love swimming. I've done the triathlon a half dozen times."

Walt turned to look out the windshield. "We have some friends who'd like to meet you at the beach. They'd like to hear a certain name from you. If you provide it, you'll live to run another triathlon. If you don't you might find the water of Lake Michigan pretty deep."

Graham heard it all. He began to run scenarios and options through his mind. *Will Leona be exposed when the van stops? What role might the helicopter play? When should I make my move?* He realized that he would need to put a stop to this before Leona could be transferred to the chopper. To make matters more complicated, this woman was coming to mean much more to him than merely an assignment. Graham studied the helicopter hovering above the shoreline.

The first Evanston Cleaners' van was now in Evanston itself, north of Chicago by a couple of blocks. To the right was an apron with thirty feet of grass and then seventy feet of sand before hitting the breakwater. A small beach area, not exactly private but relatively secluded. Lanny swung the van to the right over the grass toward the water. He slid to a stop in the sand. The helicopter hovered at water's edge. Graham remained on the highway, driving past the turn off point a hundred yards to make a U turn onto the sand. He kicked the CR-V into four-wheel drive, churning sand as he accelerated toward the off-road van. A handful of sunbathers in the area were startled by the unexpected vehicle activity; they screamed and scattered.

The kidnapper's van had come to an abrupt stop. Walt leaped out. He flung open Leona's door and leaned down to unfasten her seat belt. At this Leona split her hands free from the plastic ties, refolded them, and then came down on Walt's neck with a rabbit punch. Walt drifted into a faint, collapsing on the ground. Leona slid out the panel door and dropped to the ground as well. She crawled toward the van's rear, peering beneath the undercarriage to see what might be going on.

Neither Lanny nor the white guy saw this. They had exited on the van's left side and their attention was diverted to Graham's car bearing down on them. Each took a spread-eagle stance with two hands on their weapons. They fired their handguns at Graham, putting holes and spider webs in his windshield.

The helicopter, rocking while suspended above their heads, provided cover fire. Bullets from the sky punched more holes in

Graham's windshield. At this Graham stopped. He exited the car and used his open driver's door as a shield. He continued firing, alternating between the chopper and the two gunman at the van.

By this time Everett sized up what was happening. He swerved his van to his right and drove eighty feet before stopping at water's edge, just south of the other van. He instinctively had created triangulation: his van, Graham's car, and the gun blazing chopper. The three tams exited on the passenger side and took up positions with guns drawn, looking over the van's hood.

Scorp reminded himself that Leona had exorted him to refrain from using a weapon except... Scorp fired. He hit the helicopter window closest to the gunman. The helicopter gunman panicked at being caught in a near crossfire. He frantically jerked his hand upward to signal to the pilot to rise out of range. The craft headed up and north.

Leona found herself in the eye of a hurricane of roaring vehicles, gunshots, and human chaos. She turned her head skyward to study the helicopter. It looked to her like a Long Ranger, a duplicate of the president's. Only, this one was white. The president's had been dark blue.

Walt, now awakening, took advantage of Leona's diverted attention. He grabbed her from behind, locking his left arm around her neck. With his right hand he pressed his Glock 17 to Leona's temple. They stood up, slowly. With her under his control, he eased her around the rear of the van, taking small side steps. Like a rabbit disappearing into the thicket, the copter disappeared into the distance.

In the meantime, on the left side of the CUB van, the white guy was rattling his MAC 10 automatic at Graham's car. From behind Graham a SUV appeared, also in four-wheel drive, fishtailing through the sand toward the action. It was aimed like a missile at the parked van. The top of Shmoo's torso hung outside the back seat window. Shmoo was firing his Steyr Tactical Machine Pistol. The white guy took a bullet in the chest. He was thrust backward against the van, dropping his weapon and sliding down into a quiet slump on the ground. Blood re-colored his gray and maroon clothes.

Then Lanny stood up with both hands on his handgun, only to be downed by one of Shmoo's bullets through the forehead. Shmoo ceased firing. The SUV stopped. Shmoo jumped out. He and Graham stepped cautiously into the cloud of lingering gun smoke. They crept cautiously toward the apparently pacified Evanston Cleaner's van.

From the van's rear Walt emerged, holding Leona hostage. A tense showdown situation commenced. Everyone became quiet. Walt waved his gunhand so that all could see that he was the one in control. Leona would die immediately if Graham or Shmoo or the two men still in the SUV's front seat made a false move. It was a frozen moment.

Graham and Shmoo looked at each other. Their faces were asking, "Can you get a clear shot?" Their eyes answered, "No."

Walt raised his voice. "I want you all to drop your weapons and walk toward the CR-V. I want you to leave the SUV running. Keys in it. Ms. Foxx and I are going to take a little drive. Do you hear me?"

The two rent-a-cops in the SUV opened their doors and stepped out. Each held his hands up, shoulder high. They walked timidly toward the CR-V. Shmoo and Graham paused without moving.

"Drop 'm," screamed Walt. Shmoo and Graham had no choice. Their weapons fell into the sand at their feet. The two walked backwards toward the CR-V. Within ten seconds, these four soldiers in Leona's army were grouped. Walt and his hostage took small steps toward the SUV. Walt cleverly kept Leona between himself and the four men. The four could only watch helplessly.

As the kidnapper and hostage neared the SUV, Walt whispered to Leona, "Now, you get in the passenger seat. Slowly, with your hands on your head. Understand? Move!"

Leona put her hands on her head and took one step toward the open driver's door. A second passed. A loud gun shot. The Glock dropped from Walt's hand. Walt crumpled and fell heavily into the beach sand. When all eyes turned to find the source of the lethal bullet, they saw Scorp standing there, lowering his weapon. A single, clear and deadly shot.

Leona ran to Scorp and gave him a hug. Then, like the flip of a coin, her face turned to business. "Look," she addressed the four plus Scorp, "we have not yet drawn police attention. Let's vacate and let any bystanders guess what happened. We'll meet at the church parking lot. I'll ride with Shmoo. Scorp, clear the van and abandon it. It's too easy to recognize on the road. Make sure you get my Kimber. The three of you Stoners ride with Graham. Now, get going!"

Shmoo walked toward the two of the three bodies lying on the left side of the Evanston Cleaners' van. He raised his gun at the white guy.

"What are you doing, Shmoo?" yelled Leona.

"Gonna finish 'm off. We don't want any witnesses in court."

"No, Shmoo. Get back into this car."

Shmoo looked up puzzled. He shrugged his shoulders and did what Leona asked him to do.

A siren shrieked in the distance. Soon everyone was in their vehicle. The two vehicles took off, heading south. Leona found herself in the back seat of the SUV, telling the driver where to go. Shmoo grabbed her hand. Leona spoke first. "Shmoo, I can't tell you what a sight it was to see you coming on firing like Eisenhower's army on D-Day. I owe you."

"Leona, I'm just so glad that you're still with us."

Their two hands squeezed.

43 /FRIDAY, CHICAGO, 3:21 PM

"Let me get this straight," said Jarrod Grimes into his mobile telephone. "Lanny is dead. Walt is dead. And that local guy with the beard is dead. All dead. How could this be?"

Grimes nodded grimacing as he listened to the recounting of the afternoon gunfight on the Evanston beach, an eyewitness account reported from someone aboard the hovering helicopter. "Where is that pastor, that Reverend Foxx?" A minute passed.

"Oh, shit!" Grimes muttered. The two muscle men studying their iPads in the sitting room did not look up. Grimes listened to more coming from the phone and then commented, "I think we both know what this means. But before taking any action, let me check once with the boss. Call me back in a half hour."

Grimes hit the off button. He turned to look with disgust at his two comrades. Then he walked to one of the two closed doors in this Palmer House suite. He rapped on one. A gruff voice bellowed, "Enter!" A loud exchange blasted through the closed door. When Grimes stepped out, he spoke to his two henchmen. "It's clear. Our only option is the alternative plan: 9/11 the 2nd."

44 /FRIDAY, CHICAGO, 6:30 PM

THE RIDE SOUTH from Evanston provided a moment of relief, a moment to reflect. The four in the SUV engaged in a discussion of the details of what had happened. Leona learned that the two rent-a-cops were Hammer and Wade. Hammer and Wade had never been in a gun battle like this. They had never confronted this much life-threatening danger. Yet, the tone of victory seemed to satisfy a yearning they had been only obscurely aware of.

Leona was double-minded. The machine-minded Leona deemed what had happened to be a well-executed assault. They had decimated the enemy. She retrieved the information she had wanted regarding terrorist Plan B. Or, at least she thought she might have gained this information. And CUB would have become aware that it faced a formidable enemy in Leona and her rag tag army.

On the other hand, heart-minded Leona felt depressed. Once again, the earth was strewn with dead bodies, bleeding into the soil. *Why do our lives have to be so violent? Why do I have to be so sensitive? Why can't I be like Shmoo and take violent death as simply part of a day's work?* Leona tried to limit her thinking and re-thinking to what had just occurred. There was no time for sentimentality, for licking her wounded conscience. Events were moving fast. The possibility of a

Plan B brought a sense of urgency. Strategies needed to be discussed. What next?

Leona asked, "Do you guys want to eat?"

A chorus of "yeahs" could be heard.

Leona found her Droid and called Graham. "We slew the dragon, didn't we, Graham!"

"Sure did. But Lee, how do you feel?" responded Graham with both triumph and tenderness.

"No time for my feelings right now. Would you stop at Jewel on the way and pick up some steaks? Maybe some sweet corn? Beer? And I need some charcoal for the Weber. No matter how traumatized we might be by what happened, we need to plan our weekend strategy. We might need to conscript our newfound soldiers-in-law."

"Do you guys want something to eat?" Graham asked over his shoulder.

The three tams voiced enthusiasm for the idea.

By six-thirty that evening the Weber was spitting smoke, the steaks were sizzling, and the buzzing vigilantes were juggling beer cans in the parsonage front yard. Hillar joined the throng but got his hand slapped when he reached for a beer. Buck introduced himself to everybody; everybody took a turn holding Midnight.

Leona needed a breather. She went to her room, dropped her dirty clothes into a hamper, and put on a fresh tee shirt and jean shorts: a subconscious ritual of purification.

She paused to examine her face in the full body mirror. Her eyes shone with tears. A prayer rose up almost to her lips. *How many did we kill today, God? Have you called me to be a blood-shedder? Wherever I go, I meet death, violent death. Is this what you've called me for? Is this my vocation? I wanted to bring love where there is strife. I wanted to bring light into the darkness and wisdom into ignorance. I wanted to bring peace on earth. Short of that, I just wanted to bring moments of grace into people's lives. But whether I like it or not, somebody else will have to be the Messiah. Amen."*

As she was finishing her short prayer, she noticed that Buck had joined her. He was seated silently next to her left leg, apparently looking in the mirror. *But dogs don't recognize themselves in mirrors,* she said to herself. Yet, Buck seemed to be content as her sidekick, duplicating her action. "Is there a wolf inside you, Buckie?" she asked the canine. Buck looked up. "I think we're a lot like each other," she added. If dog's eyes could smile in acknowledgement, they did.

Back downstairs, she re-entered the hubbub of the yard. "Lift up your beers!" Leona shouted. "I'm just a sniveling damsel in distress. And all you big guys rescued me. I want to drink a toast to my protectors!"

Everyone was laughing as they toasted. "You don't need any protection, Lee!" said Shmoo so the group could overhear. "Thanks for faking it so that we all could feel like knights in shining armor." They raised their Bud cans and Sam Adams bottles to drink another toast.

As individuals passed through the living room to transport dinner items to and from the kitchen, they caught the evening television news with Bill Kurtis. "Our top story: a gunfight on an Evanston beach." The TV watchers were transfixed as the camera panned the beach with the two abandoned Evanston Cleaners' vans. An on-site reporter summarized: "Some witnesses report they saw a helicopter in the area, but they could not tell whether it was defending or shooting at the three killed. It was estimated that an additional eight people were engaged in the gun battle, possibly one woman. No one could identify the shooters leaving the scene, but they do report that three of them were African Americans wearing red tams."

The reporter turned to David Ragland in his wrinkled brown suit and loose necktie with the wreckage visible over his shoulder. "We have no idea who these dead men are, who killed them, or why," he told the interviewer in a voice registering puzzlement.

"What about the red tams?" asked the reporter. "Doesn't that suggest the Woodlawn Stoners? Could this have been gang related?"

"I don't know what Woodlawn Stoners would be doing on the north side," said Ragland. "That'll be part of our investigation."

During the commercial break, Everett offered the first reaction, giving voice to displaced anxiety. "Boy, we sure know how to trash a beach, don't we!" His comrades laughed.

As the news program shifted to matters of the global economy, the group dissipated. Scorp asked Leona for a moment to talk. "Pastor Lee, I killed one of those three men today. I never killed nobody before. Yeah, I'm a gangbanger and tough and all that, but I never done this. He's dead. I did it."

Leona looked him in the eye and communicated her understanding, and her patience. She waited.

"Is God gonna git me fer this?" A pregnant pause followed. Leona waited for this thought to be gouged into their shared consciousness before she began to speak.

"Listen to me, Scorp. First, you pulled me to safety so I wouldn't die on the Cheltenham Metra platform. You're not a killer by nature. Second, would it help if I mentioned the obvious? He was a dangerous man. If you had not shot him, I would probably be dead instead. You pulled the trigger to protect me. I'm alive because of what you did. You have saved my life twice. Isn't there something right about what you did?"

"Yes, I know that. But it don't help. That man never gonna drink a beer no more. I'm responsible."

"Sometimes, Scorp, we have to choose between two not very good choices. Neither one permits us to be innocent. Would it help to know that I struggle with this as well? I find I just have to make a decision and sin boldly."

About this time Shmoo walked into the conversation. "Are ya bothered about blowing that guy away, son?"

"Yeah. I ain't done that never before."

"The bastard needed the bullet he got. Somebody had ta git rid of that scum bag."

"Shmoo!" interrupted Leona. "Scorp's speaking from his heart. Taking a person's life is about the worst thing any of us can do. Even if Scorp was justified, still, the man is dead. It's tragic!" Leona put her hand on Scorp's shoulder and touched her left cheek to his.

Shmoo waved his left hand dismissively, muttering, "Bah."

As Leona turned around she faced two figures standing nearly motionless, staring at her. It was Hillar and Owl. Owl's large penetrating eyes closed as she turned her head downward.

"Owl's got something to say to you, Pastor Lee," said Hillar.

Owl couldn't speak. A tear rolled down her left cheek.

"Owl," said the pastor, "are you thinking that you almost got me killed today? Are you thinking that for a little bit of spending money you put somebody's life at risk? Are you thinking that I could be dead right now?"

Owl's slumped head shook up and down in a small but clear arc.

"If I had been killed...."

"Oh, God, I'm so sorry," said Owl interrupting the interrogation. She was cryng. "I didn't know...."

"It's okay," said the pastor softly, wrapping both her arms around the sobbing teenager. They held a mutual embrace. Owl could feel forgiveness pass from Leona's heart to her own.

Leona pulled back her head while holding on to Owl. "I want you to go home right now, Owl. I want you to know that you're always welcome here, at the church, in my house. But right now, we've got an emergency to deal with. I don't want you involved any further. Tomorrow, Owl, come help us with the children at Saturday Morning Club. Tomorrow we'll see each other. Okay?"

Owl nodded affirmatively. Then, after a brief look at Hillar, Owl turned and walked out.

Graham had been standing near enough to witness the tender interchanges. *What a remarkable woman this is.*

After a hasty clean-up, the shepherd thought it was time to reassemble her flock. "Everyone in the dining room. It's okay to bring your drink."

In a few minutes, all were seated around the table. Buck and Midnight were standing by in case something might drop floorward.

"Listen carefully," Leona said, raising her voice and emphatically demanding their attention. "Let me see if I can put this together in a way that makes sense. None of you know the background to what's happening that Graham and I do. I'm not going to—I can't!—fill you in on everything. All you need to know is this: the three kidnappers we fought today are part of a larger group. These guys most likely have had special forces training. They are deadly! Understand? Deadly!"

Silence engulfed the room. Leona scanned each face, each one in rapt attention.

She spoke softly. "The bad guys are planning an act of terrorism. As far as I can tell, we might be the only hope for preventing a disaster. We can't ask a secret service agency to take over, because it may have been compromised by a mole. That leaves us. We've got no time to waste. Let me ask: who here is willing to throw in with Graham and me to try to stop it?"

Hillar was the first to put his hand up. Leona only glared. "I want volunteers," she said. Graham raised his hand with a smirk on his face. "You're stuck with me, Graham. You've got no choice."

Scorp, Everett, and Quint whispered to one another. "We're in," announced Scorp.

"I'll not want to miss the excitement," said Shmoo. "It's been a few years since I got my sidearm hot. I kinda liked it today. But we're paying our rent-a-cops by the hour. Combat pay might be a little steep."

"What about it, Hammer and Wade?" asked Leona. "You'll get paid for today. But Graham can't put you under contract for what we're going to do tomorrow."

Hammer spoke. "This is out of our league. We're used to safety patrol. We watch kids cross the street or CEOs walking through picket lines. We ain't seen nuth'n like this gun battle today." Hammer looked at Wade.

Wade queried with a furrowed brow. "Terrorism, you say?"

"Yes, international terrorism right here in Chicago. That's what we're up against."

"Well," Wade continued, "this could be important. I don't think we should chicken out, Hammer."

"I'll take that as a 'yes,'" said Leona. "Now, listen as I try to draw the strategic picture." She paused to think. "We can only guess what they're planning. We don't know. We've got to make an educated guess and we've got to get it right the first time. No second chances."

Leona ceased speaking for a moment. Midnight now sat on the table, sheltered in the arms of Scorp. Buck still sat on the floor, his nose nuzzling Hillar's lap. All watched.

The table buzzed until Leona signaled for everyone's attention. "We've got to ask about four things: time, place, motive, and means. We've got the time: eight o'clock tomorrow evening. We've got the place: the John Hancock Building, 85th floor. We've got the motive. They failed to obtain a secret that I hold—and I'm not telling any of you. Their motive is to create a disaster and blame Iran. My bet is that they're planning an act of terrorism that looks something like 9/11, even if on a smaller scale. What they want is a public spectacle that will shock our nation with fear. This will prevent any immediate rapprochement with Iran and keep contractors sucking the mammaries of America, the cash cow. Are you with me?"

"My gosh!" gasped Wade. Others murmured disbelief and dread.

"The president and his entourage will be in the Hancock tomorrow," announced Leona.

"How does the president fit in here?" asked Hillar.

"Perhaps it'll be an assassination attempt," interjected Graham. "The president is on record for working things out with Iran before they get a deliverable WMD."

"Yeow," shouted Hammer. "Look at us! Wade and I are just rent-a-cops. We've got a teenager and three gangbangers at this table. Maybe Graham and Shmoo know what they're doin', but this army's bein' led by a minister, a lady minister of all things. No offense, Pastor Lee. Maybe we should turn this over to someone else, someone bigger."

"There's not enough time to tap someone bigger," snapped Leona. "And, as I said, it's possible someone bigger's got a mole. So, we're the only hope. If you're gonna whimper, Hammer, you're certainly welcome to count yourself out. Wade, you too. I understand your reluctance. What we lack in experience and firepower needs to be made up with courage and cleverness. I think we need to proceed because we may be the only ones at this point who can figure out what's about to happen. If it's not us, then it just might be nobody. It's time to show a little patriotism, you guys."

"We're in," said Hammer.

"We're in," added Wade.

"Okay. Here's what I want you to do. Wade and Hammer, you take the three Stoners back home tonight. Drop 'm off in Woodlawn. Exchange cell phone numbers. Be prepared to open up a conference call with each other tomorrow. Hillar and I will meet you at 5:00 pm on North Michigan Avenue in back of the old water tower. That will give us a three-hour countdown to the blast. Got it?"

"Yeah," said Wade and Hammer.

"Okay?" asked Leona looking at each of the three tams singly. All nodded affirmatively. "You five can leave now."

"But who's gonna finish clean'n up here, Pastor?" asked Everett.

"Now, aren't you the gentleman! You know how to win a woman's heart, Everett. If you'd gather up the trash into a plastic bag and place it by my side door, that'll do. Close up the Weber and put the utensils in the kitchen. I'll take if from there. Thanks."

The five went about their work and eventually those inside could hear car doors slamming and the SUV departing. While this was going on, Leona turned her attention to Hillar. "Tomorrow, please come to church a half hour before Saturday Morning Club begins. Help set up. As soon as it's over, go home and change. Put on your Cubs tee shirt and sneakers. Into a backpack please put two bottles of water, binoculars, a roll of Scotch tape, and your helicopter."

"My helicopter?"

"Yes. And make certain the batteries are fresh. We're going to the Cubs game. Got it?"

"Okay, but..."

"Okay, right. Time to get home and hug your mother."

"Okay," said Hillar. He gave Buck a final nose nuzzle. He left through the side door.

Leona turned to the two remaining. "Shmoo, I want to make a Skype call. I might need you. When I'm finished, you can go home.

Graham, would you please stay until Shmoo leaves? Then, I've got something for you to do too. It's gonna be a short night, I'm afraid."

The two nodded with nods vigorous enough to be salutes.

"Get yourselves another beer. I'm going into the living room to call David Ragland."

45 /FRIDAY, CHICAGO, 8:55 PM

LEONA DIALED David Ragland's cell on the big screen. He answered. "I've got Skype," said Leona. "Want to talk 'n' see?"

"Any chance to see you I'll take," Ragland said. In a moment Skype connected them visually. The detective was holding his cell with camera close to his face, but Leona could see the inside of his car behind him. Leona was comfortably seated on her couch across the room from the LED camera, providing a full room view.

"We saw you on the TV news, Mr. Ragland."

"Call me Rags. That's what my friends call me."

"Does this mean I'm a friend now?"

"Indeed," said Ragland, taking over the conversation's lead. "You'll be happy to hear something. I've been thinking about becoming religious. In fact, I'd like to come to your church Sunday. I want to sit right below the pulpit. I want to drool over the prettiest pastor in Chicago."

"Your motives don't sound too holy," Leona responded, smiling.

"I guess, then, I'll have to come and see you in one of those little confessional booths. I'll confess my unholy thoughts."

In the next room both Graham and Shmoo heard everything. Graham's face registered disturbance, the kind of disturbance that signals jealousy. Shmoo grinned and then frowned, expressing paternal disturbance.

"You'll need to confess to God, not me," said Leona.

"You didn't need me today," said Ragland, changing the subject, feigning a whimper.

"No, as it turns out, I didn't. But I need you now. Would you do me a favor?"

"No can do. I don't do favors for gorgeous women unless they come to talk to me in person."

Leona did not answer right away. Shmoo stood up and walked from the dining room into the living room. He sat down on the couch next to Leona and placed his arm loosely around her, dropping his hand on her far shoulder.

"Is that you, Shmoo?" shouted the detective.

"It sure as hell is, Rags. I'd like you to know that I think of Leona as one of my daughters. I protect her like a father. Do you catch my drift.?"

"Gotcha, Shmoo. Now, Leona, just what is that favor?"

"Are you attached to the president's detail in any way?"

"No, I gotta stay available for my usual."

"Good," Leona went on. "Would you be able to check on reports for me? Since last Sunday, has the department had to deal with anything unusual involving either Iranian nationals or Iranian Americans? Robbery? Murder? Kidnapping? Anything?"

"Yes, I can poke around. Why do you need this?"

"I cannot say right now. But it could be important."

"How fast do you need this?"

"Five minutes."

"What!?"

"ASAP. It could be important, I said."

"Okay. I'm close to the station and on coffee break. I'll get back to you by text or phone."

"If you find something, I'd like details. Everything. Can you scan and email documents?"

"Boy, you ask a lot."

"It could be important, Rags."

"I'll see what I can do. Oh, by the way, Shmoo, you've got a good-looking daughter."

"It's time for us to hang up," said Shmoo

"I'm hanging up," said Rags, while Leona was laughing.

They said their goodbyes. Leona thanked Shmoo and called a taxi to take him home. They agreed to the rendezvous at the Chicago Water Tower the next day. Then, she told Graham it was time for his assignments.

GRAHAM SAID, "I'm tired of this beer. I think I'll find some of your good wine and pour myself a glass. May I pour you one?"

"No, Graham. I suggest you don't. You've got a lot of work to do tonight. You need to be able to drive and think straight."

"Why drive?"

"Because you're not staying here. I've got a list for you."

"Are you my wife, my boss, or my drill sergeant?" Graham placed both his hands on Leona's shoulders. He looked her squarely in the eyes. He shook her very gently, then kissed her on the forehead. She twisted her neck just slightly and lifted herself up so that their lips could meet.

Still holding her arms around Graham, Leona withdrew slightly and whispered. "Sorry if I'm barking orders. I feel a sense of urgency. I guess I've just taken over here, haven't I?"

"Yes, you have. But it's really okay, Lee. You're rising to the challenge. You're a damned good leader." Graham withdrew from the embrace and reached for his beer bottle. He emptied the last drop of his Sam Adams and looked to the side. "Did Detective Ragland flatter you?"

"I don't have time to enjoy flattery right now. Give me your attention, please." She slapped Graham on the shoulder as if she were a doctor with a newborn. He turned to look directly at her. Then, she continued. "Let's think this through together. What kind of event is

CUB planning? If we're right that it's going to take place at eight o'clock tomorrow at the John Hancock Building, most likely on the 85th floor, then what? Are they going to send a party up the elevators or fire stairs to assassinate the president? Are they going to yell 'fire' and pick off important people from sniper windows? Or, are they going to set a real fire? If so, where? On the first floor? The 85th floor? Assuming the streets and sidewalks will be blue with cops, how will they make it happen?"

"Something tells me you've got a theory."

"Yes. I wonder if it's reasonable."

"Try me."

"A strike from the air."

"What do you mean?"

"The Twin Towers were taken down by airplanes flying into them. The president's surmise is that CUB would like to imitate 9/11 on a smaller scale, mainly because CUB wants to elicit the kind of national fear of Iran that took us into the wars in Afghanistan and Iraq."

"Mmmmmm. So, the worst case scenario would be a combination: an assassination of the president combined with a terrorist attack blamed on Iran. Right?"

"That's what I'm thinking."

"And it would take place tomorrow evening at eight o'clock on the 85th floor of JH, right?"

"Right.

"But Leona, you've got some holes in the bottom of your theory boat. It's leaking. Here's one. Because JH stands between so many other buildings, no one could fly a plane into it. No way to copy 9/11."

"Right. How about this? Suppose CUB flies a suicide helicopter right through the president's 85th floor window."

"A helicopter?" Graham thought for a moment. "One more hole in your theory. Where will CUB get a suicide bomber to fly that helicopter? I presume no fanatical Iranians belong to CUB. And suicide bombers are not exactly for hire."

"Yes, this is a hole in my theory. Here is how I plug it up. This is a long shot. If Hillar can fly a helicopter with a remote control and make Buck go crazy, couldn't CUB do the same thing with a full sized whirlybird? Recall that Jarrod Grimes oversaw the flying of drones in Pakistan."

"Lee, you're getting somewhere. Let's look at one more hole, though. How will CUB blame Iran?"

"Hey, my theory is almost airtight. Yes, this may be a leak. Will it sink my boat?"

At that moment Leona's Droid sounded. In seconds David Ragland appeared on the living room LED. Leona introduced Graham. "What have you got for me, Rags? It's okay to talk in front of Graham. He's my partner."

"You married?"

"No, Rags. He's my partner in crime, so to speak. We work together. Did you learn anything?"

"Not much. Just one item. Late Monday night two young men—Iranians on green cards—disappeared. They're brothers, one twenty and the other nineteen. We have a missing person's report from their mother. The boys have been living at home while attending college. Circle campus."

"Young men that age could simply wander away for weeks and then come back. So, is the mother a worrywart?"

"She has good reason to worry. It was a balmy evening. The whole family was up late. The boys were playing Ultimate Frisbee under the street lights. A panel truck tooted its horn to pass through. The boys separated to make room, but the van stopped. Gunman got out and whisked the two into the van, which then sped off. The younger sister witnessed the whole thing. The mother called the CPD immediately. No traces."

"Is this *your* case?"

"No. Another detective has it."

"Did the little sister give the police a good description of the van? License plate numbers? Anything?"

"No license plate numbers. But she did see what was written on the side."

"What was that?"

"Evanston Cleaners."

"Oh, ouch!" said Graham.

"Ouch, ouch," said Leona.

"Names!" demanded Leona.

"Jafar and Mohammad Golshani."

"Golshani!? That's Iran's president's name. Any family connection?"

"Don't know. But there's a little note in the file that might interest you. It appears that the father is a member of the exiled People's Mujahideen of Iran, called the PMOI. Does that mean anything to you?"

"Not in itself. We'd need to know more," responded Leona. "The PMOI are a pain in the ass to the Iranian government. They expose human rights violations and such. But I would not think that members of the Golshani family would support the PMOI. So, it's not clear what all this means. Nevertheless, this abduction could mean that you've struck oil, Rags. Thanks a million."

"Not so fast, you two. I've got a question. You said you saw me on TV. Behind me were two vans, both with 'Evanston Cleaners' written on their sides. So, what's the connection?"

"We'd like to thank you for getting us this information, Rags," said Leona.

"Pastor Foxx, I've investigated three separate criminal acts resulting in death this week. You have a connection to each one. Why do I get the feeling that you know more than I do?"

"Just coincidences."

"No, Lee, they're not coincidences. Don't bullshit me. I wonder if I should have you brought in for questioning."

"That would be okay with me, after church on Sunday. You'll be there for worship, right?"

Ragland smiled. "Anything else I can do for you tonight?"

"Not tonight. But I might need to find you in a hurry tomorrow."

"That's what you said yesterday. And my heart was broken when you didn't call me. Will it break again tomorrow?"

Graham sneered. "Maybe both of us will see you tomorrow, Detective Ragland. We'd appreciate you keeping your phone on, especially late afternoon and evening."

"Okay. Bye."

"Bye."

"Graham," Leona said, "I've got a feeling that if we're right about the helicopter, then I bet the Golshani boys will be aboard when it crashes into the Hancock. If they're PMOI fanatics, maybe they'd become suicide bombers. Maybe." Leona paused. "Maybe we have just plugged the hole in my theory. I wonder if I should call Bishop Hurley."

"Why on earth would you want to call him?'

"Because he's spent considerable energy in the last couple years on Christian-Muslim dialogues, both in theology and community cooperation. Maybe he could use his connections to answer a question: Are the Golshani boys likely to pilot that helicopter or should we presume it will be remote controlled? We need to sort this one out, and fast."

Graham agreed. Leona found the Presiding Bishop's number in her iPhone.

"Hello. Hurley here."

"Good Bishop, this is Leona and Graham. Can we flick to Skype?"

"Yes, I'm in my office." In a moment, Graham and Leona on the couch were looking at Justin Hurley sitting at his desk. The middle-aged prelate sported a well-trimmed mustache and a salt and pepper beard.

"Bishop, you know that works righteousness will not get you into heaven. So, why are you working so late?" asked Leona.

"Just got out of a committee meeting. It went on and on. These committee meetings can be a foretaste of hell, you know. I've earned more than enough merit to go to the other place."

The presiding bishop asked for a "how's it going?" report from Graham. Graham told the bishop that things were going well, neglecting little items such as the afternoon gunfight on the beach.

"We've got a matter of utmost urgency," said Leona. "Can we talk to you about it?"

Graham interrupted by whispering into Leona's ear, telling her that it was likely that CUB was probably monitoring her iPhone and even the bishop's phone.

"Hey, no smooching on the job," said the presiding bishop.

Leona took over. "We must talk in person, Justin. Immediately. If Graham and I jump in the car right now, we could make it to your office in 45 minutes. No traffic this time of evening. It's important. Could you wait for us?"

"Oh, I've got plenty on my desk to keep me busy. I'll alert security downstairs. Come in through the door at 8755 West Higgins."

"We're on our way."

46 /FRIDAY, CHICAGO, 10:16 PM

THE TWO SPED through the night in Graham's Honda toward the northwest side of Chi-Town. Leona pressed Graham on what his assignments would be. "I know it's late," she said. "But I want you to contact Holthusen. In person. No phone. Tell him our theory, including the helicopter possibility. Now, here's the delicate part. Recall that the copter which landed on the beach today was a Long Ranger IV. It was white. Suppose CUB plans to use this very bird. Or, suppose this bird is one of a fleet, all of the same model. Here's another tumbler that might fall into place: the Long Ranger IV is the same model the president's security used to transport me to the ship. That one was blue."

"Perhaps I see how this tumbles into place," interjected Graham. "This could mean that on the president's ship they have what they need to guide the copter, like we guide a drone. Could the homing device on the ship be modified to take over the controls of the terrorist bird? From the ship could they intercept and override the controls of any Long Ranger IV that approaches the JH?"

"We're on the same page, Graham. And if they fail to take control, maybe they could shoot it down without making too big of a mess. "

"Yes," added Graham. "I wonder..."

"You need not wonder alone, Graham. Persuade Holthusen to

authorize whatever he needs to get control of the craft that approaches the Hancock. They might have to work all night tonight to ready the technology. One more thing. With Holthusen's authorization, set up a monitoring team near the foot of the Hancock. Track messages coming in and going out. Be unobtrusive. CUB will have its observers on site, maybe even someone influencing the direction of the copter. I'll want to have constant communication with the monitoring team."

"Gotcha."

"By any chance, Graham, do you have another one of those untraceable phones?"

"Yes, by chance. I got a handful of them. They're not all hooked up yet for me to trace, but I've got a couple in the trunk."

"Could you give one to Justin when we meet him? We'll need to communicate without any eavesdropping."

"Good idea. I'll get one from the trunk and take it up with us. I'll set it up."

GRAHAM DROVE his CR-V into the circlular driveway in front of the three building complex on West Higgins Road. He parked in the middle, at 8755. Graham opened the trunk and slipped a Droid into his pocket.

The only building door open to visitors during night hours was watched by a security guard, a college-aged African American woman in a blue uniform. Slender and delicate, she sat within an imposing square desk area, a fortress twenty feet in length, with a nearly chin high front facade. Her eyes peered over the front edge.

"Good evening," she said with a smile of greeting. "It's nice to have visitors this late. Get's kinda lonely here."

"We're here to see Bishop Justin Hurley. He's working late too, " said Leona.

"Bishop Hurley phoned and told me you'd be coming. You can go right up." She pointed to the hallway leading to the Lutheran Center.

"We know the way," said Graham. "Thanks. My car will sit there for only a few minutes."

"Okay."

Graham and Leona walked the halls to the Lutheran Center and entered the elevator, pushing the button for the 11th floor. En route up, Graham and Leona took each other's picture and Graham entered their photos and cell numbers into the new Droid's directory. The elevator door opened at the 11th floor. The two were greeted on the opposite wall with a full-sized print of Satao Watanabe's painting, "Pentecost." The 11th floor belonged to the Evangelical Lutheran Church in America.

The presiding bishop's corner office included giant windows on two sides looking out over a forest, beyond which O'Hare International Airport could be seen. In the moonlit night, landing flights were visible at half-minute intervals. First the shadow, then the plane itself.

"How about a good cup of Lutheran gasoline?" asked the bishop.

The guests agreed and in moments the bishop was back with coffee for all three of them. Graham was ready for small talk. "Leona told me that she drinks coffee only in the morning. Wine is her evening drink of choice. I think she's trying to look good for her bishop."

"Got any wine, Bishop?" asked Leona. All three laughed. Leona continued. "Tonight I need Lutheran gasoline to keep me going." She sipped from her cup.

Graham placed the new Droid on the desk. "This phone is for you, Good Bishop." The presiding bishop reached for the phone and pulled it toward himself, looking curiously at the faces of his two guests.

"By any chance do you know Jafar Golshani and Mohammad Golshani?" asked Leona.

"No. I don't recognize the names. Why do you ask?" said the bishop.

"They belong to an Iranian family. They've been kidnapped. Graham and I need to find them, and quickly. By any chance, Justin, might you have contacts among Muslim leaders who have an Iranian constituency?"

"Yes, I do."

"Can you call them late at night?"

"That would be bad manners."

"It's an emergency, for the sake of Albany, Justin. Would they respond if you conveyed to them the urgency of this situation?"

"Well, I should hope so."

"Here's what we need to find out. First, is the Chicago Golshani family related in any way to Akbar Golshani, Iran's president? Second, were the kidnapped boys political? Could they be persuaded to become suicide bombers? Third, does either of them know how to pilot a plane or a helicopter?"

The presiding bishop's face reflected both intensity and a touch of confusion as he listened.

"And, I'm afraid, we need this information ASAP. Tonight, if possible," added Leona.

Graham spoke. "I have given you a phone that cannot be monitored. I've put our exclusive numbers on speed dial. Call one or both of us anytime during the night. Okay?"

All agreed on how Justin Hurley would be spending the next few hours. He said he'd fill up on Lutheran gasoline. Then he walked the two to the elevator.

Once the elevator doors had closed and they had a moment of privacy, Graham picked Leona's right hand up into both of his. He drew it to his mouth and kissed it. Leona allowed this without resistance. Their eyes met. "You are a marvel, Lee," he said. "When Holthusen and Hurley asked me to protect you, I had no idea how rich a treasure I'd be guarding." He kissed her hand again, as if dubbing her royalty. With her left hand she reached the back of his neck and pulled him slightly in her direction. Once more they kissed. Their embrace broke with the opening of the elevator doors.

Walking through the halls from the church wing toward the central building in the complex, Graham and Leona rehearsed their theory, looking for more holes.

"Let's go over the motive thing again," said Graham. "So far the logic goes like this. CUB wants to perpetuate the image of an Iranian threat associated with the development of a nuclear weapon. If, on the one hand, they obtain from you the name of the Tehran saboteur, then CUB would divulge that name to his own government. He would then be eliminated. If, on the other hand, they fail to get that name, CUB will sponsor an act of terrorism that can be blamed on Iran. And American opinion will demand we maintain a hostile posture even without a nuclear threat. This will mean more business for the contractors. Right?"

"Right."

"So, why are you in danger? Either CUB executes Plan A or Plan B. If you foil them on Plan A, why is your life threatened?"

"You came to me, Graham. You're the one who believes I'm in danger. It's your turn to plug up the hole."

"Here's my guess. CUB's long range goal of keeping themselves in business could not be met if publicly exposed. Maybe CUB suspects that you're on to them, or that you just know too much. CUB could not afford a terrorist act and then have the contractors investigated for it. Nor could the CIA for that matter. You've become more than merely a source of information; you're now a threat. They gotta shut you up whether it's Plan A or Plan B."

Leona paused. "Had I been taken away in that helicopter on the beach, I probably would never have returned, whether I divulged the name or not."

"That's the way I look at it too. If CUB has given up on getting the name from you, then there's only two options left."

"Two?"

"Yes, two. Either CUB follows through on the terrorist plan or they find Number Thirty, you know, the one other living member of the Tehran death march."

"I'm the only one that knows who that is."

"Well, if the shoe fits. Now, don't Budenholzer and Holthusen know Number Thirty?"

"Actually, yes. They know who, but not where. Only I am in

contact with Number Thirty. No one else is. The CIA provided this person with a complete identity change and with a single financial account that appreciates in value so she...I mean he or she...will be supported indefinitely. The records were destroyed. So, Number Thirty is not going to be found. Even so, Number Thirty does not know what I know about the saboteur. This leaves me alone in CUB's crosshairs, whether CUB knows it or not. And if I won't divulge the Tehran saboteur, then I certainly won't endanger my compatriot either."

"If CUB gives up on you as a source, then that leaves only one option: terrorism plus eliminating you. And maybe me, if CUB knows who I am yet."

"I know who you are. And I don't want you eliminated." said Leona.

"Why, Lee, that's bordering on the affectionate. Watch yourself."

47 /FRIDAY, CHICAGO, 11:54 PM

PASSING through the central lobby of the Higgins Road building, the two approached the security desk. They stopped briefly to chat. "What's your name?" asked Graham.

"Monica."

"Monica. Are you in school?"

"Yes, I'm a student at Wheaton College. I work here nights," she smiled showing appreciation of Graham's interest in her.

"Oh, by the way," she added, "after you guys left to see Bishop Hurley, a second car pulled up. One of the men in it walked over to your car. He got in the driver's seat."

"How did he get in? I locked it."

"I don't know. But he just did. He might have left something for you. He waved at me. I waved back."

"Did any of them in the second car come in? Did you get a good look at them?"

"Nope. No one came in. Too dark to see them clearly. They put something in your car and left. I assumed they were friends."

Graham looked at Leona. Leona looked at Graham. Then Graham spoke, "Monica, would you please call for a cab. Tell them to come immediately."

"Sure." Monica dialed and ordered a taxi. She turned to Graham and said, "Eight minutes."

"Now, Monica, I'd like to ask another favor." Graham walked around the desk to the back and entered the fortress' enclosure. Leona followed. Monica looked puzzled, though she welcomed the two guests into her desk enclave.

In a strong yet controlled voice, Graham issued an undeclinable invitation. "Okay, let's turn our backs to the front." The three turned around with their backs facing the front door. "Now, down," Graham shouted in a whisper. Once all three were on the floor, Graham lifted up his electronic car key above the desk's front edge. He punched the "open" button.

A thunderous explosion! A giant fireball shot forty feet straight up from the car, spraying sparks in all directions. The entire CR-V was engulfed in flames. The building's heavy front doors burst open. Thirty foot ceiling-to-floor windows fissured and crackled. Then the glass plunged, splattering on the marble floor. Shards streamed in all directions.

In their protected cave below the desk fortress, the three had avoided injury. As the sound subsided, Graham and Leona turned to look at each other. Graham squeezed Leona's hand.

"Somebody's late for the Fourth of July," commented Leona.

Graham hit the speed dial for Bishop Hurley on his Droid. No answer. "Oh, shit!" He said with frustration in his voice and fear on his face.

Graham turned to Monica, who was still trembling. "Okay, please listen carefully. First, call Presiding Bishop Hurley on the house phone. Tell him what happened and that his guests escaped injury. Tell him that like the three kings, *he* must go home by a different way. His car might have a little gift just like mine did. Second, call the police. It's okay to tell them everything you know. Then, call your boss. But please wait to make these calls until we've left. Got it?"

Monica replied with a jitter in her voice. "But I don't remember your names."

"I said, it's okay to tell the police what you know. Don't worry about what you don't know. Make sure the bishop has left before any detectives show up. Okay?"

"I think I've got it," said Monica, stammering.

Once in the taxi Leona directed the driver to the Drake Hotel on Chicago's near north side.

"Why the Drake?" asked Graham sitting across the back seat from his pastor friend.

"You need a headquarters close to, you know, close to where the action will be tomorrow. If you get hold of you-know-who, then you might even meet there."

"That worries me, Lee. Who'll protect you?"

"I can take care of myself, Graham."

"I'd feel better if you called Shmoo and asked him to spend the night...in my hide-a-bed."

"Graham! I'm going to be okay," Leona insisted.

Graham looked out the taxi window. Then he turned again to Leona. "Here's another problem with your plan. The Drake's expensive."

"Come on, Graham, you've got a virtually unlimited budget. Get out the plastic. Think of what your boss will save if he doesn't need to pay CUB any more. He can spend that on you. One more thing. When we stop at the Drake, would you please pay for my trip back to South Shore?"

"Now, I can see why you don't want me eliminated."

"Ah, Graham." Leona moved her hand over and placed it on top of his.

48 /SATURDAY, CHICAGO, 5:59 AM

AFTER THE PROFANITY of the long day—nearly losing her life twice—in a beach gun battle and an exploding car—Leona sought the sanctity of her home. Buck greeted her with a wagging tail and Midnight demanded lap time.

Leona found "call me" messages from Angie on her iPhone, but ignored them with only a tinge of guilt. She welcomed the Sand Man without jumping rope and without either a bath or Bach and even without calling Angie. Rather than store the Kimber in her protected drawer, she bedded it along with the Droid under her pillow. She slept soundly.

Shortly before six o'clock, the doorbell rang. Buck, who was sleeping on her bedroom floor jumped to his feet. Bleary-eyed, Leona donned her fleece robe and stumbled down the stairs to the front door with Buck at her side. Midnight remained in bed. After seeing no danger through the peep hole, Leona cautiously opened the door and looked down. Buck looked up. There stood a dainty African American girl, looking up at Leona with wide open eyes.

"Is it time for Saturday Morning Club?" she asked.

"No. It's only six o'clock. Saturday Morning Club doesn't start until nine o'clock. Come back then."

"Okay," said the little girl. She turned and descended the porch steps, one at a time.

While closing the door, Leona noticed a car in the parking lot, one she did not recognize. She stumbled back up the stairs and flopped on her bed. She was out in seconds. Buck resumed his tummy lie on the rug between the bed and the door. Midnight, looking perturbed at having been disturbed, gently curled up on Leona's chest. In moments all three were sound asleep once again.

At 6:45 the doorbell rang. Leona grumbled. Still wearing her robe, she and Buck headed down the stairs. Buck did not bark, but he showed intense interest at who might be at the door. Once open, Leona saw the same sweet face smiling up at her. Buck muscled his way through the opening and raced down the porch steps, brushing the delicate human figure standing there.

The little girl showed no reaction to the freight train husky that had just whizzed by her. "Is it time for Saturday Morning Club yet?"

"No. It's only quarter to seven. I said come back at 9:00."

The little one continued to look up at the pastor.

"What is your name?" asked Leona.

"Cupid."

"Did you say Cupid?"

"Yes. I'm Cupid."

"How old are you, Cupid?"

"Five."

Leona thought for a moment. "Do you know how to tell time?"

Cupid's eyes turned downward. "No."

Leona paused "I've got a kitty."

Cupid's eyes came back up.

"Would you like to come in and pet my kitty? Her name is Midnight."

Cupid didn't say a word. She just made her way into the living room. By this time Midnight was making her regal appearance descending the stairs. Leona grabbed the cat and asked Cupid to sit on the couch. She placed Midnight on Cupid's lap, much to the child's delight.

"Cupid, I'm going to make breakfast. Would you like some?"

Cupid nodded her head up and down. Then, the image of the strange car in the parking lot popped into Leona's mind. She returned to the front door. She could see Buck circumambulating the strange vehicle, sniffing the left rear tire. A driver's head was now visible. The face turned toward Leona.

"Shmoo!" Leona hollered. "Breakfast in a few minutes!"

The veteran cop registered surprise. Then he departed the car and migrated into the parsonage, Buck following.

"Been there all night?" Leona said to him.

"Gotta protect my Little Lee, yaknow."

"Get yourself freshened up and then meet Cupid."

Leona smiled and headed for the kitchen. She brewed and poured herself some coffee, then bit off the arm of the last gingerbread man in her cookie jar. Foraging in the fridge, she pulled out a carton of eggs along with a piece of steak from the night before. She poured a glass of orange juice for Cupid and a cup of coffee for Shmoo to keep them busy while Leona took her private coffee time to wake up.

When back in the living room, the pastor flipped on the LED and went to 'Bible Works'. *Let's see*, she said to herself. *Tuesday it was Psalm 31. Wednesday; Thursday; Friday. Today must be Psalm 35.* The cursor brought the thirty-fifth Psalm to the screen. Leona sipped her coffee and ate the other gingerbread arm. She read the psalm out loud with Cupid, Shmoo, and the two animals watching and listening.

Leona re-read selected verses of Psalm 35. "Let not them that are mine enemies wrongfully rejoice over me: neither let them wink with the eye that hate me without a cause. For they speak not peace: but they devise deceitful matters against them that are quiet in the land.... This thou hast seen, O Lord: keep not silence: O Lord, be not far from me. Stir up thyself, and awake to my judgment, *even* unto my cause, my God and my Lord."

If you can't even give Hank Greer a lousy single, Lord, it would be a waste for me to petition for a mighty act of salvation today. I guess your omnipotence has gone on vacation. Amen. She prayed almost out loud, as if talking to her two-legged and four-legged audience instead of God. She finished the prayer and the coffee and headed back to the kitchen.

Her iPhone sounded. It was Hillar, asking if he could have some breakfast. "Of course," she said. In moments Hillar arrived, met Cupid, greeted Shmoo, and set the table for four. He admitted he had been anticipating steak 'n' eggs for breakfast. No wussy cereal or even pancakes would do for a day such as they were expecting. Each of the animals watched intently, waiting for some tidbits to be placed on their tongues. Unofficially, it was a table for six.

Leona was sipping her post-breakfast coffee when Hillar took command of the living room computer and the giant LED. Soon he was engrossed in a video game.

"What are you playing, Quaz?"

"*Call of Duty Black Ops.* I'm a U.S. Special Forces agent shooting Cubans. We're gonna assassinate Castro."

"Hillar, don't you know all that video violence warps your mind?! Stop it."

"Oh, Pastor Lee. It's fun. It's got nuth'n to do with real life."

"But Hillar, it desensitizes you to killing other human beings. Castro is a human being. And you want to kill him. Why?"

"Pastor, it's only a game. I don't really want to kill anybody. Honest. Ya gotta understand the difference between actual violence and play violence. When I play with violence in a video game, I'm safe. Nuth'n bad can happen. It's fun, sometimes even funny."

Leona took a sip of her Major Dickason while watching bodies on the screen hit by tracer bullets fly every which way. Leona studied Hillar's face, amazed by his total absorption in the game. The pastor picked up a ballpoint pen. She reached over and lightly stuck the pen's point into Hillar's nose ring. Then she pressed down until the pen was lodged. Still concentrating on the video screen Hillar waved a hand briefly, as if swatting away a pesky fly. The annoying "fly" did not depart. Finally, he stopped. Sat back. Removed the pen. Leona was doubling up with laughter. "Are you laughing at me?" he asked.

"Oh, Quaz, you're soooo cute."

Hillar winced at the word "cute".

Leona caught her breath. "Would you mind taking Buck out for a romp in the parking lot?"

Hillar cheerfully shut down the game and hollered, "Here Buck." Out the front door trooped boy and dog. Cupid and Shmoo followed to the porch, the little girl still holding Midnight. Leona, with her MSU cup in hand, stood at the door to watch the yard show. Buck raced around. Where the parking lot meets the alley, Buck stopped at a telephone pole. He raised his right leg to mark his territory.

Cupid looked up at the pastor. "Why's Buck doing that?"

"Doing what, sweetheart?" she said, just to buy a little time for her to think of an answer.

"Why's Buck lifting his leg against the pole?"

By this time Leona was prepared. "Well, Cupid, back at the beginning when God was creating the world, God made dogs. The dogs were happy. They ran around together, playing. One dog walked up to a telephone pole to, well, go to the bathroom. All of a sudden, the pole fell down and killed the dog. Some of the other dogs saw it. They were scared. So they ran to all the other dogs and told them what they had seen. From then on, whenever dogs need to go to the bathroom near a pole, they lift their leg up to protect themselves."

"Oh," said Cupid. She continued to pet the kitten. Shmoo bid all goodbye, and with a promise to connect again at 5pm, he drove away. Leona went upstairs to ready herself for the big day ahead.

Hillar headed for the Fellowship Hall to prepare for Saturday Morning Club. He was joined shortly by Owl, offering to help. Leona and Cupid arrived a few minutes before 9:00. The pastor greeted the arriving children, a mixture of Caucasians, African Americans, and Latinos. The mothers who had volunteered to lead Crafts and Bible Stories were busy setting up their tables.

At 9:00 sharp Leona stood up and demanded everybody's attention. She welcomed all to the Saturday Morning Club and introduced Mr. Chadwick who would lead them in the official Saturday Morning Club Song. The children gathered in a circle as directed. Leona seated herself on a folding chair. Cupid made her way over to where Leona was sitting. She climbed up onto the pastor's lap and looked toward Charles Chadwick, who was smiling and strumming his guitar.

> Young folks, old folks, everybody come.
> Join Saturday Morning Club, 'n' have a lot o' fun.
> Please check your chewing gum and raisins at the door,
> "n" we'll tell you Bible stories you've never heard before.

After the second time through, Charles stopped playing. He directed a question to the group, "Would you all like to learn a new song?"

"Yeah! Yeah!" the kids shouted.

"What city do we live in?" asked Charles.

"Chicago!"

"That's right. Chicago. So we're going to sing the Chicago Fire song. Anybody know it?"

Nobody responded. "Okay. Listen to me," announced Charles, starting to play chords on his guitar. He taught the children what to them was a new song, though an old one to Leona.

> One dark night, when we were all in bed.
> Ol' Mother Leary lit a lantern in the shed.
> When the cow kicked it over, she winked her eye and said,
> "There'll be a hot time in the old town tonight.
> Fire! Fire! Fire!

In Leona's own mind she was thinking, *I hope we can avoid a repeat of the Chicago fire tonight.*

49 /SATURDAY, CHICAGO, 12:57 PM

IT WAS NEARLY one o'clock by the time Leona and Hillar were seated on the Metra headed north. Both were wearing their Chicago Cubs shirts. Leona's had the name Hank Greer with the number 42 on the back. Hillar toted a backpack with sundries, including his remote helicopter.

The pastor-spy carried both phones, her iPhone and the Droid. She took a deep breath and then checked her Droid messages. As she had hoped, Justin Hurley had left her a voicemail.

"It's 4:30 am, Saturday," he opened. "I've been up all night. Can't drive my car, in case it's got a bomb. If you think attending a committee meeting is meritorious, working for you is a work of supererogation. St. Peter'd better pat me on the back on Judgment Day. Here's the poop. After numerous phone calls with appropriate apologies for calling so late, I struck oil with a Muslim colleague. He knows the Golshani family well and was aware of the kidnapping. The Golshanis are worried sick. Yes, the father is a first cousin of President Akbar Golshani. Yes, he was active in the PMOI. The two cousins had a row over their disagreement. Even though they're blood relatives, the now Americanized Golshani feared reprisal in Iran. So he brought his family to the states. They want asylum. There is no reason to believe that this family here in Chicago has anything to do with the current government in Tehran. No, the two boys are not radical Muslim ideologues. The older one, Jafar, has even filled out an application form to join the U.S. Army. Doesn't look at all like we have a terrorist here. That's the best I can do. I'm going to bed. I hope this helps. Good night. I mean, good morning."

Noting how Hillar had left this world for that of his iPad, Leona took some moments to think this through. *If the American Golshani family is not politically allied with the president of Iran, then why would kidnappers want the two young men? The two young Golshanis would not likely volunteer to become suicide bombers. The kidnapping indicates they have been taken against their will. Why the Golshanis? Maybe the answer lies in the name. Should the name come up in the media, people will immediately associate this name with that of Iran's current president. Maybe that's all these terrorists need: a simple name association. Mass opinion does not depend on facts, only loose associations. Is this what CUB is counting on?*

The next message was from Graham, delivered at 9:30 am on the Droid. Leona tapped her screen for an audio message. "Lee, this is Graham. I connected with Holthusen. In fact, I'm calling you from the ship in the harbor. We went over and over your theory. He could not find any holes that we had not already considered. We've got to bet that your boat will float. Holthusen has put some techies to work preparing to take remote control of any Long Ranger IV that flies into the vicinity. They can make happen what you've asked for. We decided not to tell Chicago's finest what we're working with. Can't risk a leak. We think this theoretical scenario would make very little change in their strategy anyway. Also, Holthusen and I discussed at length the possible role of Budenholzer. Because there's enough suspicion, Holthusen has ordered some intelligence gathering from CIA Internal Affairs. We're working on that now. We need to know what you're planning to do on the ground. I missed you last night. Call when you can."

Leona disconnected from her Droid and picked up her iPhone. She dialed. "Edna here." Edna and her husband lived on the 85th floor of the John Hancock Building.

"Edna, this is Leona Foxx. How are you and Marty doing?"

"Fine. How are you?"

"Actually, Edna, I need to cut to the chase. Are you guys affected in any way by the president's visit?"

"Yes, indeed. He and his security have taken over the three apartments next to ours. The president's in the middle and security in the two on each side. And, they've taken over the entire 84th and 86th floors."

"Why are you still there? Why didn't they move you out?"

"Because Marty and Andrew Dodge are good friends. Marty was one of Andy's supporters back when he was a Chicago Alderman. They have already had a cup of coffee together this morning."

"Edna, could I come to visit you?"

"Yes. We have to come down to the door on East Delaware and vouch for you."

"Twenty minutes. Hillar Talin and me. No, on second thought. Just me."

After disconnecting, Leona dialed Angie. She told Angie that she did not have time to talk. Angie said she understood, but urged Leona not to wait too long to get back to her. Hillar could overhear Leona saying, "Terrorists come and go, but a girlfriend lasts a lifetime."

50 /SATURDAY, CHICAGO, 1:10 PM

AFTER DISEMBARKING the train and walking up the Magnificent Mile, the two stopped near the nineteenth century water tower. Located at 806 North Michigan Avenue, the Chicago Water Tower had been built in 1869, designed by architect William W. Boyington. It stands 154 feet tall. The tower helped rescue Chicagoans from the Great Fire of 1871. Was it really Mrs. O'Leary's cow that started it?

"This is our rendezvous point, Quaz," said Leona. If we get separated for any reason, this is where we'll meet. Got it?"

"Yeah, sure."

"I need to go upstairs in the Hancock Building. Security will be tight. I don't think I can make it through with what I've got."

"What've you got?"

"Quaz, please open your backpack so I can discreetly put something in it." Leona proceeded to remove from the back of her waistband her Kimber. She dropped this and extra ammo into the backpack. Hillar's eyes doubled in size. Leona spoke. "I'd thought about bringing my Glock 19, which is an Austrian high capacity pistol built from carbon-fiber plastics. Most X-ray machines cannot detect it. But the barrel and part of the bolt are still steel; and that could trigger a security detector. So I thought I might as well bring my

Kimber. I feel at home with this baby. Please take care of it until I get back."

Hillar had never heard his pastor speak this way. He was momentarily dumbfounded.

Leona continued, ignoring Hillar's reaction. "While I'm gone, shoot Castro for me."

"Okay" muttered the confused teenager.

Leona walked north on Michigan and right onto Delaware. Edna, with her perfectly styled graying hair, greeted her warmly in the lobby.

"You look fabulous, Edna," exclaimed Leona.

"So nice of you to come and visit. Marty's waiting upstairs."

Leona was quickly cleared by security and received a pass card to return to security upon departure. They took an elevator up to floor 44, transferring then to a second elevator. This took them up to floor 85 in what seemed like a jet-propelled rocket. Martin Townsend greeted the two at the apartment door. The small talk did not last long. Leona marched to the large picture window to view the stunning landscape and seascape to the south. She studied the location of various buildings.

"Where is the president staying?"

"He's two apartments to our left," said Martin. "Immediately next door is where security sleeps, if they sleep at all."

"Mmmmmm." She scanned the landscape again. She imagined herself in the cockpit of a flying terrorist craft. *How would I approach? How could I make a square hit with minimum angle deflection?* She ascertained that most likely the craft would come from the southeast, from Lake Michigan, past the Parkshore and Harbor Point. *I would probably fly over the Water Tower Plaza just prior to impact.* This could mean that enroute it would fly in the vicinity of the president's ship. The president would be here, of course, probably entertaining the mayor and guests. He would not be on the ship. But *the ship would be alive with Holthusen's techies. Mmmmmm.*

"Is the presidential apartment as deep as yours?" asked Leona.

"Actually," Edna said. "It's deeper. I've been in it many times. It's more than twice as large as ours."

"Large enough for a cocktail party?"

"Oh, yes. More than ample."

"Have you been invited to this evening's reception?"

"Yes, of course," replied Edna.

"Look, Marty and Edna. I need to ask you to leave. By seven o'clock don't be here. Even if the president urges you to join him, don't go. Spend the night somewhere else."

"Lee, what are you saying?" asked Martin.

"I can't explain. I can say it's a matter of life and death. Take my word for it."

The earnest expression on Leona's face was persuasive. Without too many more questions, the Townsends agreed to vacate for the evening.

WALKING BACK toward the water tower, Leona called David Ragland. "Where are you right now, David?"

"Why should I tell you?"

"Do you want to see the Cubs play the Cards?"

"Why are ya ask'n?"

"I'm on my way to Wrigley with my friend, Hillar."

"Your *friend*, eh. Do you and your friend live together?"

"Hillar's only fourteen, for heaven's sake. He's my helper at the church."

"Just checking."

"You're not very subtle, David."

"Rags."

"We'll meet you at Wrigley in twenty minutes. Gate F on Addison. I'll buy your ticket if you can flap your badge and get all of us through security."

"Are you pack'n heat, Reverend?"

"Never mind. Is it a deal?"

"See you at Gate F in twenty."

51 /SATURDAY, CHICAGO, 2:04 PM

Rather than take the L, Leona and Hillar caught a taxi and were delivered to Wrigley Field in front of Gate F. The game had already begun, so lines were short. Leona hastily bought three tickets in Section 122, Field Level Infield, just to the visitors' side of home plate. Rags arrived as expected and guided the party through security. Leona led them to their seats.

Ragland talked all the way. "Wrigley Field was built in 1904, the oldest professional baseball stadium still in use by the Major Leagues. Its charm is exceeded only by the lack of comfort of its now too small seats. Over a century fan bottoms increased in size while the seats remained the same." Leona and Hillar listened with appropriate head nods.

Despite the big breakfast, Hillar immediately asked for a Chicago dog with all the trimmings. The detective bought the snacks, including an Irish stout for himself and the pastor.

"So, your name is Foxx, eh," Rags said to Leona. "Any relation to Jimmy Foxx?"

"I don't know if I'm genetically related. But I think I share some of the Foxx spirit."

"They called him 'Double X' and 'the Beast'. Is that the spirit you mean? When he played for the Cubs, he played right here at Wrigley.

When he quit, he'd hit 534 home runs with a lifetime batting average of .325. He was the 'Right-Handed Babe Ruth.'" Rags paused. "When were you born, Lee?"

"July 27. I'll keep the year secret. Woman's prerogative."

"That makes you a Leo. 'Leo' means lion, you know."

"Oh, yes, I'm aware. My name, Leona, makes me a lioness."

"So, you're a foxy lion, eh. Let me ask you: are we working or are we on a date?"

"Working, Detective Ragland, strictly working. Got it?" she said firmly.

"Rags."

"What do you think of the president and his entourage?" asked Leona without much expression. Looking toward the field, they could see the president in the front of Club Box 20. Leona removed the binoculars from Hillar's backpack and studied the arrangement. To the right of President Dodge sat Mildred. To his immediate left was Sugar Daley. Sugar had been a dark horse during the mayoral election, even though she represented a new chapter in the long story of the Daley Machine. She won on the Democratic ticket when the opposing vote was split between Republicans and Independents. In the same election, curiously, one member of the Woodlawn Stoners, Ruben Wallace, had been elected Alderman. Wallace was not among the dignitaries behind home plate. Security agents, large muscular men too big for their clothes, were obvious. Rex Allen was calmly talking into something in his hand, most likely a mobile phone.

From her jeans pocket, Leona withdrew her business card. She turned it over to write a note. Hillar and David were absorbed in the game. The Cubs had runners on first and second. All eyes were on the field. All eyes except Leona's. On the back of the card she wrote, "Stay away from your window. Danger."

She reached into Hillar's backpack and pulled out the helicopter. She fastened the card securely to the bottom of the craft with Scotch tape. She tapped Hillar. "Please get this ready to fly."

"What?"

"You heard me. We'll wait for the crowd to stand. Then, launch this baby. Lift it up, over the crowd. Then drop it right into the president's lap. Can you do that?"

Hillar's eyes lit up. "Really?"

"Really."

The crowd's drone rose in pitch and volume as a walk loaded the bases. "Greer's up," exclaimed Rags.

"Oh, I gotta watch this," said Leona. The first pitch was a ball. Outside.

"He's afraid of 'm!" screamed Rags.

The second pitch was just as far outside as the first. "Scaredy-cat!" screamed David. Hillar was half watching and half readying his craft for take-off.

"This one's gotta be a strike," said Leona, nodding to both Hillar and David.

It was. The pitch sizzled right down the middle, letter high. Greer's swing came from the heels. He connected. The crack of the Louisville Slugger issued a heavenly sound for ears of Cub fans. The ball shot up and up. Everyone in the stands sprang up, watching the white pellet sail over the brick wall in left center field. Leona leaped up and off her feet, punching the air with her right hand. "Grand Slam!" she screamed. When she came down, she dropped into a crouch and gave a loud whisper to Hillar, "Now!"

Hillar pressed a button on the remote and the helicopter took off straight up. With the jumping and roaring of the crowd, the flying object was hardly noticed by anyone. All eyes were fixed on Hank Greer rounding third base. The baseball star paused after touching home plate to receive high fives from fellow Cubbies. The crowd's applause grew even louder before the roaring fans settled back into their seats.

By this time the small silver craft was forty feet in the air and making its way toward the backstop. Leona and Hillar tracked its flight. Rags was becoming somewhat curious, but nothing prompted him to look in the direction of the flying object.

"Careful," Leona whispered nervously. Hillar gripped his remote guidance box. Soon the copter was hovering just above the president. "Lower it slowly, Hillar."

"Yes, I know."

"Slower."

"I'm okay, Pastor Lee. I've got it."

"Okay. Sorry."

Gently the remote whirly bird descended. Hillar flicked the off switch. It dropped into the president's lap.

"Perfect!" exclaimed Leona.

"What are you doing?" demanded Rags.

"Oh, nothing," said Leona, sitting back. "Just watching the president." By this time Hillar had picked up the binoculars and admired the fruits of his labors.

"Look what I've got," said Andrew to both Mildred on his right and Sugar Daley on his left. He fondled the treasure, examining it from all sides. At first, he did not notice the business card taped to the bottom. One of the security agents quickly came to the end of the row, just to Sugar's left. "Perhaps I should take that, Mr. President."

"Sure," said Dodge. As he lifted the object to pass it to the agent, he spotted the note. Without revealing what he was doing, he unobtrusively peeled off the card and handed the copter to Sugar who, in turn, handed it to the agent. "We'll examine it," said the agent as he departed.

Dodge turned the card from side to side. He could not help but smile as he read, "Rev. Leona Foxx, Pastor. Trinity Lutheran Church." He turned the card over. There he found written, "Stay away from your window. Danger."

The president thought for a moment, asking himself, "What window is Lee talking about?" The only window he could think of was the screen that protected him and other fans from fowl balls.

"My helicopter's now gone," complained Hillar.

"I tell you what, Quaz. Next time you file your income tax, deduct the cost of the helicopter from your tax liability."

"I don't pay income tax. I'm too young. Remember?"

"Oh. In that case, I'll buy you a new one."

Through the binoculars Leona followed Andrew's movements as he placed the card into his pocket. *Success.* She couldn't help but watch beyond what she needed for confirmation. It appeared from the jostling and smiling that the entire presidential party was enjoying the game. Occasionally, Mildred would flip her hair back. Then she would lay her head on her husband's shoulder. He would pat her tenderly. For most onlookers this appeared to be a charming insight into the personal life of the nation's leader and the First Lady. For Leona, however, it was depressing.

"I think it's time for me to leave the game." Hillar and David protested. But she held fast to her decision. "Hillar, we rendezvous at five o'clock, remember?"

"Yes."

"Rags, where will you be there at five o'clock today?"

"Dunno. Depends on who kills whom."

"If you have no murders to solve, you could meet me and my friends at the Chicago Water Tower. If you don't come, you'll miss some fun. In the meantime," Leona leaned toward Ragland and whispered in his ear, "I'm thinking about your buddies at the Chicago PD. You might tell whoever is in charge of presidential security one little thing."

"What's that?"

"Tell him to clear East Chestnut just under the John Hancock Building before 8:00 this evening."

"What? Why?"

"Falling debris."

"What the hell? Why should I do that? What do you claim to know? Why should I act on your authority?"

"It's up to you, Rags. You can ignore me. Keep what I said all to yourself, if you like. Bye."

Ragland was befuddled. He pulled out his cell phone while watching Leona disappear up the concrete stairs toward the exit..

52 /SATURDAY, CHICAGO, 4:01 PM

LEONA HEADED for the L train. She phoned Graham, who reported that the intercept plan was now in place. It included two units, the primary one on the ship and an auxiliary one on the roof of the John Hancock. Graham also said he'd returned to shore. In fact, Holthusen was with him. They were catching a late afternoon coffee on State Street at the north end of the Loop.

"Graham, did you also set up a monitoring station?"

"Yes."

"Where?"

"Near the foot of the Chicago Water Tower. Look for a white van. I'll meet you there a little before five and introduce you to the techie team."

"Perfect," exclaimed Leona. "Put Holthusen on."

"Hello, Lee," said the CIA director.

"Do you know where Budenholzer might be right now? Washington? Chicago? The Middle East?"

"No, I don't. He's a *secret* agent, you know. He has no official reason to be in Chicago, as far as I can tell. I've not heard from him in a few days. But recall the photo at Gatwick."

"What are the chances that he's the mastermind of CUB?"

"As of yet, no evidence. Just to be careful, though, I've kept him out of your loop. As far as I know, he's oblivious to your activities."

"He preceded you as director. Maybe he's hurting because he lost that position. He may be resentful toward Dodge for demoting him. To whom is he most loyal: the CIA or his contractor buddies?"

"All of those questions have crossed my mind. To date, however, we have no persuasive evidence that he's involved."

"It may be relevant to remember that he was director when I was a full-time operative in Iran. He knows me. He knows my case. He would know that I possess the knowledge that CUB wants. In fact, I don't know how CUB could find out about my knowledge without Budenholzer divulging it."

"You've got a point there, Lee. What about Number Thirty?"

"I believe only three people in the world know who Number Thirty is. I do. The president. And Budenholzer. Maybe you."

"Yes, I know, because Budenholzer passed this information on to me during the director transition," said Holthusen. "That makes four. So, of the four of us, who told CUB about you? And would that person tell CUB about Number Thirty as well?"

"Gary, is Number Thirty safe? Did you check recently?"

"Now, Lee, we both know that only you know the location of Number Thirty. How could I check? Even so, the office has received no indirect reports of searches, let alone threats. And, as far as I know, Number Thirty still does not know what you know about Iran's nuclear program; unless, of course, you shared this information. So, that could explain why CUB is after you and you alone."

"Maybe we should learn just where Budenholzer is. What do you think?"

"I'll put a call in to him. Let's see."

"May I suggest you place that call just a few minutes after five. Ask the monitor team to locate his phone. This'll tell us where he is."

"Good idea."

"Will you be with the president tonight?"

"No. He's hosting the Daley family and some other Chicagoans at his John Hancock condo. Our agents are among his security force. I'll be in touch with them constantly, but I'll remain off-site."

"Where?"

"Well, Miss Leona, tell me where you'd like me to be."

"With Graham. Protect him. I kinda like him."

"Should I tell Graham that?"

"Tell him whatever you want to. Let's keep each other on speed dial."

"Gotcha."

She dropped down the stairs from the L platform and headed for North Michigan Avenue's Magnificent Mile. Leona noticed the shadows created by the late afternoon sun. One of the shadows mimicked her own.

She hit Angie's speed dial. "Angie, I just want to say that I can't say much now. I'm still in the middle of things."

"Is Graham in the middle with you?" asked Angie.

"Yes and no. He's with another guy. I'm by myself. But I'll see him soon." She studied the shadow following hers. "In the meantime, Angie, there's good shopping where I am."

"That's my Lee, always the bargain hunter."

"Gotta go. Call ya later. Bye."

"Bye."

The two shadows continued to march in sync. She walked with the assumption that she was not alone.

She opened the door to Saks Fifth Avenue. Once in, Leona immediately turned right and flattened herself against the wall. Seconds later the store door opened again. In walked Rex Allen. She grabbed the agent from behind. She thrust her right hand under his right armpit and up his chest to the left shoulder. With her left hand she grabbed his left forearm and yanked it around toward her own back. Neither of Allen's hands could reach for a weapon.

"Why are you following me?" she demanded.

"It's not what you think, Reverend."

"Tell me what to think."

"President Dodge sent me. He wanted me to follow you to protect you."

"It's the president who needs protection, not me." She loosened her grip. The two turned to face one another in civil conversation.

"Another thing," Rex Allen went on. "The president wants to know: which window is dangerous?"

"The window in his condo on the 85th floor of the John Hancock," she responded. "Tell him not to stand there at eight o'clock, better from 7:30 on. He and everybody else should get back toward the hall, the building's center." *I bet he knew all of this but sent you anyway, Rexie. Maybe Andy wants to look chivalrous to me.*

"Why the caution?" asked Allen.

"Only a theory," she said. "Will you be with him after seven tonight?"

"Yes."

"Then, you can make certain he's safely away from the window before eight, Okay?"

"Yes, Reverend."

"You can go. Thank the president for me. Maybe I'll see you when this is over."

"When what's over?"

"Just get back to your duties, Rexie. Bye."

Rex Allen left, heading toward the Hancock. The wheels within Leona's mind began to turn again. She walked. She thought. *CUB wants one and only one thing: to make Iran look like a threat to the American people. What does this imply? If I were Grimes or even Budenholzer, what would I want to do? I'd want to make certain the media would record the worst of the worst.*

Leona ran through alternative scenarios. *How could CUB get the media in place and ready by eight? With a dummy event at seven,* she answered herself. *If something would draw the media to an area near the John Hancock Building just prior, then cameras would be in place to watch the terror on the 85th floor. A fire? A shooting on the street? A suicide jumper? Whatever it was going to be, it would take professional orchestration.*

53 /SATURDAY, CHICAGO, 4:58 PM

IT WAS NEARING FIVE O'CLOCK. Leona headed for the water tower, circumambulating the small block with geometrically segmented lawns separated by wide sidewalks. On the north side, on East Pearson where horse carriages pick up tourists, she noticed something unusual. Parked halfway on the sidewalk was a large panel van, white, slightly smaller than a bus. Antennas decorated the roof. It appeared to be a media van with "Channel 007" written on the side. Leona could not resist a smile. No such channel exists. But somebody's humor does.

Leona rapped on the shotgun door window. The door opened and she identified herself. After a verbal exchange within and Holthusan's voice giving her permission, she entered. The door shut behind her. She was amazed by the array of electronic monitoring equipment. "Looks like you're ready," she announced.

"We're ready," said Graham. "The CIA shares equipment like this with the FBI."

Leona was introduced to the two techies, Tom and Ted, younger men, perhaps in their late twenties. Both were with the FBI.

"I just had another thought," said Leona, addressing Graham and the two techies. "Is there a way you could tune into TV stations and listen in on incoming calls? I bet that some will come in around seven announcing something dramatic happening in this area. We'll want to trace the origin of those calls."

"Can do," said Tom. "We'll take care of that."

"Want some coffee?" asked Graham. "I'll pour it."

"Thanks. Half a cup," said Leona. "Black." Leona sipped. Her eyes peeked over the cup and caught Graham's eyes.

Through the windshield Leona noted that Hillar was nearby. He was seated on a concrete post playing his video games. Soon, she thought, the others will be arriving. Time to become a field marshal.

Shortly after five all had gathered on the water tower lawn: Hillar, Graham, the three Stoners, Shmoo, and the two rent-a-cops. Holthusen watched through the vehicle window, admiring Leona's organizational abilities. "I wish we still had her with us," he said to the first techie.

"It looks like we still do," Ted responded.

A moment later Holthusen was gone, disappearing into the crowd of pedestrians.

54 /SATURDAY, CHICAGO, 5:02 PM

THE JOHN HANCOCK BUILDING was constructed in 1970. With its 100 floors and antennae its height reaches 1500 feet. But it is still a bush when measured by the world's forest of skyscrapers. The JH looks up to the Burj Khalifa in Dubai, the Taipai 101, Shanghai's World Financial Center, Hong Kong's International Conference Center, Petronas Towers in Kuala Lumpur, and Chicago's own Willis and Trump Towers. Even so, the John Hancock is an impressive architectural icon which houses condominiums, business offices, a radio and television broadcast facility, and a 94th floor observatory. Its elliptical-shaped outdoor plaza includes a twelve-foot waterfall. The JH is located one block north of the Water Tower at 875 North Michigan Avenue.

On the Water Tower apron Leona addressed her army. "I think the fireworks will begin earlier than eight," she said. "Maybe as early as seven."

Hillar removed Leona's gun from his backpack, and all watched unobtrusively as she placed it in her waistband. Leona, now turned field marshal, shared her theory about a staged media draw. "Here's what I would like you all to do. Hillar, I want you stationed here. Get to know the techies in the van. Stay as connected as you can with all of us, using your iPhone."

Hillar nodded his head in agreement. Leona continued to direct.

"We're going to fan out and locate where we each can see what's going on. Quint and Wade, walk one block north and position yourselves on the steps of the Fourth Presbyterian Church. From there you can see any action on the west side of the John Hancock. You've got Hillar on speed dial, and you can text him. Hillar will orchestrate what needs to be communicated."

Quint and Wade gave Leona a mock salute.

"Shmoo, you take Hammer and Scorp over to the northeast corner on East Delaware Place, where it intersects with Mies van der Rohr. There's a Hilton Suites on the corner. From that point you can see what goes in and what goes out of the door at 175 East Delaware. Remain outside the police perimeter. But Shmoo, when you have a chance, sidle up to your cop buddies and see what you can learn. Keep in touch with Hillar."

"Aye aye, Captain," said Shmoo smiling.

"Graham, I want you and Everett to come with me down East Chestnut. Water Tower Place will be on our right. Hancock on our left. We'll settle somewhere in the vicinity of the Broadway Playhouse."

Graham and Everett also saluted, grinning.

"Hillar, again, you stay here at the Water Tower. Outside. If you need anything, go talk to Tom or Ted in the van. Otherwise, stay on the Water Tower lawn. Keep your eyes open. You can see the upper floors of the Hancock from here, but you won't be in any danger if things start falling. Got it?"

"Yeah," said Hillar.

At about 6:00 the group disbursed with an unsettling mixture of eagerness and apprehension. Leona, Graham, and Everett marched east. They surveyed the JH façade, looking for suspicious activity. They saw none. Police motorcycles had arranged the safety perimeter, blocking off nearly the entire street. Leona concluded that David Ragland had placed an important phone call.

When the threesome arrived at the Broadway Playhouse, they positioned themselves under its large awning. From there the Hancock and the street were in clear view. They waited for the drama to unfold outside the playhouse. Time passed. The three studied their surroundings very carefully, reviewing out loud with one another details about buildings, windows, awnings, traffic, police, and suspicious pedestrians. More time passed.

"I could sure use a hot dog—one of those Chicago-style Vienna beefers," announced Graham. "There's a hot dog cart up the street. Over by the Cheesecake Factory. See it, Everett?"

"Oh, yeah."

"I'll buy if Everett will run over and get them."

"Yer on," said Everett. "The works?"

Leona looked at Graham with furrowed eyebrows, then nodded at Everett. "Everything."

"Everything for me too," said Graham. He dished out a twenty. Everett headed up the street.

Graham looked into Leona's eyes. "I don't really need a hot dog, Lee." Both smiled. Graham's left hand picked up Leona's right. He drew it to his mouth and touched it lightly with his lips. Then he slowly lowered the clasped hands until dropping hers at her side. Nothing was said. Nothing needed to be said.

THE TWO HEARD a rustling among pedestrians to their left. Feet shuffled. Voices murmured. Many in the crowd were craning their necks upward, watching some sort of commotion on the roof atop the Escada Plaza clock tower. Graham and Leona ran quickly toward, and then across, Michigan Avenue. Everett spotted them running by and joined the chase. Atop the clock tower was a fenced balcony where silhouetted figures swayed back and forth. The activity was hard to make out, but it felt ominous to the crowd. Then, a limp human form tumbled off the balcony, spinning through the air, bouncing off jutting roofs. The body fell on the concrete within a few feet of Leona and Graham.

"I'll try to head them off," said Graham. He took off running. Everett spotted Graham and sprinted to catch up with him.

Leona was the first to kneel at the side of the body, which lay prostrate and still. The collision of a falling human body with a concrete side walk is one where the body suffers damage, not the sidewalk. Blood flowed like the Mississippi. She rolled the man over. Rex Allen. It took a moment for Leona to collect her thoughts. *Oh God. Into your hands I commend his soul. Amen.* A note pinned to Allen's shirt then commanded her attention.

"Death to America," was her translation.

55 /SATURDAY, CHICAGO, 7:08 PM

Graham and Everett dashed around the Escada Plaza toward its rear. They took positions behind a dumpster. Within seconds, the building's rear door flew open and three men in drab gray sweatsuits with maroon trim burst out, each carrying a weapon.

"Halt," yelled Graham.

All three twisted their heads towards Graham. They raised their weapons and started shooting. Shots were fired from both directions. Graham's semi-automatic kicked up heat and smoke and death. It was all over quickly. Two down. One with hands up. Everett stared at the gun in his hand, grateful that he did not need to fire.

Graham and Everett approached the quelled enemy. So did three running policemen complete with battle rattle and drawn guns. Graham flashed his CIA credential to the lead officer. "Cuff 'm," he said. "They're part of a presidential assassination team. We've got more to go after. Can't tell you more right now. Please excuse us."

A second patrolman grabbed Everett and started to handcuff him. "No," said Graham. He's with me. He's with the CIA." The cop immediately released him. Graham and Everett disappeared, heading back toward where they had left Leona. As they were running, Everett took a look at Graham. "So, I'm CIA, eh." Both laughed.

THE FRONT SIDEWALK of the Escada was now in the public spotlight. Pedestrians and police converged. A fire truck pulled to a stop. An ambulance right behind. Leona drifted back, out of the hubbub. Her Droid struck up a tune, "Gimme Mo' Town." Ted was calling her from the listening van. "Got something for you," he said.

"Good. Gimme," she said.

"We've traced some of the phone action. Someone in your area phoned Channel Five to report a suicide jump from the Escada. Then, a minute later, someone else phoned 911 to report the same jumper to the police. First the media, then the call for help. Got it?"

"Got it," said Leona. "This does not surprise me. I see a media van with roof antennae approaching on Chestnut. Soon a camera crew will be filming."

"It looks like you nailed it, Reverend," said Ted.

"Ted," she said. Then she heard a deafening blast through the phone as well as with her naked ear. She looked south and saw black smoke billowing from the Water Tower plaza. "Ted?" she yelled with dread into the phone. "Ted!" No answer.

WHAT HILLAR on site had seen was a green SUV, perhaps a Jeep Cherokee, pull up next to Channel 007 on Pearson. The Cherokee stopped for a few seconds, then drove on, turning south. When the SUV was a block further south on Michigan Avenue, the FBI van exploded. The sound of the detonated bomb was deafening. The vehicle catapulted ten feet in the air. Then it turned to fall on its side. The entire van was burning. A startled Hillar hid behind a tree until the debris settled. Then, he ran to the burning van, concerned for Tom and Ted inside. The heat was so intense he was forced to keep a distance. Hillar felt as helpless as he was terror-ridden.

From the church two blocks north rushed Quint and Wade, running past the Escada activity at full speed. Leona seemed invisible as they ran by her. The two breathed a brief sigh of relief as they came to a stop next to Hillar. The helpless spectators watched the now transparent van disintegrate in the flames and heat.

"Did you see who did it?" Quint asked Hillar.

"It must've been that green Jeep Cherokee." gasped Hillar. "I noticed it behind the horse carriages, maybe waiting for the right moment. I saw it stop next to the van."

Within seconds two policemen were on-site. Within minutes a fire truck arrived. Traffic was beginning to jam up.

Wade offered an idea. "Suppose you're right about the green Cherokee. Do you think the bombers might take a spin around the block and come back? Won't they want to check on their handiwork? Could we ambush them?"

Hillar and Quint nodded in agreement. Wade and Quint took up positions at curbside, watching traffic moving east on Pearson. Traffic crept along Michigan Avenue at five miles per hour as their drivers rubber-necked the Escada and the fire scenes. Wade and Quint spied the green Cherokee approaching. Prophecy fulfilled.

"Let's hold back until they're waiting at the corner to turn onto Michigan," said Wade. "Then we jump in through the back doors. You on the right. Me on the left. Got it?"

"Got it."

"Just before we jump in, fire a bullet into the right front tire. I'll do the same on the left. With two flats, they won't be going anywhere we don't want them to go."

"Got it."

"What if the back doors are locked?"

"Then we'll point our weapons at them through the front. But let's try the back doors first."

"Got it."

As the Cherokee crawled passed the devastation, the driver and the shotgun rider admired their handiwork, exchanging high fives, oblivious to the sneak attack about to take place.

Suddenly, gunshots! The back doors swung open. Now four were in the car. Wade shoved a gun barrel into the neck of the driver, who could already feel the drag of two flat front tires. Quint creased the neck of the right front rider with his pistol. "Turn right and up the curb," demanded Wade. "Drive on the sidewalk, slowly. Very slowly."

The driver did as he was told. In a moment the Jeep halted on the Water Tower plaza. Wade and Quint gingerly exited the Jeep and stood carefully pointing their pistols at their respective captives. One of the policemen approached. Wade hollered,"These are your arsonists, officer."

After showing the cop his security credential, the policeman accepted Wade's account and put the two firebombers under arrest. Hillar corroborated the story and volunteered to be designated a witness. They explained to the officer the urgency of the situation, that this FBI truck was part of a larger attempt to prevent a terrorist action. The policeman excused Leona's soldiers to continue their operation. Hillar remained at the fire site while the other two raced back to Escada, looking for Leona.

56 /SATURDAY, CHICAGO, 7:53 PM

ANDREW DODGE and Sugar Daley found themselves talking to one another at the picture window of the president's temporary apartment. Sugar was holding a martini. The president a single malt Scotch. From the 85th floor they admired a staggeringly beautiful vista: Lake Michigan, the Chicago skyline, the orange and pink afterglow of a setting sun on the clouds.

"I was warned by a friend to stay away from a window," Andrew told Sugar. "I wonder if this is the window."

"But the City of the Big Shoulders is so irresistible! Thank God for such a window," said the mayor. "Why the concern? Terrorism?"

"Probably."

The two continued their engaging conversation, eye-to-eye with profiles parallel to the window. Mildred and guests clinked and chatted elsewhere in the apartment's living room.

"I know you're always on the alert for terrorism, Andy. Do you think this warning might include an assassination attempt?" asked the mayor.

"Actually, this matter has been on my mind since I first sat down in the Oval Office desk chair," said Dodge. "I've studied the history of my office and asked: Just what does it mean to attempt to assassinate a president of the United States? Abraham Lincoln was shot to death by

John Wilkes Booth, angry at the Union's victory in the Civil War. President James Garfield was assassinated by a frustrated and delusional political hack. William McKinley was killed by a loner. Franklin Delano Roosevelt, whose paralyzed legs left him unable to run for cover, was shot at five times by an unemployed Italian immigrant, Giuseppe Zangara."

"But Roosevelt wasn't assassinated," interrupted Sugar.

"Right. Roosevelt survived the attempt. But John Kennedy, didn't. He died when snipered by Lee Harvey Oswald. Ronald Reagan successfully ducked the bullets of John Hinckley, who was obsessed by a movie he saw about assassinations. Now, we might ask: what could this pattern mean? Does it indicate that America's international enemies are constantly threatening the life of our nation's head of state? Not in the least. It means that Americans kill Americans. I need to fear most the very people I serve."

"Now, that's a downer, Andy."

57 /SATURDAY, CHICAGO, 7:56 PM

AT FIRST, they did not notice it. It began as a small speck on the horizon, approaching from Lake Michigan. It glistened in the sunlight, so it was difficult at first to make out what the object was. Few bothered to study it closely until it passed the beach and was flying over land. It kept a low altitude. Had the mayor and president been looking, they would have seen a white helicopter traveling at eighty miles per hour coming in their direction.

The Long Ranger IV slowed as it entered the air space above the Water Tower Place apartment and business building. It hovered above Chestnut Street, almost asking for attention. The already positioned television cameras at the Escada Plaza were re-aimed at the aerial visitor. After pausing in an almost stationary position, the helicopter reversed direction. It rose and darted southeast for a half mile. News cameras followed its flight pattern. The chopper reversed its direction again. It picked up speed and altitude, bulleting toward the Water Tower Plaza, but this time higher. The copter's altitude matched that of the 85th floor of the John Hancock, aimed like a cruise missile right at the president's window.

By this time the president realized he was standing in front of *the* window. Dropping his drink, he turned and hollered, "Everyone! Out! Get to the center hallway!" Andrew stumbled over a coffee table. He was immediately grabbed by a secret service agent and escorted to safety. Mildred screamed. Another agent took her by the arm. Soon she, the president, the mayor, and other guests were sequestered in the building's center hallway.

Terror filled the street below. Even though a large space under the Hancock building had been cleared by the police responding to Ragland's warning, those at the perimeter ran further away out of fear of falling debris. Screams rose up from ground level. A collision seemed imminent.

Rubberneckers on the ground witnessed a sight as uncanny as it was dramatic. As the guided missile raced towards its target, its speed decreased. It slowed asymptotically, until it came to a mid-air stop only a few feet from the building's façade. One of the blades scraped the apartment window. Glass shards sprayed like a fountain, raining down on Chestnut street. The pulsating sound of the chopper's engine doubled its roar as window fragments shot inward, toward the walls barely protecting the huddled presidential party. The insiders flinched to protect themselves from the hurricane of flying glass fragments. One stout and strapping security agent, standing directly between the president and the window, felt one shard rip through his left sleeve. Blood spilled briefly, staining his clothes. After brief flinch, he turned to the president with a smile.

"Your red badge of courage," said the president with a grateful glisten in his eyes.

The helicopter withdrew from the building slightly and stabilized. There it hung. Rotors moving. No change in location. The craft tilted to the left. It tilted to the right. Without warning, it began to fall. Straight down. It plunged past the sixtieth floor. It passed the twentieth floor. The engine roared. By the twelfth floor it leveled off. The rotor pitch rose. So did the helicopter. Up and up until its altitude exceeded that of the John Hancock Building. It slowly reversed direction. Then, it meandered south and east.

Those on the upper floors watched the once dangerous attack vehicle retreating toward Lake Michigan. No one other than the agent had been hurt. Relatively little damage had been done. No assassination of a president or a mayor had taken place. No act of terrorism had demolished the bronze skyscraper.

The casualty count? Tom and Ted were dead. So was Rex Allen. Two bodies of CUB commandos lay behind the Escada building. Three CUB attackers were under arrest. Was it over? Would it be over soon? No one knew.

58 /SATURDAY, CHICAGO, 8:18 PM

SHOULDER TO SHOULDER with everyone else on the street, Leona had witnessed the acrobatics high above. Like others, she was relieved over what did not happen; but she alone knew the depth of terror that had been avoided.

Leona was on the phone with Hillar when Graham and Everett found her in the crowd. Hillar recited quickly the events surrounding the van explosion and the arrests. Leona admonished the teenager to sit tight at the Water Tower.

"My God, I'm glad you're safe!" exclaimed Graham. All three hugged.

Leona smiled, but only for a fraction of a second. "We've got to find the droners."

Graham responded, "Because they threw the body from the roof of the Escada building, I bet no droners are up there now. Anyway, Everett and I wiped out the fleeing killers."

"Somewhere south of the Hancock, I bet," muttered Leona. She dialed Shmoo to explain what happened on her side of the building. She spoke quickly. "Shmoo, we've got to find the location where the CUBies have their guidance equipment. I bet they're close by. They needed a site where they could see both the chopper and their target.

This suggests the southeast side of the Hancock. The Seneca Hotel might be a good candidate. Can you find the bastards?"

"We're on our way," said Shmoo. His band of three worked their way south through the blockade and crowd.

"More than likely they shopped for higher ground," added Everett. "What about Lake Point Tower?"

"Is that close enough?" asked Graham.

"I don't know. Probably not," responded Everett.

Leona paused to think. "Graham, maybe we should get a bird's eye view from atop the John Hancock. Call Holthusen to get clearance and then take Everett to the roof. Shmoo's threesome will take the Seneca. Here come Quint and Wade. I'll ask them to try Water Tower Place."

"Okay," said Graham. He and Everett disappeared, heading for the 175 Delaware door of the Hancock. Leona sent Quint and Wade to scout the roof of Water Tower Place.

Her phone sounded. It was Shmoo. "I think we may have spotted something on the Seneca roof. We're going in. And we're going up. Maybe you should guard the front door in case some of the rabbits scurry through our fence."

"Gotcha," said Leona.

Through the hotel's interior and elevator three of the soldiers in Leona's army made their way to the Seneca roof. They were quiet and cautious as they entered the roof area.

By this time Wade and Quint had made it to the Water Tower Place roof. No signs of activity. They surveyed the Seneca roof below them. They spotted signs of movement on the Seneca roof.

Graham and Everett were still riding a sequence of elevators up a hundred floors to the top of the Hancock.

On the Seneca roof, there was in fact movement. Shmoo saw it. He whispered to Hammer and Scorp to take cover positions where they could see well. Three suspicious men were folding up electronic equipment and placing it in suitcases.

"This is where they must've guided the chopper," Shmoo said to his comrades in a soft whisper. "You two get behind that lattice over there, the fence by the air conditioner unit. I'll get behind this janitor's utility cart. I'll step out first. Then, you two peek around with guns aimed." All three took their positions.

Shmoo stood up with his gun aimed. "Drop your weapons and put your hands on your heads," he yelled. The three men at the roof's edge were caught by surprise. None complied. They defiantly pulled their weapons into shooting position. Shmoo fired. So did Hammer and Scorp. Smoke and noise reigned. In the bullet exchange some shots passed through the openings of the lattice, injuring the legs of both Hammer and Scorp. Both went down. Suddenly, quiet.

Shmoo was now safely behind the janitors' utility cart, gun drawn. He scanned the rooftop battlefield. One body lay across a suitcase. The other two were not in sight. *Where are they?* Might they be crawling invisibly toward him, ready to get a clear shot at the retired cop?

Time to smoke 'em out, he thought. Like a street hooker, Shmoo showed a little leg around the utility cart. Three quick shots rang out, pinging the janitors' utility cart. The smoke revealed that the shooter was secure behind a large heating duct.

Multiple bullets, but only one shooter. Gotta do something quick. Hammer and Scorp might be bleeding badly. How can I flush out that shooter? And where's the third guy? Shmoo hit speed dial for Graham. At the click, Shmoo cupped his hand around the mike and whispered, "Where are ya?"

"I'm just arriving at the Hancock roof. I've got Everett."

"The roof?! Great! Look down at the Seneca roof. Look carefully. You'll see a green janitors' utility cart. I'm behind it. Between you and me you'll see a horizontal heating duct. Large one. A shooter is behind it. He's got me cornered. Scorp and Hammer are down. Can you give me backup?"

"Shmoo, I'm a couple hundred yards away."

"Got any sharp shooters up there?"

"Yeh, lots of 'em."

"Do I need to say any more?"

"No, of course not. Hold on, buddy!"

Graham ran to a Secret Service sniper with weapon in hand. "Is that a Remington 24 you're holding?" Graham asked.

"Yeah," said the sniper.

"I'm with the CIA. I've got an enemy shooter on the Seneca roof. Can you sight him?"

The gunman looked through his scope. "Actually, there's more than one on that roof," he said to Graham, with a questioning look on his face.

"Let me look through your scope," Graham asked.

The gunman handed Graham the weapon. Through the scope Graham sized up the situation immediately. He found the shooter in the crosshairs. Slowly and deliberately he squeezed the trigger. Two rapid fire shots. The target had just moved before the trigger pull, and Graham did not pause to watch the target. It was a hit, but not lethal.

The marksman scowled and screamed, "You're not allowed to fire my weapon!"

"Sorry," said Graham as he grabbed Everett and raced toward the down elevator.

BACK ON THE SENECA ROOF, Shmoo realized the situation had changed in his favor. "Thanks, Graham," he muttered to himself. *Now, is it safe to step out into the open?* Shmoo could not be sure, as long as the third enemy combatant was not accounted for. But he felt he could wait no longer to clean up. He hesitantly stepped out, first with a little leg and then his entire body. No shots from any direction.

Shmoo checked his two comrades. Both had taken flesh wounds, but nothing seemed life threatening. Then Shmoo walked cautiously into the open toward the bodies of his foes. Shmoo knelt at the first body lying on the roof. He was dead. Shmoo carefully pulled himself over the heating duct to where the second body should be lying. Shmoo spotted a puddle of blood, but no body. Spots of spilled blood provided the trail of a crawling man. It led behind a bank of air conditioning exhaust fans. Shmoo took cover and then crept slowly, not knowing which end of the air conditioning bank hid the gunman. Should he follow the blood trail or circle around and come in from the other end?

Shmoo listened for a clue. Silence. It would be a fifty-fifty gamble. Could he split the difference? Could he run toward the bank, leap on top, and surprise the gunman from above? Perhaps 30 years ago. Not today.

He decided to follow the blood. He sensed that his movement was quiet, too quiet to be heard. Perhaps he could still take the enemy by surprise. Suddenly he was on his feet and running. He turned to the back side of the air conditioning bank and found his target at the other end, with his back to him. "Freeze!" hollered the retired cop.

The gunman spun around with a raised weapon. Shmoo let go with the full clip. Hit, the gunman bounced up and backward, falling to the roof surface.

Shmoo walked carefully to the now unmoving body. He could see where Graham's two shots had pierced the torso, and where Shmoo's own clip had turned his heart into spaghetti. *What a shot that guy Graham must be,* marveled the ex-cop, as he felt through the dead man's clothes. He found a wallet, including a driver's license with a name. Jarrod Grimes.

Shmoo hollered over the duct, "Scorp, call Leona. Tell her we've got Jarrod Grimes. Dead." As soon as they connected, Scorp blurted, "Three bad guys on the roof. Two dead. One named Jarrod Grimes. We don't know where the third one is."

Wade and Quint, still atop Water Tower Place, knew. They watched the third rappelling down the Seneca wall from floor to floor. "These terrorists must have prepared in advance with an escape rope," said Wade. "As Special Forces vets, they're trained for this." He wanted to fire his pistol from the Water Tower Place rooftop. But at that range the chance of hitting the flying escapee was virtually nil. The circus act ended when the fleeing CUBie disappeared through a hotel window.

Wade dialed Leona to announce that the prey would soon appear at the hotel's entrance.

59 /SATURDAY, CHICAGO, 8:49 PM

WITH THE SUN having set and darkness beginning to fall, Leona took up watch directly across Chestnut from the Seneca entrance. Hotel lights provided adequate illumination to study the faces and clothes of those passing through the Seneca's front doors. With Grimes dead, she was not sure for whom she was looking. If Grimes was the chief, was she looking for a brave? What does an assassin look like? Iranian? American? Man? Woman? Uniformed? Plain clothes?

After watching a dozen or more people shuffling in and out, Leona grew impatient. Finally, one man caught her eye. A man dressed in a familiar gray and maroon sweatsuit stepped through the front door and paused. He looked around. *Could the white guy and this man shop at the same Big 5?* She walked warily toward him.

At twenty feet, their eyes met. She recognized his face: Karl Budenholzer. Leona's right hand slipped deftly to the rear of her waistband to grip her pistol handle. But she did not draw the gun.

"So, the mouse catches the cat," Budenholzer said coolly to Leona.

"What would you have done if the cat had caught the mouse? Played with me? Tortured me?" said Leona.

"I would have performed a secretectomy. I would've surgically extracted what I want and donated the rest of your body to science. I suspect your hand is on your gun, Leona," he said.

"You've got that right," she said. "Keep yours where I can see them."

"I'm finding you to be quite an annoyance, Leona. You won't tell me the name I want. You won't let me kidnap you. You won't let me fly a helicopter into the building over there. Is this the way you treat your former superior?"

"I can be quite cooperative with the right people, Karl. I hope you'll cooperate with me now."

"I was once your boss."

"Oh, yes. I remember. I also remember how you treat those who work for you. They're like fish food for piranha."

Budenholzer laughed.

"Now, let me read your mind, Boss. Because I wouldn't share my secret, you thought you'd assassinate our president. Is that right?"

"Right."

"For you somebody's gotta die: either a nameless man in Tehran or our head of state. If not one, then the other. Right?"

"Right."

"What for? So you and your CUB buddies can keep raking in the money? You'll shed blood for profit? Anybody's blood? Is that what you're up to?"

"You got it. But that's not all of it, Miss Goodie Two Shoes. I'm also fighting for a cause."

"What cause?"

"I'm fighting against unemployment. These contractors are my guys, my buddies. They've been trained to become professional spies, professional soldiers, professional adventurers. That's what they know how to do. That's the only thing they know how to do. I keep 'm working. That's how I serve my country."

"Well, it's over, Mister Patriot."

"It ain't over yet, Miss Pollyanna."

Budenholzer rubbed his arm on the side of his body. Something dropped on the pavement. Leona reached for her pistol. Before she could aim it with two hands, a magnesium flash blinded her. Her hands covered her eyes, but too late. They smarted and welled up. Seconds passed. She removed her hands and wiped her eyes, then saw that the space where Budenholzer once stood was now filled with smoke. She coughed, as did the confused bystanders. She looked to her right. She looked to her left. Down the block on the left she thought she saw rapid movement. Someone running. Yes. It was Budenholzer. Leona sprinted southward. *He may be sixty*, she thought to herself; *but he runs like he's twenty*. This did not discourage Leona. She was used to running a dozen miles on a morning jog. She was confident she would not lose the CUB leader.

With a large number of Chicago's finest manning the president's perimeter, police motorcycles were parked everywhere, some with keys in the ignition. Budenholzer hopped on a Harley and was soon speeding west on Pearson. Leona followed suit, stealing an idling motorcycle and following Budenholzer's lead. The two swerved left onto North Michigan Avenue. They sped south toward the Loop. North Michigan Avenue became South Michigan Avenue.

The bikes raced passed the Chicago Art Institute. Then, left onto Jackson. A right onto South Columbus. Budenholzer thought he could shake her at Buckingham Fountain. The fountain spray drifted over onto the pavement, leaving a thin damp slick. Budenholzer extended his left leg and circled the fountain, cautiously enough to avoid a skid. Leona followed, just as cautiously. Both sped. Neither skidded. Pedestrians screamed and scattered to make way for the speeders.

A bright light picked them up at Buckingham Fountain, but lost them momentarily. *Maybe a police chopper is tracking us*, thought Leona. *I bet the cops want their Harleys back.*

Budenholzer led the bike duo out to South Lakeshore Drive, turning right with Leona tight on his tail. The Harleys revved and whined and sped. South and west of Soldier Field, with Leona keeping her distance at less than fifty yards. The lead cycle turned left onto East 18th Drive, and then again onto Museum Campus Drive. The second cycle took the same two turns, both racing north. Budenholzer and his tail turned sharply to the right onto East Solidarity Drive, passing Shed Aquarium on their left. Tourists and picnickers and those exiting the museum complex watched the loud chase.

As the two approached Adler Planetarium, Budenholzer skidded up onto the central mall, stopping short of the monument to Copernicus. With a jerk, he parked his bike sideways and pulled out his Glock. Hiding behind his motorcycle for the ambush, he watched Leona's bike jump the curb and rocket toward him on the grassy mall. Budenholzer fired at the oncoming Harley. His bullet hit the front tire. It exploded and went flat. The quick-thinking Leona did a wheely and cut her engine. The front fell with a thud, throwing its rider over the handle bars and onto the planetarium lawn. While Leona was still rolling, Budenholzer mounted his Harley and sped off to the south of the Adler building. He disappeared from Leona's sight.

Where could he be going? she asked while picking herself up. *Scrapes, but no broken bones.* She listened carefully. The sound of Budenholzer's bike quit short. *Must be on the other side of Adler.* Her Kimber lay in the grass where only seconds before her body was splayed. She picked it up, checked the ammo, and holstered it into her waistband.

Leona decided to make her way toward the east side of the Adler via the north waterfront. The grassy apron led down to a series of concentric concrete rings from the lawn to water's edge. At water's edge the cement walkway was girded by steel supports, providing a ten-foot margin between the lake's surface and that of the balustrade. If she could move stealthily along the concrete walkway at the foot of the lower wall, perhaps she would not be seen as the tall mercury yard lights flickered on. Leona headed east, glancing occasionally at the lapping of Lake Michigan against the rusted steel supports.

Stooping and crawling for nearly a hundred yards, she passed the sundial. Leona heard the rumblings of an engine on the lake. She raised her head a few inches and spotted the arrival of a power boat, a Baja 35 Outlaw with two men, one standing at a steering wheel. Off to her right, Budenholzer was inching his way down the cement steps toward the arriving V-hulled craft. For balance, his arms were stretched out like a high-wire walker.

Leona's mind went to work. *A prearranged rendezvous, eh. Can I pick off the boat driver with a single pistol shot? Perhaps, but not at this distance. Gotta be closer. Can I get closer without being discovered? Could I get closer soon enough to intercept the disembarkment?*

When the Outlaw docked at the steel support, one of the boat's sailors hoisted a ladder. Its top hooked securely on the concrete balustrade. As Leona crept toward the landing site, she thought through the question: *dead or alive? Maybe it would be best to take Budenholzer alive. He would know which contractors had joined the CUB union and which were either excluded or voluntarily remained clean. Like Santa Claus, Budenholzer knows who's naughty and who's nice. Questioning the mastermind would be easier than tracking down each contractor with an independent investigation. Regardless, the followers as well as the leader should be brought to justice.*

Budenholzer was now within fifteen feet of the boat landing. The boat's engine had been silenced for boarding. It would be only seconds and the CUB chief would be aboard. Then gone. If she was going to act, now would be the time. The huntress spread herself out on the ground at water's edge. Her stomach pressed into the concrete. Leona lifted her Kimber in both hands, with elbows anchored on the concrete. She sighted the man standing at the steering wheel. A trigger squeeze. Through the smoke in front of her Leona watched the body lurch and then fall to the far side and splash in the water.

Instantly the second man bolted to his feet to fire his automatic weapon at Leona. He sprayed the area where he had seen Leona's gun smoke. Leona heard bullets ricocheting off the cement wall behind her and the steel girders below her. She remained unscathed. Once again taking aim, the prone sharpshooter squeezed the trigger. The second man catapulted overboard. The boat was now unmanned, yet still secured.

Budenholzer was close enough to grab the ladder's top rung. He tried to maneuver himself for boarding. In a flash Leona was bounding down the balustrade like a lion chasing a wildebeest. She dropped the Kimber. Airborne, she aimed her body like a rocket at Budenholzer. Both flew into the water with a splash. The Lake Michigan water at fifty-two degrees felt like ice. Under the surface they struggled, pulling and tugging. They rolled. Water prevented punches from hurting. At first neither gained advantage. Then, Budenholzer smashed Leona's head on a subsurface rock. His hands felt the smack of flesh on stone. Leona's body went limp. She lost her grip and lost her consciousness. The once attacking tigress had become defenseless. She floated listlessly, face down.

Might Leona be dead? If not, she certainly would be out for a while. No longer a threat, thought the relieved Budenholzer.

60 /SATURDAY, CHICAGO, 9:44 PM

THE SURVIVING BUDENHOLZER pulled himself into the boat, exhausted and panting. He breathed deeply to steady himself. He assessed the situation. Believing that Leona was no longer the huntress, the game thought himself free to return peacefully to his lair. With one foot on the ladder, he kicked the boat away. He climbed. When again on terra firma, he looked toward the boat. It had drifted beyond reach and looked like it was already on its way to Milwaukee. Budenholzer turned toward the Adler and stumbled his way up the concrete steps toward the motorcycle, still parked on the lawn just above the top cement ring.

While standing on the top concrete level, the bike's wheels met him chest high. He searched through a saddlebag. He removed a .40 caliber Beretta, police issue. After checking it for ammo, he put the pistol in his large wet sweatshirt pocket. Then, to his surprise, Budenholzer heard a voice.

"Leave it in your pocket and turn around slowly," he heard. It was the voice of Leona, coming from behind. He turned slowly. After 180 degrees, he could see his wet adversary, lying on the concrete right in front of the ladder. Her fiery eyes were looking straight at him. Propped up on her elbows, her two hands were aiming the Kimber at his chest. His right hand still touched the Beretta in his sweatshirt pocket. Could he shoot through the sweatshirt? No. He could not aim at this distance. He would have to have his hand free. Could he beat Leona to the trigger pull? This would be his gamble.

Budenholzer whipped out the gun and began firing repeats. Leona squeezed the trigger once. A three bullet burst. All three hit the same place: Budenholzer's chest. His body whirled. His left hand gripped the top of the stone wall. He steadied himself momentarily. Then, he fell. He fell in such a way that he was sitting when his backside dropped on to the concrete.

Leona stood up. She walked toward Budenholzer, aiming her pistol at his head as a precaution. Budenholzer was not moving. After kicking away the wounded CUB leader's weapon, Leona knelt down on his left side.

"You're badly wounded," she said softly in his left ear.

His eyes turned toward her. "Very badly," he said, choking.

"You told Andrew Dodge to let me die in Tehran," didn't you?'

"Yes."

"Did you want all thirty of us dead?"

"Yes. Nothing personal, Leona."

"It was personal to me." Then her eyes turned glassy. "But why? Why did you do this?"

"Important...(wheeze)...feared public opinion...(cough)...nice people like you might ask our nation to clean its hands...(cough)...to cut out the dirty work. I like dirty work, don't you know?"

"What did you say to the president?"

"I told him the best strategy...(cough)...told him not to negotiate with terrorists such as Golshani...(pause)....Hang tough, I said. Everyone who volunteered for this kind of dangerous work knew the risks. That applied to you too...(cough)...You knew the risks. The president was not required to wipe your nose with a tissue just because the operation caught a cold...(cough)."

"Twenty-eight people died because of this White House decision. You're responsible for it. How could you?"

"It's my job. It's my work. In the long run, it was best for the country." Budenholzer coughed up some blood. He spat it out. It created a small red pool on the concrete.

"Again I ask: how could you?"

Budenholzer looked up at Leona's face. His open eyes met hers. He tried to speak, but nothing came out. His eyes closed. His head dropped onto his left shoulder.

61 /SATURDAY, CHICAGO, 10:11 PM

Leona leaned against the cement wall to ponder what had happened. Her gun hung listlessly at the end of her relaxed arm. On the edge of consciousness she realized that she was no longer alone. Human voices in the distance were growing louder, approaching. A crowd was gathering.

A voice shouted, "drop that weapon!"

Leona turned in the direction of the voice. She spied a police officer approaching with gun drawn. It was Brad Kuhn.

"Brad!" she said loudly.

"Pastor Lee, is that you?"

"Yes, Brad."

"What's happening?"

"He's dead. Nothing's happening now."

Brad bent over to study the corpse.

From above a noise demanded their attention, the drone of an engine becoming increasingly louder. Then, an intense blue-white light shone down upon her, Brad, and Budenholzer's corpse. A helicopter was descending rapidly. The light was so bright that at first she could not discern whether or not it was a Long Ranger IV. It was.

Once the blue chopper had landed on the lawn near the sundial and the rotors slowed to a stop. The door opened. Out stepped the president, Andrew Dodge. Dodge ran to Leona and embraced her. She put her arms around his neck. Their cheeks brushed each other. The expression on Dodge's face indicated he wanted frantically to kiss her; but realizing they were being watched he hesitated. At this hesitation, Leona withdrew her arms. He continued to hold her shoulders in his two hands, almost defying his growing audience. Dodge spoke with glassy eyes, "Oh, Lee, I'm so glad you lived through all of this."

"Thank God *you're* alive," she exclaimed.

"That helicopter came so near to wiping out the 85th floor of the John Hancock!" he said. "It could've been my end! My life is now a gift. And I've got you to thank for it."

"It's your moment of grace, Andy. I had mine in a Tehran prison. Both were rescues. But look at Budenholzer there. Look at his blood leaking onto the concrete. It seems that grace for us means death for others. That's the part that will grieve me until I finally go to my grave."

Despite being in public, they hugged one another and shared another fragment of eternity. Within seconds Leona continued. "What happened?"

"Holthusen's tech team finally took control of the flying torpedo at the last second. Two radio teams fought to control the same drone. We won. The CIA had sites both on the ship and on top of the John Hancock. We redirected the helicopter back to the ship's heliport. It landed safely. When Holthusen opened the doors he discovered containers of wired explosives."

"Potent?"

"You can say that again! Once the copter hit the Hancock, fire would've spread everywhere. In the seats were the two kidnapped Golshani boys. Their IDs were on them. They were unconscious and strapped in. They had been drugged. My White House physician on the ship is attending to them now. His prognosis is positive. I plan to phone Akbar Golshani in Tehran and tell him what's happened. He should know, I think."

"Lasers!" said Leona in a whispered shout, arching backward.

"What?"

"Lasers. Think: lasers. When you phone Golshani, tell him you want to end the tensions. Our planet's time is running out, Andy."

"What're you talking about?"

Leona stood silent for a moment. She fell toward the president, and he wrapped his arms around her once again. "Is it over? " she asked with eyes closed.

"Holthusen assures me that it's over. Leona's army seems to have totally defeated the enemy. Now, I want the heroine to come back to the ship with me. It's a short helicopter ride. I want you to be where you belong, Lee, with me. At least for tonight. I'll have my doctor examine your injuries."

Leona paused. She looked up at the president. "Will Mildred be aboard?" She hesitated again. Before he could speak, she added with emphasis, "No, Andy, don't answer that. It doesn't make any difference." She thought for a moment while she hugged him. "I need a cliché. Here it is: no, Andy, I can't come. I've got a sermon to write. You know how it is for a pastor on Saturday nights. A preacher's in hell until the sermon's done. I haven't even started. I'm going home. Thanks anyway for the invitation."

"But you look scraped and bruised, and your skull is bleeding a little."

"I've got a first aid kit at home. Actually, I'm feeling fine. A long warm bath is all I need. Thanks just the same, Andy. I'll miss you desperately, but you've got your work and I've got mine."

Leona withdrew completely from his shoulder grip. Then she realized that the two of them were being watched by a large number of people arrayed on the Adler Planetarium lawn. They had gathered when the commotion had begun. The onlookers were curious about the police chopper and now the landed presidential helicopter. They were buzzing about what might be happening. Police were examining the debris from the battle. Leona said to Andrew, "I think I've got to escape before any questioning begins. Can you cover for me?"

"Certainly," said the president. "I'm really going to miss you tonight. Do you have to go?"

"Yes. I must. But don't think I won't be missing you."

Leona turned to leave while the president motioned for Brad Kuhn to come and confer. The bright lights of the helicopter shone on the crowd. The pilot remained in the craft. The president did the talking.

Leona picked out Graham and Hillar in the crowd who were being joined by Shmoo, Everett, Quint, and Wade. "What happened?" is a phrase that could be heard repeatedly above the buzz of the crowd's conversation.

Leona paused in front of Shmoo. "That's what I want to know. What happened to Scorp and Hammer?"

"They took a little lead," said Shmoo. "Only leg wounds. They'll heal."

"Where are they now?"

"Ambulance taking 'm to Cook County as we speak," said Shmoo.

"Cook County? Shmoo, why are you not going there to be with them. You gotta go."

"Nah. They'll be OK. Just flesh wounds."

"Shmoo, no. You get your ass over to Cook County. Hold their hands. Comfort them. They need you right now. They need you like any little boy needs a father."

"For God's sake, Leona!" stammered Shmoo, stomping his left foot. He paused. His eyes watered slightly. "I feel like I'm *your* father, Lee. And I'm so proud of you and so thankful you're all right."

"You heard me, Shmoo," Leona said while hugging the graying man. She kissed him on the cheek. Her tender body language did not match the sternness of her commanding voice. "Now, get out of here."

Shmoo left immediately. Leona cocked her head and said plaintively, "Graham, please take me home." Turning to her assembled army she said, "You're all given an honorable discharge. You're dismissed."

Before any of them could take a step, the crackling of a loud speaker drew the attention of the crowd. From the helicopter a megaphoned voice trumpeted: "Attention, please. This is your president speaking, Andrew Dodge."

A hush fell over the crowd. All eyes turned to the brightly lit craft on the Adler lawn. The president's voice continued. "This is an extraordinary moment," he said. "You have witnessed the thwarting of a horrendous terrorist attack. Had our enemies been successful, they would have taken my life, traumatized the city of Chicago, shattered the confidence of our nation, and placed the world once again into a state of nuclear fear. Like David standing up to Goliath, one woman stood up and felled a giant. This courageous and brave woman along with her friends are responsible for preventing a disaster of untold consequences."

The spotlight from the helicopter scanned the crowd. Finally, it settled on Leona, Graham, and her comrades. Now, all could see the persons about whom the president was speaking.

"I will withhold her name for the time being," he continued. "But do not underestimate the amount of gratitude each of us here tonight owes her and her volunteer army. Open your eyes wide. Right now you are looking at a patriot. More. You are looking at an icon of patriotism whose shoes I am unworthy to untie."

A pair of hands clapped. Then a second. Soon the entire crowd burst into vigorous applause. Ill at ease, Leona's mouth dropped open. Her eyes registered confusion and fright.

"Please, Graham," Leona whispered impatiently. Graham put his jacket over her head. Photographers were arriving. With his left arm on Leona's left shoulder, he led her through the crowd to the Shedd Aquarium parking lot. Hillar followed close behind. All three stepped into a taxi and headed for South Shore.

"How did you know where to find me?" Leona asked Graham.

"The GPS beacon. I bet you didn't lose your cell phone."

Leona looked out the windshield, then down at her shoes. "I shed a lot of human blood tonight," she said mournfully.

"I gather your machine mind has turned off," said Graham.

Leona looked up at Graham with glistening eyes.

Hillar peered through the back window and watched the president's helicopter rise and disappear into the night sky.

62 /SUNDAY, CHICAGO, 6:00 AM

It was 6:00 am when Leona's alarm sounded. She had roughed out her sermon outline during the previous night's late bath. As was her custom, she rolled out of bed and headed downstairs for the coffee pot. Midnight stood up and stretched but remained on the bed, watching her mistress shuffle out the door. As Leona walked through the living room, Buck, who had been sleeping with Graham on the downstairs hide-a-bed, looked up at Leona as she passed. Graham did not stir.

After her morning liturgy of orange juice—the last gingerbread man had been eaten the day prior—and pouring a full cup of Peet's, she passed through the living room once again. Buck's nose was flat on the blanket in sleeping position, although his eyes were open and he was aware of Leona's presence in the room. Graham's body under the blanket was still. Leona bent down and softly kissed Graham on the forehead. She whispered, "Thank you, Graham."

Buck's body did not move. Yet, his eyes shifted to look at Graham's. Graham's eyes were also open, even though he did not move. Buck and Graham acknowledged their shared awareness through eye contact.

Leona tiptoed up the stairs to flop once again on her bed. Midnight resumed her curled position on the pillow. Leona was nearly awake and almost ready to face a Sunday that would begin with worship. She took a moment to go online and book a flight for Monday to Oakland, the airport nearest to Berkeley, nearest to Professor Elliot.

Time to check my emails? It would take a minimum of mental energy to skim through and pick out the urgent ones. Sipping her coffee, she opened her AOL.

One email caught her eye: Re: "For God and Country." She opened it.

Dear Rev. Lee Foxx,

I looked up your church on the internet. You are the pastor of Trinity Church. Perhaps you were once a Boy Scout. If so, you remember the award that scouts must earn before they can become and Eagle: Pro Deo et Patria (For God and Country)>

My son, Tommy, is ready to begin work on his Pro Deo et Patria. He needs a clergyman to evaluate his work and approve his credit. Would you be willing to work with my son?

Sincerely,

(Mrs.) Jacqueline Simonson

Leona pondered the contents of this email. Then, she hit "reply" and wrote:

Dear Mrs. Simonson,

Thank you for your inquiry. You should be proud that your son, Tommy, wants to work on his Pro Deo et Patria. This may be one of the most noble awards. It testifies to loyalty, our loyalty to God and to our nation as well. Unfortunately, I am not qualified to help. I wish you well as you look for a pastor who is.

Sincerely,

Rev. Leona Foxx

The moment she hit "send"' the parsonage phone rang. She reached for the bedroom extension quickly, hoping the ringing would not wake Graham downstairs. A man's voice spoke to her. "Reverend Foxx?"

"Yes."

"This is Doctor Solomon Wieder at the South Shore Hospital. I have someone here who would like to speak with you. Will you take the call?

"Yes, of course." She could hear the transfer of the phone from one hand to another.

"Pastor Foxx?"

"Yes."

"This is Victoria Walker. I'm Cupid's mother."

"Oh, hello!"

"Cupid told me all about you. She is so fond of you. I already feel like you're one of the family. Thanks for what you do for Cupid."

"Well, Mrs. Walker, Cupid is a doll. I enjoy having her here. She can visit me anytime."

"That's *Miss* Walker, Pastor. I'm here in the South Shore Hospital. I just had a baby this morning, in the middle of the night, actually."

"Congratulations."

"Could you possibly get over here today to *ooh* and *ahh* about my new baby? After all, you're my pastor now.

Leona chuckled. "Yes, of course, I'll come. I've got church this morning. I'll try to get there in the afternoon. What room are you in?"

"I'm in five fifteen. Thanks, Pastor."

"Bye."

"Bye."

Leona hung up the phone. She took a sip of her Major Dickason. Then, she spoke to herself out loud. *I'm her pastor. Wow. Gotta call Angie.*

ALSO BY TED PETERS

Click HERE to continue the adventure!

Leona Foxx is a killer with a conscience.
She kills like a machine, yet loves with a heart.
Sometimes violence is Leona's only path to love.

The black op with the white collar, Leona Foxx, takes on renegade Transhumanists making themselves kingmakers by selling espionage technology. Leona's strategy is to turn superintelligence against itself in order to preserve global peace. Can a mere human prevail against the posthuman?

If you want to grasp the promises and risks of enhancing human intelligence in a world riddled with competition for supremacy, buy this book.

Get Cyrus Twelve Today!

at **www.books2read.com/cyrustwelve**

ABOUT THE AUTHOR

The Leona Foxx series of espionage thrillers is the fictional creation of Ted Peters, a Berkeley scholar and author of non-fiction books dealing with science and religion. Although distinctly a fictional character, Leona is a synthesis of a number of real life people on both sides of the violence fence. On one side, like her real life model, she has been a CIA operative undercover in Iran, experiencing imprisonment, interrogation and the threat of execution. Leona is both a victim and perpetrator of violence. On the other side, again modeled on someone in real life, she is conscience-driven to pacify, negotiate, heal, love, and care. As a pastor in a racially tense neighborhood, she gives total devotion to her God of grace while pulling the trigger on her semi-automatic. Leona is a killer with a haunting conscience.

Ted Peters has served as a pastor on the south side of Chicago, as well as a professor of theology at Pacific Lutheran Theological Seminary, a member school of the Graduate Theological Union in Berkeley, California. His first-hand experience with violence in the inner city, combined with academic teaching, has led him to wrestle with the nature of human nature and with the question of why we human beings kill one another in the name of some higher good.

Made in the USA
Columbia, SC
06 July 2022